GAP YEAR

Twelve Months That
Changed Two Lives

Helen Chislett

ISBN-13: 9798884103399
ISBN-10: 1477123456

Cover design by: Sarah Callender
Library of Congress Control Number: 2018675309
Printed in the United States of America

To Christine

CONTENTS

SEPTEMBER

As they pulled into Gare du Nord, Isobel noticed it was raining. They waited for the other passengers to disembark, then she and Grace heaved the enormous case off the train and dragged it up the platform. There it was: the unmistakable rise and fall of the SNCF theme. Long ago, it had been more like a series of bongs, but now it was the voice of a young chanteuse that trilled through the four notes, creating a soundscape that was as evocative of Paris as Le Tour Eiffel itself.

By the time they reached the taxi rank, there must have been a hundred or so people in front of them. Neither she nor Grace said much as they huddled together, trying to shelter from the rain under the canvas roof below which the queue snaked. Eventually they were ushered forward and she gave the address to the driver in the best accent she could muster, conjuring up an image of the quiet tree-lined avenue in the eighth *arrondissement,* where her daughter was to live for the next ten months.

Sitting in the taxi, she looked out at grey, rain-soaked Paris and thought about the journey she and Grace had made together a few weeks earlier. They had been introduced to Madame Chirol via Robert's old boss, whose own daughter had studied in Paris a few years previously. Madame Chirol was a formidable widow who let out a few rooms within her own once legendary, family residence. Isobel had been reassured by the deep respectability of the Élysée neighbourhood, ten minutes from the Champs-Élysées. She had left Isobel in no doubt that it was *c'est pas normale* for her to welcome a tenant as young as Grace, but the room was free and the rent was guaranteed, so terms were quickly agreed. She'd felt a sense of pride, of job-done satisfaction that she'd sorted out her daughter's new life within just forty-eight hours. They celebrated with a glass of champagne at the Ritz's Bar Hemingway – one of her old haunts - before heading back to the Eurostar. Now she had no idea why she had thought champagne appropriate. What on earth were they doing here?

Grace said very little, staring out of the window as they weaved through the city traffic. Isobel made a few upbeat comments about the weather and the architecture, suppressing the feeling of panic that threatened to overwhelm her. Her precious child was not just being tipped out of the nest, but thrown deep into an unfamiliar, urban jungle. Would she cope?

"Mum?"

"Yes, sweetheart."

"Do you think I'll be all right?"

"Are you worried?"

"A bit."

"About being homesick?"

"S'pose so."

"It would be odd if you weren't, Grace. This is a big step. You'll be fine though, once you settle in. Make some friends."

"What about you?"

"Me?"

"Will you be OK? Without me around?"

"Don't worry about that. Granny and Grandad are good at taking up my time, remember. I'll have lots to do." And all of it dull, dull, dull.

When they arrived at the house, she rang the bell to the apartment and tapped in the code she'd been given, so that the door opened onto the internal courtyard around which generations of Chirols had lived and died. There wasn't room for both of them and the suitcase in the tiny, wrought-iron lift, so a white-faced Grace braved the journey with her luggage and Isobel began the climb up to the second floor where Madame Chirol's maid, Antoinette, was waiting to welcome them in. A formal tea was laid out in the salon, with its views over the rooftops to the Eiffel Tower a mile or so away.

Madame Chirol rose from the deep-buttoned velvet couch to greet them, apologising for the fact she couldn't entertain them for long as she was expected at her regular Bridge party in an hour's time. Isobel had forgotten how tiny she was. She looked like a beautifully dressed wren.

She waved them towards the pair of gilt *bergère* chairs facing the sofa, before lifting a silver teapot and pouring China leaf tea into tiny porcelain cups decorated with loops of roses and lilies, offering miniature silver tongs to add finely sliced slivers of lemon. Madame Chirol spoke English with confidence, just occasionally slipping into French when a phrase was not immediately to hand. Isobel had the sense that she'd decided at their first meeting that neither of them was up to holding a conversation over tea in French, unless they were to be confined to the sort of stilted phrases a shy thirteen-year old might utter. In fact Grace had achieved an A in French at A-level, having sailed through her oral with a discussion on Zola's '*Au Bonheur des Dames*', but sitting in Madame Chirol's imposing drawing room, it seemed she could manage no more than the occasional '*merci beaucoup, madame*' or '*oui, s'il vous plaît, madame*'. Isobel found this vexing. She tried once or twice to interject with some phrases carefully rehearsed in her head, but was left with the distinct impression she too had simply confirmed Madame Chirol's low opinion.

The cakes had been artfully arranged onto a three-tiered, porcelain stand painted with rotund cupids. Here they were invited to choose from thin slices of Caneles de Bordeaux, fairy-light pastries of crème and choux, sugary pink macaroons and cubes of *fondant au chocolat*. Grace looked delighted to see traditional French butter cakes – *madeleines* – on the top tier. Isobel knew what she was thinking. Proust. Grace was ridiculously romantic.

"May I?" Grace turned to Madame Chirol. Her French had clearly flown out of the window.

"Of course." Then, as if by telepathy, "Would you like to dip one into *your* tea?"

Grace smiled. For the first time, the atmosphere relaxed a little.

Isobel could feel herself becoming seduced by these elegant surroundings. It was all so perfect, a time warp preserved in amber, with the tall, panelled walls, magnificent crystal chandelier, parquet floor and gilded cornices. While they chatted amiably – Madame Chirol was most complimentary about the 2012 Olympics that had taken place in London that summer, although of course *désolée* that Paris had lost the original bid – she allowed her eyes to rest momentarily on the huge, faded tapestry that hung on the wall behind her hostess. Aubusson maybe? For a moment, she imagined it new and vivid with colour, as it must have been when a style-setting Chirol of the eighteenth century had first commissioned the bucolic scene.

With her petite figure and perfectly coiffed, white hair, Madame Chirol seemed to Isobel the embodiment of Parisian chic. No matter that she was far from young – seventy-five? eighty? – she held herself beautifully, sitting upright on the sofa, a perfectly knotted Hermès scarf camouflaging any sagging of the neck skin. The cut of her deceptively simple black dress spoke of couture, while the solitary brooch she wore was encrusted with rubies and diamonds.

Once Isobel had owned a wardrobe that was the envy of her friends, but she had long ago ceased to care much about clothes and make-up. These days her mainstay were print dresses and cardigans that had been through the washing-machine a few times too often. What did Madame Chirol make of the underwhelming black trousers and cream shirt she was wearing today? For that matter, what must she be thinking of Grace's scuffed ankle boots, ripped jeans and unruly hair? No doubt she thought their dress sense as lamentable as their French.

The inscrutable Madame Chirol conducted herself with a disciplined politeness that gave no indication whatsoever of her inner thoughts. It was soon time for her to leave for her Bridge party: no doubt she had planned this departure well in advance. She apologised once more, "But of course you are welcome to stay here as long as you like. Antoinette will make you fresh tea."

Isobel took the hint, politely declining the offer and suggesting to Grace they began unpacking immediately. Madame Chirol led them through the double doors at the other end of the salon where the tenants' rooms were located, making a good show of concealing any embarrassment she may have had about the contrast between the eighteenth-century grandeur of her own rooms and the coldly-lit starkness of the tenants' wing. Another of the tenants fluttered in to say hello, introducing herself as Nina before fluttering away again.

American. Seemed sensible enough, but who could tell? She and Grace set to work unpacking the huge case and recreating a bonsai version of Grace's bedroom in the little French cell.

Grace knew her mum wanted to make the evening as upbeat as she could, but it was hard to pretend she wasn't dismayed that tomorrow Isobel would catch the Eurostar home and leave her here alone. Her course at the Cours de Civilisation Française de la Sorbonne was due to start next week and she couldn't get her head around the fact she would be expected to turn up there alone. It had long been her dream to live and study in Paris, but now she wished she could persuade her parents to relocate there and look after her while she studied. It was pathetic. She hated herself for being such a wimp.

"Shall we share a bottle of wine, Grace? White?"

"Thanks. Lovely."

They were sitting in a small bistro that Madame Chirol had recommended, "Tell Marc-Pierre I sent you." Her name clearly carried weight. When they'd walked in, nobody had paid them any attention at all. When the *maître d'* finally sauntered over and Isobel had identified them as friends of Madame Chirol, the transformation was immediate. He escorted them with smiles and bows to a table he clearly considered superior, with waiters summoned with clicks of his fingers to pull out their chairs and arrange linen on their laps. Grace was embarrassed by the attention. Hated a fuss.

"Thank goodness for Madame Chirol," Isobel was smiling to herself.

"What do you mean?"

"Look by the door. That would have been us."

Looking over, she saw a couple who were obviously English – hair, clothes and embarrassed demeanour all underlining this fact – whom Marc-Pierre was pointedly ignoring. Every time they tried to catch his attention, he looked the other way and spoke to one of the waiters. It was obvious they didn't know what to do: patiently wait, or give up and find somewhere else to eat.

"Why's he being so mean?"

"You'll have to get used to that."

"What?"

"Not all the French love the English. Quite the opposite. Particularly here in Paris." Great. Now she told her.

She was relieved when Marc-Pierre relented a few moments later and led the couple to a table. It was next to the loo, but at least they were being allowed to eat something.

"Know what you want to eat, Grace?"

"Sea bass, please."

"Me too. Shall we share *frites* and spinach?"

"Sounds good."

Over dinner, she found it hard to relax, but Isobel seemed determined to lighten the mood with witty observations about the afternoon.

"Make friends with Antoinette if you want to know what Madame is really like."

"Why do you say that?"

"The staff always have the best gossip."

"Really?"

"Really."

Grace knew that Isobel had worked as a secretary for someone rich before marrying her dad and had visited Paris on many occasions, but she'd never thought much about her mum's job, secure in the knowledge that she, Grace, came before any career. For the first time, it struck her that Isobel had once existed as a person independent of Robert or herself.

"What was your job like?" The question seemed to take Isobel by surprise.

"Why do you ask that?"

"That thing about staff having the best gossip. Did you have the best gossip when you were at work?"

Isobel smiled, "I suppose I did."

"Like?"

"I probably shouldn't tell you."

"Mum, don't be ridiculous! It's centuries ago!"

"Not quite that long, Grace. Well, I knew which perfume to buy the wife and which to buy the mistress."

"Mum!"

"I knew what to say to one when he was with the other."

"Go on!"

"I knew he was also shagging Linda from the corporate team, but that he wasn't shagging Meryl in accounts who boasted they were an item."

"It's like a Jackie Collins novel."

"If you'd ever read a Jackie Collins novel, you'd know they're a lot more racy than that."

"Sounds pretty racy to me."

"Just the age-old story of a man with too much money confusing his net worth with his sex appeal."

"Did he ever try it on with you?"

"Grace!"

"He did, didn't he?"

"It would have been rather insulting if he hadn't, but I was firm in my refusal."

"Sure?"

"Sure!"

"But you came to Paris together?"

"We did, but usually not just the two of us. Kelly often came too."

"The mistress?"

"How did you guess? He was the sort of man who equated Paris with mistresses. Very traditional."

"What did you do here?"

"Stayed in lovely hotels, ate in lovely restaurants, went shopping to buy lovely underwear with Kelly . . ."

"That's not work."

"There were business meetings too. Property to manage. Sometimes, he wanted me here to make up foursomes at dinner."

"What do you mean?"

"Business is social too, Grace. He would arrange to have dinner with associates who would invariably bring their wives – all of his associates were men back then – and he didn't like to take Kelly to that sort of thing."

"Why not?"

"Let's just say he hadn't picked her out as his mistress for her intelligence."

"So he took you instead?"

"Exactly."

"Weird."

"Not really. Just how it was. Sure things must have changed by now."

"Hope so!"

"Me too."

"Do you miss it?" Until that moment, it had never occurred to her that Isobel might.

"Sometimes."

"Oh. Which bit?" The hotels and the restaurants presumably.

"Being good at something. Knowing you're good at it."

"You're good at being *you*. My mum."

"I'll take that as a compliment."

"You could go back to work?" Impossible to imagine.

"Now that you're here, you mean?"

"Exactly. You get your life back."

"Thanks, but you can't go backwards in life."

"Another job then?"

"Maybe."

"You could move here! Do a course at the CCFS with me!" She wasn't joking, but she hoped her mum thought she was.

"Tempting! But this is your gap year, not mine."

"We could share it."

"Don't think dad would be very happy about that."

"He could come too!"

"And leave Miss Mapp? Never!" Miss Mapp was the name of Robert's bookshop in Rye, the town where they had lived for nearly all of Grace's life.

Over coffee, Isobel leaned across the table and took Grace's hand in hers, "You are happy to be here, aren't you?"

Anxiety made her callous, "Of course I am. It's all I've ever wanted."

Isobel hated good-byes at the best of times, so she refused to let Grace accompany her to the Gare du Nord. They clung to each other tightly at the door the apartment, almost unable to speak for fear of one of them crying and setting off the other.

"Call us tonight?"

Grace nodded.

"And you know the code for getting in and out?"

Again a nod.

"And you will be very, very careful?"

"Of course, I will." Grace's voice was small and tinny. Isobel needed to go otherwise she would break down and so would Grace.

In the taxi to the station, she stared blankly out of the window, while her brain raced through all the dangers that now awaited Grace. She would be murdered, raped, kidnapped, beaten-up, robbed. She would step in front of a bus or car, not used to the fact that traffic flowed from the opposite direction. She would become addicted to drugs, take up with an abusive boyfriend, be trafficked for sex. She would make unhealthy friendships and bad decisions. What kind of mother was she to leave her only daughter alone in such a dangerous city?

Somehow she managed to make herself board the Eurostar, but as the train pulled out of Paris, she felt as if she were undergoing an amputation. She needed to calm down and stop being ridiculous. Grace was an adult and this was her choice. She wasn't back-packing through Thailand or South America like so many of her friends. She was only two hundred miles away from home; Scotland was further from Sussex than that. She could ring or Skype whenever she wanted. There was absolutely no reason to fear the worse. She must get a grip.

But when she got off at Ebbsfleet and was safely in the car, she switched on the music system to find that Robert had left Joni Mitchell's 'Blue' in the player. She began to cry noisily and messily. Once she could see well enough to drive, she drove home with the volume up, singing and crying in equal measure. By the time she turned off across the Romney Marsh, Joni was singing 'River' and her own heart was shattering into tiny shards of glass.

I'm so hard to handle,
I'm selfish and I'm sad.

Now I've gone and lost the best baby
That I've ever had.
Oh, I wish I had a river I could skate away on
I wish I had a river so long,
I would teach my feet to fly.
Oh, I wish I had a river I could skate away on.

Her face was pink and blotchy face in the rear view mirror. She couldn't go back looking like that. Instead, she turned off towards Camber Sands and walked through the dunes to the fast expanse of sand beyond – the sea a distant line. After half an hour of listening to the cry of gulls and feeling the breeze in her hair, she had regained composure enough to get back in the car and drive home.

When she arrived at the house, she could hear Robert talking to someone in the study. They weren't expecting anyone, so she listened at the door to see who it was, before realising he had the phone on loudspeaker talking to her mother.

"Have you got the list there, Pam?"

She had asked him to do the weekly online shop for her parents, but he'd clearly forgotten about it yesterday. He was probably in a rush to get it done before she got back, hoping Pam wouldn't complain to her.

Taking care of the shopping was Isobel's way

of trying to compensate for the fact that her father was finally off-road, but Robert wasn't usually asked to get involved with this particular head-ache. She couldn't resist listening at the door. He was hopeless at this sort of thing.

"Carry on, Pam and I'll type in what you say."

"Ok dear – now - tuna fish, cheese, rice, pasta, tomato puree . . ."

"Hang on."

" . . . onion, kitchen roll, white wine vinegar . . ."

"Could you slow down a little, Pam?"

"Those are things we don't need."

"What?"

"We have plenty of all of those."

"You don't need tuna or Cheddar?"

"No, as I said we have those, Robert."

"Do you think you could just read out the things you *do* need – less confusing on the computer?"

"Well I'm just coming to that, Robert. It's all on my second list."

"Could you possibly just read out that list then, Pam?"

It was no good. A bubble of laughter erupted.

"Bel, is that you?"

She opened the door, Robert rolling his eyes at her dramatically. "The online shop", he mouthed. "Bit bloody late!" she mouthed back.

"Hi Mum", she called. "How are you - is Dad OK?"

"Isobel?" came the voice, now slightly plaintive. "I thought you were in Paris with Grace."

"I was. Just got back."

"Is Grace all right?"

"Fine. Settling in well." She had to hope this was true.

There was a pause while she could hear this information being relayed to her dad and more mumbling between the two of them before she came back on the line, "Well we hope she is *safe* out there, Isobel. We would not have allowed you to do such a thing at her age."

Time to change the subject, "Have you got your list there, Mum?"

"Yes, but I think Robert is struggling a bit with the computer. You're always so quick when we do this."

She gestured at Robert to move. Typical he hadn't done the one thing she'd requested.

"Don't worry, I'm here now – you and I can do it together. Now where had you got to – doesn't look as though there's anything in the basket yet?"

"I *knew* he wasn't doing it properly".

"Ok I'm ready now. What would you like?"

Behind her, Robert made his escape. She hadn't even had time to take off her coat.

When Grace was six, her parents had taken her to Paris. They'd travelled by elevator to the third floor of the Eiffel Tower and looked out at the panoramic view, but she'd cried because she couldn't see the Eiffel Tower.

"That's because you're on it," said her mum.

"But you said, we could see the Eiffel Tower from anywhere in Paris."

"Not if you're on it, Grace."

"But you said!"

Her mum had started to laugh, which made her furious, but her dad had knelt beside her and explained that sometimes we couldn't see something, because we were simply too close to it. Remembering that now, she thought how right he was.

Paris. She'd thought it was such a good idea a year ago, but now she was here it was overwhelming. What had appeared inviting and exciting in the abstract had morphed into terrifying reality. Why had she thought spending her gap year there was such a good idea? She could have taken the easy route and gone back-packing with her friends round Thailand. They would be having a brilliant time over the coming months: nothing but beaches, boys and clubs. She must have been mad to insist on spending a year improving her French before going to Durham to study Modern Languages. She would be in classes doing assignments while they would have nothing more to think about than where the next high was coming from. Might as well have stayed in school.

She was such an idiot. It was easy to pretend to her family this was all she'd ever wanted, but her friends thought she was crazy – and rightly so. How was she going to cope in a new city when she could barely get herself to Hastings and back? Her friends might be thousands of miles away, but they would have each other. Going clubbing in Ko Sumai wouldn't be that different to going out in Brighton. They would meet the same crowd, but with the benefit of more sun and no parents. In Paris, she knew no-one at all.

She heard a knock on her door and Nina peeped in. As Grace had thought, the walls between these small partitioned bedrooms were thin. Nina must have been all too aware of the sobs she had tried to muffle in her pillow.

"You OK?"

She nodded.

"Really?"

"Yes, sorry."

"No need to be sorry. Must be hard."

She sat up and attempted a smile. "I don't usually cry. Honestly."

"It's fine. Just didn't want you to feel neglected on your first evening alone. Fancy going out for a drink? We can't smoke in the flat – Madame Chirol would go ape."

"I don't smoke anyway, but I'd love to go for a

drink. Thank you!"

Fifteen minutes later, they were walking past the Miromesnil metro towards a small bar Nina liked on the Rue d'Anjou, "quite close to Buddha Bar".

Nina managed to smoke two cigarettes in quick succession before they arrived. "Why France had to get so uptight about cigarettes I will simply never understand – if there is one place made for smoking it's Paris. They even invented Le Smoking jacket for chrissake".

She broke into a few lines of song,

"Je ne veux pas travailler
Je ne veux pas déjeuner
Je veux seulement l'oublier
Et puis je fume".

"Pink Martini!" said Grace.

"How do you know that?"

"It's on one of mum's Hotel Costes CDs. The last line is a bit of a family joke. You know, something happens - like the toast burns or the printer runs out of ink - and one of us will say, '*Et puis je fume*'. Although actually none of us do."

"Christ", said Nina. "You English really are nuts."

Once in the bar – Pernod for Nina and white wine for Grace – Nina started to fill her in on Madame Chirol.

"How old do you think she is?"

"About seventy-five?"

"Nope – you are at least ten years out.

Antoinette says she's eighty-six".

"Wow – well she's in good nick for eighty-six."

"Combo of money and good genes, I suppose."

"Is she very wealthy?"

Nina laughed, "You kidding? She doesn't just own the apartment. She owns the whole damned lot."

"You mean the whole building? Around the courtyard? But that's huge."

"You bet. Must be worth squillions. I reckon there are at least sixteen apartments as big as hers – and they're all full of Chirols. We might be in the year 2012 but the whole set-up is like seventeenth-century Versailles with Madame Chirol as queen bee, although I think of her more as a spider in the centre of her web."

"You don't like her?"

"I'm not sure 'like' comes into it. I admire the old cat, but I don't find her very lovable."

"How long have you lived here?"

"Since June. I moved over from Miami, because I needed to sharpen up my French."

"Why? What do you do?"

"I've been studying Fashion Merchandising at Miami International, but I always said I would work for one of the big French couture houses, so I need the language skills."

"So it's a sabbatical?"

"Exactly."

Grace plucked up the courage to get the second round of drinks in while Nina stepped outside for another cigarette.

"How old are you anyway?" she asked as she sat down again.

"Eighteen."

"You're such a baby! Oh god, I feel old now."

"Why, how old are you?"

"Twenty – but that's younger than Katja."

"Who?"

"Our other roomie - Katja."

"What's she like?"

"Ha! Least said, the better."

She said it with such a wicked smile that Grace felt a wave of anxiety.

"Meaning?"

"Meaning nothing. You'll find out."

Over the third round of drinks, Nina asked a lot of questions about Grace's parents and home, fascinated by the description of the Miss Mapp Bookshop and the cobbled streets of Rye. When Grace said her own half-timbered home was thought to date in parts to medieval times, she was wide-eyed,

"How old is that?"

"About 1400 – but that's just one small bit of it, the rest is more like 1780."

"You've got to be joking!"

"No really."

"You have a house that goes back over six hundred years?"

"Yes. But only in parts."

"Jeez. George would love to see that!"

"George?"

"My dad. I always call him George. He was only twenty-one when I was born – still at college – he says he couldn't get his head round being labelled dad back then."

"What's your mum called?"

"Maria . . . but she's dead."

"Oh I'm sorry."

"I know. Everyone always is."

Later, walking back arm in arm, they sang "*Et puis je fume*" over and over, giggling as they did so. But once back at the Chirol residence, Nina put a finger to her lips,

"And now we creep like mice. Like little tiny *souris*. We do not want Madame to hear us, OK?"

Grace nodded, stifling a laugh. Through the deserted salon they crept, the Eiffel Tower illuminated in gold against the velvet sky. The door to the third bedroom was closed and in darkness.

"Katja's probably in bed, whispered Nina. "But not here, I think. *Bon nuit ma petite*." And with those words, she kissed Grace full slap on the mouth before heading down the corridor to her own room.

Lying on her bed with the lamp on, Grace noticed the ceiling was spinning. Not a good sign. She needed water, so she crept out of her room and into the tiny kitchenette that the lodgers shared. The lino was cold underfoot and she was shivering in her cotton pyjamas, anxious not to disturb the other girls or, worse, Madame Chirol. Just as she was putting glass to mouth, she heard a noise behind her that made her jump, nearly sending the tumbler crashing to the ground. In the doorway stood a thin, black-haired girl in jeans and black T-shirt with tattoos climbing up both arms and lips pierced with rings.

"Who the hell are you?" She spoke in English but with an eastern European accent of some kind.

"Grace. I just moved in."

"Oh right."

"You're Katja?"

"Sure. How come you know that?"

"Nina told me."

"Right."

There was silence. Katja stared intently, unsmiling. Grace felt like a *souris* cornered by a *chat noir*.

"Well, goodnight then." Grace edged towards the door, clutching her glass carefully.

For a moment, it seemed Katja wouldn't move out of her way, then she turned sideways just enough to allow Grace to squeeze past, all the time fixing her with her dark gaze.

Back in her room, Grace climbed into bed. The ceiling was no longer spinning so noticeably, but her brief conversation with Katja had left her feeling unnerved. She wondered why the other girl had not once smiled. Yet thinking about it, she couldn't imagine Katja smiling at anyone.

◆ ◆ ◆

Isobel went to see Dani the day after she came back from Paris. Her best friend was also Grace's godmother and had gifted Grace a generous sum of money to help her through her gap year. Dani led her through to the kitchen where her ginger cat, Linden, was sunning himself in the September sunshine. Saskia was up at her studio.

"My happy space," said Isobel. Saskia had painted the kitchen in hot Mexican pinks and oranges and filled the antique dresser with brightly coloured majolica pottery that she'd collected over the years. On the table was a huge vase of dahlias and asters that she'd clipped from the garden that morning, while on one of the majolica plates was a fluffy lime cake that she'd baked the day before. Not for the first time, Isobel wished that she had a wife as good at home-making as Saskia.

"Coffee?"

"Lovely. I just wanted to say thank you for Grace's money. Very generous of you." Particularly as she and Robert were so stretched for cash.

"Well, when you don't have children of your

own, it's nice to have someone else's to spoil."

"Even so. Much appreciated."

"Cake?"

"Yes please. Looks amazing."

"A Saskia special."

"How is she?"

"Great thanks. She's progressed from rodents to birds." Saskia was learning the art of taxidermy, a new skill for her artistic palette. Isobel found it hard to imagine petite, pretty Saskia doing anything so gory.

"Doesn't she come home covered in blood?"

"Not at all. Do you end up covered with blood if you peel the skin from a chicken."

"No, but . . . ."

"Well then. It's the same principle."

Isobel envied Dani and Saskia their life of ease, living in the house in Rye that Dani had grown up in and which she had inherited aged twenty, with a substantial nest egg, when her parents died prematurely in a car crash. She had a successful career as a self-employed graphic designer, but had lived her whole adult life free of mortgages, debt or the demands of employers. Hard to imagine how that must feel.

"Is Grace excited?"

"Not sure. She seemed very quiet, to be honest." Surely she wasn't regretting the whole thing?

"It's a big step."

"It's an expensive one."

"Poor you. Money well spent hopefully."

"Bloody hope so."

"Well it sounds to me as though Grace has landed on her feet – with the apartment?"

Isobel hesitated, "The apartment's like the curate's egg – nice in parts. Nice if you're Madame Chirol."

"A great location by the sounds of it."

"It certainly has an air of privilege. Lots of embassies on the doorstep."

"And Madame Chirol?"

"Not warm by any means, but I bet she has some stories worth telling."

"Go on."

"She has a very regal air. Amazing poise. Must have been a knock-out back in the day."

"Sounds like the Queen."

"Much grander than the Queen."

"How old do you think she is?"

"Hard to say. Late seventies maybe."

"Did you meet the other girls?"

"Only one of them – Nina. American, but looked more South American."

"What do you mean? Dark and exotic?"

"That sort of thing, yes."

"Maybe she's from Cuba or somewhere?"

"Could be. Anyway, she seemed very lively and friendly. Hope the third girl is as nice."

"Great if she and Grace became friends."

"That would put my mind at rest."

"Are you worried? About Grace?"

She was sick with worry, but it sounded stupid to say so, "A bit. She looked so little and lost when I went."

"She'll soon settle in, Bel."

"Hope so."

"It's not as if she's miles away."

"I know. Keep telling myself that."

"What about you? How are you feeling?"

"Me?"

"Yes you. The fledgling has flown the nest. Must feel odd."

"I've barely had time to think about it. Will a year make any difference? It'll probably be over in a flash." Truth was she couldn't believe Grace had gone.

"You're right. She'll be back before we know it." Dani was smiling at her. She wouldn't be fooled for a moment.

"To be honest, I wish we could have called the whole thing off".

"Thought so."

"What am I going to do with myself?"

"You'll find lots to do."

"I'm going to miss her so much."

"I know you are. We all are." Dani walked round the table and bent down to give her a hug.

For a moment, she couldn't speak. Gripped the handle of the coffee mug hard.

"Don't cry, Bel."

"Saying good-bye was far worse than I would have thought."

"Can't say I'm surprised. You've always been so close."

"It's more than that, I think."

"What then?"

"Such a feeling of emptiness and loss."

"She'll soon be back, honey. No need to grieve."

"I'm not just talking about Grace."

"Go on."

"Maybe I am grieving. Sparked by a conversation we had last night."

"Tell me."

"About me. My old job. Who I was back then."

"And?"

"I think it's not just that I'm going to miss Grace, but Grace leaving home has made me miss *me*. Miss who I was. Does that make sense?"

"Possibly. But I think your current incarnation is pretty fab."

Isobel smiled, "It's ridiculous I know. Whoever would have thought I would turn into such a cliché?"

"You mean Empty Nest Syndrome? Perimenopause? Bored wife? Midlife crisis?"

"You always say the nicest things."

"Give it time, Bel. You might feel a chapter is ending, but that can only mean one thing: another is about to begin."

OCTOBER

It had been a long time since Isobel had walked through the Tuileries, with its avenues of perfectly spaced lime trees and manicured gravel paths. Robert was walking arm-in-arm with Grace, while she dawdled alongside, enjoying the burnished gold of the trees against the blue of the sky. Snatches of conversation were blown like paper above the distant growl of traffic from the Rue de Rivoli.

"Are you sure you're not lonely?"

"I'm fine, Dad. Which isn't to say I don't miss you both of course."

"But you've got the other girls to talk to . . . "

"Nina, yes."

"You haven't told us much about Katja."

"Not much to tell. She isn't exactly friendly."

"Why not?"

"No idea. It's not a question I plan on asking her either."

Just as Isobel was about to ask what she meant by that, Grace spotted something ahead, "Look! Isn't that lovely?"

Isobel had forgotten about the Tuileries'

carousel until that moment, but seeing it afresh, she marvelled at how magical it seemed, incongruous against the formality of the park.

"Do you want a ride?"

"Only if you come too!"

Clearly, she was expecting Isobel to refuse.

"Come on then. How about you, Robert? Fancy the ostrich?"

He smiled and shook his head. Isobel and Grace chose twin horses, carved and painted in the Belle Époque style. As the carousel began to move, they giggled like six year-olds.

Out of the corner of her eye, she noticed someone else had stopped to watch: a figure now waving at Grace.

"Nina!" shouted Grace as she swept past – and up – and down. Nina was laughing, as was the tall man at her side. She saw Robert walking over to introduce himself. Why had she suggested this stupid ride? A middle-aged woman acting the fool. She began to count down the minutes until the music would stop. Finally, her mount juddered to a halt.

"Hi, Mrs Peters. Grace told me you were all coming over for the weekend. Looks like you're having fun."

"Nice to see you again, Nina. Isn't it a beautiful day?"

The man beside her held out his hand, "I'm George. Nina's father. Pleased to meet you, Mrs Peters."

He could have been straight from Hollywood Central Casting. Tall: tick. Dark: tick. Handsome: tick. Younger than she had imagined. Definitely not her type.

"Lovely to meet you too, George. I'm Isobel – none of this Mrs Peters stuff, please".

She knew very little about Nina's father other than he lived in Miami. His wife, she knew, was dead.

"Dad flew over on Thursday, but this is the first time he could fit me into his hectic schedule."

Nina said this with a big smile, but George looked flustered.

"Don't make me feel any worse than I do, baby. The meetings are done and I'm all yours now!"

"When do you fly back?" asked Robert.

"Tuesday."

"A long way for such a short time."

"Yes, but I had business in Amsterdam. Only a short hop from there to here. How about you?"

"We caught the Eurostar yesterday evening," said Isobel. "We go back Monday. Also a quick visit, but we can't leave the shop too long."

"And where are you off to now?"

"The Musée de l'Orangerie – to see the Water Lilies. And then for lunch."

George turned to his daughter, "Didn't you want to do the lilies too, Nina?"

Isobel smiled, "Do join us if you like." How

very American to invite himself along.

It seemed as if Nina read her mind. "Not today. We'll go next time you're over. I thought we would head for the Rodin."

Isobel almost exhaled a sigh of relief. Robert, however, was deaf to the sigh, "Well if you change your mind, you're very welcome. Or if not, meet us later for lunch – or dinner?"

George smiled, "How about a drink later? Which hotel are you staying in?"

"I don't think you'd know it", said Isobel, for the first time taking in the expensive elegance of George's coat. "Where are you?"

"Just over there", a nod of the head towards the traffic. "Le Papillon. Know it?"

Yes, she knew it. Without even meeting Robert's eyes, Isobel knew what he was thinking. Too bloody expensive there for a round of drinks for five people.

"It's quite a place. Dali furniture and all that," Nina laughed. "He literally never stays anywhere else. You should see the room where we meet for breakfast – might as well be in Versailles."

By the look on Grace's face, Isobel and Robert knew they were beaten. It was agreed they would all meet in the bar at seven that evening. As they said their good-byes and walked away, Robert muttered under his breath, "If he offers to pick up the bill, say nothing. One round of drinks will cost a first-edition Ian McEwan, I reckon".

◆ ◆ ◆

Better make that two first-editions, thought Isobel, when they walked into the bar that evening to find George and Nina waiting with a magnum of champagne on ice.

George leapt up to greet them, "How are you? Enjoy the Monet?"

While waiters moved tables and leather club chairs around to accommodate the group, Isobel took in the wood-panelled splendour of the bar.

"Look at the ceiling, mum!" said Grace.

Isobel looked up to see clouds at sunset with the last remnant of golden light peeping through. It must be nearly twenty years since she was last in this bar, looking up at the *trompe l'oeil* ceiling with a champagne flute in her hand.

George invited Isobel to sit next to him. Once everyone had a glass of champagne in hand, he raised his glass, "To new friends!"

Grace and Nina grinned as they looked at each other, raising their glasses in a theatrical way. Before long, the group had fallen naturally into two halves: Robert, Grace and Nina discussing the challenges of life with Madame Chirol; George and Isobel swapping polite chit-chat about previous visits to Paris.

"Have you been here before?" asked George.

"You mean, *here* – Le Papillon? Actually yes. I

stayed here a few times when I was still working – before Grace was born."

"What were you doing?"

"PA. My boss owned a lot of property and I helped run the portfolio. It included a lovely apartment in the Opéra quarter."

"Miss it?"

"Work – or Paris?"

"Either. Both."

"To be honest, I didn't think I did. But Grace moving here seems to have opened up a time machine. Looking up at the ceiling just now, I couldn't quite believe where the years have gone."

George looked over at Nina for a moment, "No, what on earth happened?"

There was a sadness in his voice that disarmed her, but then he turned back to her with a smile. "I'm so glad Nina has Grace now. I've been anxious she would find it too lonely here."

"We share the same worries."

"It's what parents do, I guess."

"What do *you* do? You mentioned you flew over from Amsterdam earlier."

"Architect. I have a client with multiple properties."

"Goodness – what a coincidence – hope it isn't my old boss."

George laughed. "Unlikely. He's only twenty-eight. Tech billionaire."

"Why's he buying in Amsterdam?"

"Cool city. And he likes the cannabis culture of course."

"Ah. Should've thought of that."

"Have you ever been to Amsterdam?"

"Not since I was a child. Certainly not to enjoy a legal high."

"Did you ever smoke?"

Isobel looked at him with such astonishment, he laughed out loud.

"Sorry, I wasn't thinking. Not the place for that sort of conversation."

"What's the joke?" asked Robert.

Three pairs of eyes swivelled towards them.

"Nothing." said Isobel. "George was just telling me about his job."

George smiled and turned to Grace. Isobel took her cue and began chatting to Nina, dimly aware she was probably repeating the exact same questions Robert had already asked. Before long, she was floating on a champagne cloud of happiness, barely noticing Robert's pink face or Grace's slightly slurred speech. It occurred to her that none of them had eaten much since lunch-time. When George called the waiter over to order another bottle, her sensible side kicked in, "Thanks, but we really should be going. Shall we ask for the bill?"

"Absolutely not", said George. "It's on my tab. My pleasure."

Robert protested, but not too heartily. Ian

McEwan was safe for now.

As they stood up to say their good-byes, George held her hand for a moment, "I really hope we meet again, Isobel. I'll be visiting again before Christmas."

"Yes. Me too."

"I'll ask Nina to make sure we're all connected."

"Great. And thank you again."

"No problem at all. As I said, the pleasure was all mine."

As they stepped out into the brisk autumn night, Isobel looped arms with Grace, "George is nice isn't he?"

"Very. Nina thinks the world of him. I can see why."

She could see why too.

The next morning, she woke to the sound of bells. It took her a moment to filter the fact these were not the bells of St Mary's, Rye, but those of Sacré-Cœur. This was the same inexpensive hotel, high on the hill of Montmartre, that she and Robert had stayed in on their first visit to Paris together over twenty years ago. Robert had booked it out of nostalgia and affection, but Isobel had complained it was too far out, a Metro ride away from Grace as opposed to short walk.

But deep down she had to admit it was far more charming than the three-star place she'd stayed in off the Champs-Élysées when she first brought Grace to Paris.

She stood at the window staring down at the rooftops and the cobbled streets below. The street lights were still on, but the first grey, morning light was beginning to filter through the outline of the trees below. Incredibly, it was the exact same view that she remembered from her pre-married, pre-motherhood life. She was for a moment a time-traveller soaring back over the decades, melding briefly her former self with her present one. The sensation made her want to cry.

"Bel?" Robert had stirred and was now blinking at her, groping automatically for his glasses.

"Mmmmmm . . ."

"Come back to bed. You must be cold standing there. What time is it anyway?"

"Not sure. About seven I think. They've been ringing the bells for morning Mass."

She climbed back into bed.

"Your feet are freezing. How long have you been standing there?"

"Not sure. Ten minutes?"

"Well snuggle up and get warm. Here put your feet between mine."

Allowing herself to be enveloped by Robert's arms, she waited for the inevitable overtures.

It wasn't possible for them to stay in a hotel without sex being part of the package, along with breakfasts that were double the quantity of anything they ate at home and miniature cartons of artificial milk with which to make tea. Twenty years' ago, she and Robert would have been far more energetic and adventurous in their sexual christening of any hotel room, but this slow, thoughtful, generous way of making love also had its plus points.

Lying in his arms afterwards, her thoughts turned to George. She replayed moments of the conversation, dwelling on how handsome he was and remembering with pin-pricks of excitement how he had held her hand as they said good-bye. Did it mean anything? Did he like her? She hadn't had a crush for years, not even on an actor or a rock star. To have a crush was life-affirming. Her brain was still capable of talking to her pussy.

"What are you thinking about, Bel?"

"What?"

"You seem very deep in thought. What is it?"

"Goodness. Nothing. Just thinking about how nice it is that Grace has Nina."

"Yes. Lucky they have each other, I think."

"Very."

"And George?"

"George?"

"What did you think of him?"

"Oh George. I thought he was very nice."

"Is that all?"

"What do you mean, 'all'?"

"Well you were talking together a long time. And laughing. I thought you might have gleaned more than 'nice'."

"What exactly do you mean?" She rolled out of his arms and half sat, looking down at him. She felt a devil-rush of irritation.

"I don't 'mean' anything. It was a simple enough question."

"What was?"

"What you thought of George . . . oh, for God's sake, forget it."

"Why are you starting an argument with me?"

"I'm not. It was just a question, Bel."

"But you're implying something it seems."

"No, I'm not. Although frankly . . ."

"What?"

"Your over-reaction to a perfectly simple question might give me cause for concern."

"'Cause for concern'! What are you, my head-master? My psychiatrist? Get over yourself, Robert!"

"Isobel!"

"What do I think about George? I'll tell you what I think: he's handsome, funny, smart, sexy and has the best dress sense of any man I've met ever. He also smells glorious. I would go to bed with him in a heart-beat. At the snap of his fingers. Happy now?"

Silence.

"I said 'happy?' Is that what you wanted to hear?"

Still silence.

"Well?"

"I had no idea that 'nice' could cover so much."

He was the prince of the under-statement. She looked at him enraged, but his mouth was twitching and the absurdity of the whole situation overcame her. She started to laugh.

"Come here, lovely wife." He stretched out his right arm so she could lie on his chest and feel the soothing up and down of his breathing.

"Sorry, Bel."

"Me too."

"I was being an idiot. Schoolboy jealousy."

"Very flattering."

"The trouble is he is all those things. He does indeed smell glorious. I would go to bed with him myself at the snap of a finger."

"Idiot."

He rolled towards her so they were facing, "Only annoyingly, I am in love with my wife."

"More fool you."

"Quite."

"Love me back?"

"Not one bit." She smiled and he smiled back.

"Hungry?"

"Very."

"Come on then, you make the tea and I'll take a shower."

"Other way round?"

"You strike a hard bargain, Bel, but I'll agree on one condition."

"What?"

"Sex at the click of my fingers."

"In your dreams!"

"Well, it will be from now on."

Madame Chirol had asked Isobel and Robert to tea on Sunday afternoon, saying she would like to meet Grace's father while they were over. Antoinette was again waiting at the door, leading them through to the salon where Grace was sitting next to Madame Chirol on the velvet couch. To Isobel's annoyance, Robert was clearly a hit with the old lady from the start, complimenting her on the splendour of the tapestry behind her, "Not Aubusson but Savonnerie surely, Madame?"

"It is Savonnerie, Monsieur Peters. How clever of you to observe that."

"So it's seventeenth century?"

"Indeed. Made originally for Louis XIV in about 1670 we believe, but acquired by one of my husband's ancestors about two hundred years later."

Robert turned to Grace, "Whoever made this would have been a lot younger than you."

"Really?"

"Yes. Savonnerie famously apprenticed orphans to make tapestries, some as young as ten years old."

"That's shocking."

"Not at all, *ma petite*", said Madame Chirol. "It was a great honour to work for Savonnerie. After all, only royalty was allowed to buy a Savonnerie carpet. Such a skill offered those children a route out of poverty."

When Madame Chirol smiled, it was possible to see how great a beauty she must have been. Isobel wished she knew her better, well enough to ask about her husband, her children, the life she had once led. How old would she have been in the Second World War? Little more than a child presumably. What kind of life had she led in occupied France?

The drift of her thoughts was cut short by the bang of the front door. All heads swivelled towards a black-haired, scowling young woman standing in the salon doorway, clearly annoyed to find the way to her room impeded by visitors. Isobel saw Grace turn pink and look down at the floor rather than meet the intruder's eyes. Only the unflappable Madame Chirol seemed at ease.

"Katja. How nice to see you. These are Grace's parents. Would you like to join us?"

If looks could kill, Madame Chirol would have been blasted into little pieces.

"No? Well do at least shake hands and say

hello on your way through."

It was not a request, but a command. Isobel and Robert stood awkwardly, as Katja stepped forward, stretching out a tattooed arm to each of them in turn with a muttered, "Hi." No eye contact was made. Then she disappeared behind the double doors to the sanctuary of her own room. She and Grace had never once acknowledged each other during the whole uncomfortable scene.

"More tea?" said Madame Chirol. "Grace do pass the pastries round, *s'il vous plaît*."

Robert made a sterling effort to reignite the conversation, this time drawing Madame Chirol out on the election of President Hollande earlier that year. She was not a fan, "But so funny to see him stand in the rain during his inauguration, non? 'Wet through' as you British say! Have you ever seen the films of Monsieur Hulot? That is who we have as our president it seems!"

As one of Robert's favourite films was *'Les Vacances de Monsieur Hulot'*, he and Madame Chirol clearly had even more in common than Isobel had anticipated. Indeed, Madame Chirol was soon rocking with delight at Robert's well remembered, favourite scenes, "Ah yes! *Le tennis*. What a genius that man was!"

Grace was notably quiet. Now that Isobel had seen Katja for herself, she could see why her daughter had wanted to avoid the subject yesterday. But what was puzzling her most was why on earth Madame Chirol would give house room to a girl like that?

◆ ◆ ◆

On Mondays, Miss Mapp was closed. On Tuesdays, Isobel covered for Robert, allowing him time to restock the second-hand books' section by trawling charity shops and house clearances. She enjoyed this time, sitting in Robert's captain's chair with his father's old mahogany desk set out neatly with till, card machine, sales ledger and pens, but she was also irritated by the amount of cosseting the shop required. Why couldn't her husband take the easy path and concentrate solely on the new titles from which they had a chance of making some money, rather than pursuing his obsession with vintage Penguins and rare Folio editions? The fact was that all the tourists to Rye wanted to buy were Mapp and Lucia books or anything by Henry James. That was one advantage of living in a small town with two big literary stars. It seemed such a waste of time bothering with second-hand stock that sold for tiny amounts of money. At least a brand new edition of Benson or James had a chance of selling.

She hadn't resented giving up her job for Grace, but now her daughter was eighteen, it didn't feel as though she'd achieved much and it wasn't as if her marriage had turned out brilliantly either. When she and Robert first met, they were both going places in their different ways – she as an executive PA and he working in an antiquarian book-seller's just off Berkeley Square. Now they were diminished in different ways. She had thought they would have two or three children, but every pregnancy after Grace had ended in miscarriage. As for Robert, having his own bookshop hadn't proved as easy or profitable as he had hoped. Mother of one wasn't much of an achievement, but neither was proprietor of a failing bookshop.

There were always a few displays on the desk, which right now included Hallowe'en sticker books, colouring books and just about anything with witches on the cover. The window was festooned with spiders' webs, enormous black papier-mâché spiders, carved pumpkin heads and a primitive silhouette of a witch on a broom. Isobel had made the spiders and witch with Grace years ago, storing them with the Christmas decorations until they were needed again, but each year she and Grace had a pumpkin-carving day on the last Sunday of September. This was the first time her daughter had missed it.

Robert had stocked the windows with his personal selection of spine-chilling literature, including '*The Castle of Crossed Destinies*' by Italo

Calvino and '*Shirker*' by Chad Taylor. Inside the shop was a Hallowe'en section, which included not just horror books, but masks, slime and the same fake spiders' webs used in the window.

She'd made a brisk trade that Tuesday morning, thanks in part to the ghost walks around the town that were especially popular at this time of year. It was also one of the last days of the season for people to see around Lamb House before it closed for the winter. There were a few people browsing when she heard the bell ring and looked up to see Dani.

She stood up to give her friend a hug, "How's it going?"

"Good thanks. How about you?"

"All fine. Back to normality as you can see."

"How was Paris? Grace OK?"

"Yes, I think so."

"Think so?"

"Thinner."

"Ah."

"But she seemed happy enough."

"Any friends?"

"Only the one I met before – Nina – but it's early days."

"So what did you do?"

"A few of the touristy things – walked through the Tuileries, went to see the Monet water lilies in the Orangery . . . "

"Sounds fabulous. Lucky you!"

Isobel smiled, "And we went to a very swanky

hotel and drank champagne."

"*Really*? Goodness, I wouldn't have thought that was a Robert sort of thing to do."

"It isn't, but he didn't get much choice."

Just as she was about to tell Dani all about Nina and George, she realised a customer was hovering by the desk, a grey-haired lady in tweeds with a rather nervous manner.

"I'm so sorry – can I help you?"

"I'm looking for a book - by someone called James. A friend recommended it."

"Henry James?"

"No. It's recent."

"And you can't remember its title?"

"No." For some reason, Isobel felt this was not the truth.

"What's it about?"

Faded blue eyes darted anxiously around the shop, "I'd rather not say."

Isobel noticed that Dani had turned away and was now studying the cover of a Stephen King novel in a concentrated way, avoiding eye contact.

Of course.

"I think this might be it", said Isobel, leading the customer to the romantic section. *Romantic*? "Fifty Shades of Grey. By E.L James."

The customer was looking rather flushed, but took the copy gratefully. "Ah yes. I think that's what she meant. It's for a friend of mine – I'm visiting her in hospital."

Of course she was.

Once she'd left, with book discreetly tucked into her canvas shopping bag, Isobel and Dani looked at each other, trying not to laugh. There were still a couple of customers browsing.

"I told Robert he should make a whole window display called 'The Other James'. We just need fifty tester pots of grey paint and some chipboard to make a backdrop."

"Genius idea. Why won't he?"

"He says he doesn't want to offend his regulars. But really I think he's scared of being mobbed by ladies of a certain age."

"Anyway, you were saying? Champagne? Hotel?"

Isobel looked down at her phone, "Look, it's nearly twelve-thirty. I'll put the Closed For Lunch up – then we can catch up over a bowl of soup."

"Lovely."

"Ten minutes?"

"Perfect."

As she warmed the parsnip soup over the Aga, she told Dani about the evening at Le Papillon; about the feelings it had awakened in her for her pre-marriage life; about George – "although he's really not my type" – about the way he had held her hand, just for that little bit longer than necessary.

Dani was direct as ever, "Do you fancy him?"

"No! Of course not."

"Why 'of course not'?"

"Well, it's ridiculous to even think that way. I'm forty-nine in March."

"So?"

"So . . . I think the moment has passed for fancying *anyone*."

"What rubbish. I think you're just scared."

"Scared?"

"Yes, scared. You say you don't fancy George – maybe you do and maybe you don't – but I think he's stirred something up in you that you would prefer to ignore."

"And what would that be?"

"The fact that you're forty-nine in March. That you feel time is running out. That you're withering on the vine."

"Thanks very much!"

Dani laughed, "I'm not serious. You're as lovely an English rose as ever you were. Saskia and I both think that, as does Robert judging by the way he still looks at you. As does George no doubt. But what matters is, do you think it?"

"I think you're being ridiculous. You've probably just caught Robert with his constipated look and mistaken it for lust. As for George, he probably has a beautiful, twenty-five-year old Latino back in Miami. Now let's have this soup, while you fill me in on all the local gossip. I have to be back in the shop in half an hour."

There was definitely something odd going on between Nina and Katja. Grace couldn't put her finger on it, but a few times she walked into the kitchen with the definite sense that she'd just stopped conversation between them. Not friendly, girlish chatter, but something dark and hostile.

It happened again when she got back from the Gare du Nord having seen her parents off. She could hear voices, urgent and low, as she walked down the corridor, but when she walked in, they stopped immediately.

"Hi Grace!" Nina was sitting at the small, laminated table, smiling as if everything were fine. Behind her, Katja lent against the sink, arms folded as always. She scowled fiercely in Grace's direction.

"Fancy a coffee? The kettle just boiled." Nina was clearly determined to act as if Katja wasn't there at all.

"Thanks. Anyone else?"

Nina shook her head. Katja carried on scowling. The atmosphere was heavy, as if a storm were about to break. She wished she hadn't taken up the offer to make herself a coffee. Saying good-bye to her mum and dad had been hard: the last thing she wanted was to come back to this tension.

"I'll leave you two to it," she picked up the mug, ready to retreat.

"No, stay," said Nina. "Please."

"I think Katja would prefer me to go." No denial. Just the same sullen silence.

"Well I'd prefer you to stay."

Behind Nina, Katja muttered something under her breath.

"I really would like to go to my own room. Feeling a bit tired."

"Poor you. I'll come and see you in a moment."

"Fine."

As she walked out, Katja spoke for the first time, "That's right. Piss off, English girl."

Before she could react, Nina sprang to her feet, her face close to Katja's, "Back off, bitch!"

"Nina! Please don't."

Smiling horribly, Katja echoed her words back, "Neeeeeeeena! Pleeeeease don't."

Nina gave Katja a shove, so hard that she smacked her head against one of the kitchen cupboards. It must have hurt, but Katja didn't react, just carried on smiling nastily at Nina, "Feel better now, girlfriend?"

Grace hovered in the doorway not knowing what to do, "You OK, Nina?" *Girlfriend*?

Nina nodded, but she looked far from OK.

With a contemptuous look in Nina's direction, Katja stalked out of the kitchen. As she passed Grace, she bumped her elbow hard, so that hot coffee went all down her shirt.

"Shit!"

Katja kept walking. The door banged behind her.

"Are you all right, Grace?" Nina rinsed a cloth under the cold tap and tried to mop the worse of it off.

"Not really. What was all that about?"

"Just Katja being Katja."

"Meaning?"

"She just loves to cause a scene."

"She succeeded all right."

"Did it scald you?"

"My hand mainly."

"Better hold it under the cold tap. I'll make you another coffee."

"Don't worry. I don't fancy it now to be honest."

"I'll rinse your shirt for you."

"It wasn't your fault."

"It sort of was. I should have guessed she would do something like that."

"Why does she hate me so much?" She expected Nina to deny it.

"Probably because you're normal and happy."

"Am I?"

"Your parents love you. You love them. Those are all reasons for Katja to dislike you."

"What's her situation then?"

"I don't know all of it, but it's not like that." Was Nina standing up for her? She couldn't shake off that final 'Girlfriend'.

"Does she dislike you too?"

"We don't look like friends, do we?"

She wasn't sure how to answer that. "It's not the same. She doesn't seem as hostile to you as she does to me."

"Simple explanation for that."

"Which is?"

"I'm not normal. I'm not happy. And my mum is dead."

Soon after returning from Paris, Isobel made the short drive to check up on her parents. Pam and Jack had been the back-bone of village life since retiring there twenty years ago to be near Isobel and Grace, "But we won't be on your door-step, dear."

Jack had served on the Parish Council, the Village Hall Committee and as a volunteer for the community hospital. Pam had busied herself with organising the flower-arranging rota at St Laurence, taking on the role of Treasurer at the W.I. and being a Read Aloud volunteer at the local primary school. If ever funds were needed for church roof repairs, village green upkeep, the community shop or any other local need, Jack and Pam could be relied upon to dig deep to help out. They were the sort of people that other people describe as "marvellous."

Until a few years ago, they had been

physically well for their ages, but now Jack's health was failing in an indeterminate sort of way. He was often tired, spent whole half-days in bed, was unsteady on his feet and seemed to be losing weight at an alarming rate. However, the only concession he had accepted – angrily at first – was the use of a stick. Pam had now given up many of her activities in order to single-handedly look after her ailing husband. But at seventy-nine herself, it was obvious that this was taking a toll on her own health. All offers of professional help were stubbornly refused. Isobel, an only child herself, had long become used to their mantra of "We're fine, dear. Don't worry about us." The problem was that it was clear to everyone who knew them they were not fine. Worry was becoming the air she breathed.

As always, she tapped on the back door of the bungalow and walked into the kitchen. Her mother had her back to her and was emptying bottles of milk into the sink.

"Hello, Mum!" she said loudly, Pam's hearing not being very acute. "Oh dear, have those gone off?"

"Hello, dear. How are you? No it came this morning."

"Why are you throwing it away then?"

"Well I always do."

Isobel felt herself blind-sided by her mother's bewildering logic.

"Sorry?"

"I don't want to hurt his feelings, you see."

"Whose?"

Pam looked at her as if she were being stupid, "Paul's. The milkman."

"Sorry Mum, I still don't understand."

Pam sighed, "I buy milk at the community shop, so that I can give them a little bit of business, particularly now you *insisted* on taking over the usual shopping." This was said, Isobel noted, not with gratitude, but irritation. "But I don't want to hurt Paul's feelings by cancelling his delivery, so I buy milk from him too and throw it away."

"How long have you been doing that?"

"Since you asked the computer to do our shopping."

"Oh."

"Anyway, it's all done now, so if you could just put these on the front porch in the crate that would be a great help. I'll put the kettle on and you can tell me all about Grace."

Best be patient. Do what she was told.

When she came back into the kitchen, she smiled brightly, "So how much are you paying Paul each month, mum? For milk you don't use?"

Pam looked shifty, "Not much, dear. Not sure exactly."

This was a bare-faced lie. If you took Pam's battered, brown purse from her hand-bag, she would be able to tell you what was in it down to the last penny. But Isobel knew which battles were worth fighting and which ones to show the white flag on. The problem of Paul the milkman would have to go on hold.

Pam had set the tray out for three and Isobel carried it into her parent's cosily chintzy sitting-room.

"Where's Dad?"

"Resting, dear. I'll go and tell him that you're here."

It was 11am in the morning. Usually she came in the afternoon, a natural time to find her father napping post-lunch. This mid-morning rest was a new development.

"I'll go if you like."

"No, dear, I'll do it." It was a tone that brooked no argument.

She could hear murmuring down the passage-way, a complaining tone from him overlaid with a shrill insistence from her mother.

Pam came back in, "He's just coming, dear. He was about to get up anyway."

It had only been a week since she saw her father last, but she still felt a shock when he shuffled into the room. Once so tall and broad, he looked shrunken and grey. When she rose to give him a kiss, she could feel his bony arms through his jumper. His hair smelled unwashed. A new worry to add to all the others.

While she told them about Grace and Nina over Pam's anaemically milky tea, she tried to sound upbeat and cheerful. But deep down, she was dismayed by how quickly things were heading downhill. Her mum had always been house-proud, but now everything looked dirty, a thin layer of grime over surfaces, ornaments and paintwork. It was obvious to Isobel she wasn't coping. It was all getting too much for her. Did her father ever have a bath? She didn't see how he could get in or out of one in his current, fragile state. No doubt her mother gave him what she would call "a good wash down", but how long could that go on for?

The moment Jack finished his tea, he announced he was going back to bed. Pam looked mortified, "Must you, dear? Isobel's only just got here."

"Well we didn't know she was coming, did we? Just turned up like a bad penny."

"Jack!"

Isobel was shocked by her father's rudeness.

"I don't usually ring before I come over, Dad."

"No you don't. Well maybe you should. Can't be at your beck and call."

And with that, he shuffled out the room, stick in hand.

The two women looked at each other. "What on earth's wrong with him, Mum?"

"Don't take any notice, dear. He just doesn't feel well."

"Then we need to get him to see a doctor."

"He doesn't want to see a doctor. There's no need."

She felt the urge to shout, but managed to stay calm, "That doesn't make sense – and you know it. If he feels ill, he should see a doctor."

"He can't face it."

"Face what?"

"Sitting around a waiting-room. It makes him so tired."

"He's tired now."

"Yes, but here he can lie on the bed."

Again she felt herself slipping down the black hole of Pam's illogicality. "Mum, please, I'm worried about him. And you. You need some help with this."

Pam's tone was sharp, "No we don't. We're managing just fine, thank you."

"A cleaner at least?"

"I've never had a cleaner in my life."

"I know, Mum. But maybe now would be the time."

"Some Nosey Parker looking in my drawers and cupboards? No thank you."

"Then let me come and clean for you."

"There's no need. You've quite enough on your plate with Robert and Grace and the shop."

"No Grace now, Mum."

"Well even so. I wouldn't feel right about it."

"Then help with Dad – someone to help give him a bath."

"He's always been a very clean man."

Was. Not now.

She took a deep breath, "I think we should at

least talk about what's going to happen – in the future."

"None of us have a crystal ball."

"You know what I mean, Mum."

"Do I?"

"Yes. What are we going to do when . . . when Dad can no longer be here. When you can no longer cope?"

"You're father's not going anywhere, Isobel. This is his home and this is where he stays."

"And you?"

"What do you mean? What about me?"

"What happens if something happens to you?"

"Absolutely nothing is going to happen to me, dear. Nothing at all."

Defeated again. Her shoulders ached. It was all a waste of breath. She sat back and let her mother ramble on about neighbours and friends - their children and grand-children - people she had never met and probably never would. Her parents ate lunch early, so after an hour, she popped her head round the bedroom door to say good-bye to her dad. He was flat on his back, eyes closed, his face a frozen mask. She whispered good-bye and his eyes opened, "Good-bye, Grace dear". She couldn't be bothered to correct him.

Walking out into the crisp autumn air, someone waved at her. A neighbour from across the street. She walked over, "Hello, Mrs Dawkins. How are you?"

"I'm fine, Mrs Peters, thank you. But I have to ask – because a few of us are wondering – what are you going to do?"

"Do?"

"About Pam and Jack."

Isobel was so taken aback, she couldn't think what to say.

Mrs Dawkins looked at her sternly, "They can't go on like this, you know. We're all very worried. You'll have to sort something out soon. It's killing your mother."

"I know but . . . ."

"But nothing. Your mother always says, 'Oh Isobel's very busy with her own life', but even so, they are your parents."

Was Mrs Dawkins telling her off? And how dare her mother say that when she visited at least once a week? The implication that she was too busy to care hurt her to the core.

"Believe me, Mrs Dawkins, I do share your concerns. But it's hard to help someone if they don't want you to help."

"They're proud, I know."

"They are."

"But you'll have to do something even so. Right now, they're an accident waiting to happen."

"Thank you, Mrs Dawkins. I will bear all of that in mind."

On the drive back to Rye, she seethed with fury, irritation and anxiety all rolled into one noxious cocktail. She played out each scene. Her mother pouring fresh milk down the drain. Her father's rudeness. Her mother's stubbornness. The dirtiness of the bungalow. Mrs Dawkins' interference. It had been an hour of intolerable awfulness. She wished she were Grace. She wished she were living in Paris a world away from all of this.

Grace was walking down the Boulevard Raspail towards the CCFS. She was clouded in homesickness, upset by Katja's hostility, ruffled by her parents' visit and suffused with the sadness of saying good-bye once more. Only Nina understood how hard she was finding the move to Paris, made more painful by the guilt she harboured at what it had cost Isobel and Robert to send her there given the precarious finances of Miss Mapp. When they came to visit, she had been determined to behave as if everything was fine.

But now there was something else troubling her, something even Nina could never understand. A cold autumn wind whipped around her face, sending her hair flying and making her wrap her coat tight as she walked, head bowed to keep the city grit from her eyes. Carried on the wind, a voice called her name –

then came the sound of running footsteps and Carlos was by her side.

"*Óla, Graça* !" This was Carlos's usual greeting. He had never heard the English equivalent of her name before, so translated it always into his native Portuguese. It was an irony that barely anyone attending the CCFS spoke French other than when forced to in class. In fact English seemed to be the language of choice among students, in part because of the dominance of the American fraternity and in part because most students had acquired at least a smattering of it from school. There were over a hundred different nationalities gathered under this one roof. Grace knew of only one other British student and he had made it clear he wasn't there to hang out with another Brit. She wasn't sorry about that. Hipsters were a national embarrassment so far as she was concerned. This one even wore a duffel coat.

"Hi Carlos. You OK?"

He grinned, "Not really. Bad head."

"Out on the lash again?"

"Lash? What is lash?"

"Sorry. I mean, were you at a bar last night?"

"Many, many bars!

He announced this with such a blend of pathos and pride that she couldn't help but laugh, forgetting her sadness for a moment. This made him laugh too, crinkling up the skin around his indigo blue eyes. She liked the fact he always seemed so exuberant and happy.

"You're what my granny would call a real tonic, Carlos."

"Granny? Ah *Vovó*?"

"If you say so!"

"But why you say 'tonic'? Gin-and-tonic?

That made her laugh again, "Yes you're a real gin-and-tonic."

Carlos was delighted to add this to his English vocabulary. "And you're my gin-and-tonic too, *Graça*."

Now they were walking through the door, surrounded by the morning hubbub of students greeting each other loudly in a kaleidoscope of languages. The Tower of Babel had a lot to answer for, thought Grace, as she and Carlos pushed through the crowded lobby. She realised he was trying to speak above the melee.

"Sorry, Carlos, what was that?"

"Will you come out tonight? So I can buy you the gin-and tonic?"

"Hadn't you better give it a rest? Sounds like you overdid it last night!"

"I recover well. Please, *Graça* – say you will come."

She had known for a while that Carlos liked her, but had tried to keep things simple and friendly. She wasn't looking for complications, particularly in the context of CCFS. She had a horror of people talking about her in class or of intimacies being shared on social media. Carlos seemed nice enough, but she wasn't about to lose her head.

"Is anyone else coming?"

He looked disappointed, "Am I not enough?"

People were moving towards their classes, "It's not that Carlos." She hated it when people looked hurt.

"Fine – one gin-and-tonic – but just friends OK?"

He smiled, "OK, *Graça*."

"Grace."

"OK, Gra-y-se."

She laughed at his effort, "Got to dash. Bye Carlos!"

"*Até logo, menina linda*!"

She had no idea what that meant, but it sounded like he meant it.

Tip-toeing through Madame Chirol's salon that evening, she remembered her first night in Paris when Nina had told her to creep like a little *souris*. The memory made her want to giggle. She was too wide awake to sleep, so was happy to see a light under Nina's door. She knocked as quietly as she could. As always, there was no light from Katja's room.

"Nina?"

No reply.

She gently pushed open the door to find Nina sitting up in bed with her laptop and headphones.

"Hi, Grace!"

Nina spoke loudly, disentangling her headphones from her hair as she beckoned her to sit on the bed. Grace put a finger to her lips.

"Oops, sorry. Didn't mean to shout. Had fun?"

"Yes. Very nice."

Grace had messaged earlier to explain she would be late as she was meeting Carlos for a drink. She knew her friend would worry about her if she came home later than usual.

"And?"

"And nothing."

Nina raised her eyebrows. "Truly. He bought us both a gin-and-tonic – long story – and then we cracked open a bottle of wine. He's nice. Funny. Smart. Good-looking."

"And?!?"

Grace laughed, "A peck on the cheek when we said good-bye. Nothing more exciting than that."

"Would you like something more exciting to happen?"

She wasn't sure how to answer. "Not with Carlos, no." She paused. "I'm just not sure that getting involved with a fellow student is a good idea."

"You are so sensible, for chrissake!"

"Boring more like."

"Far from that." Nina gave her a look that was

hard to read.

"Anyway, what have you been doing?"

"Skyping with George. He's back in Miami. Sends his love."

"That's nice of him. Send him mine too of course."

"Oh you'll see him soon enough."

"How come?"

"Apparently Amsterdam is going to be even more demanding of his time than he thought. Says it makes sense to come to Paris for weekends if he's over."

"What about his other projects?"

"He has a good team of people. They're used to him flying all over the place. He'll make it work."

"Nice for you."

"Very nice for me. Champagne all round!"

The memory of the evening in Le Papillon made them both laugh.

"How about your mum?"

"What about her?"

"Will she be coming over again soon?"

"Not sure. Why?"

"We could go out as a happy foursome." Grace felt her heart dive and her skin turn clammy.

"What is it? Are you ill?"

She shook her head miserably.

"I wasn't serious about setting them up – your dad's an absolute legend for one thing."

"I'm not sure that's how mum would describe him."

“Oh. Marital stuff?”

“Nothing we discuss. More a feeling I have.”

“Sorry. Didn’t mean to put my foot in it.”

“You didn’t.” She forced a smile, “Ignore me. There’s probably nothing wrong at all. Gin and wine just don’t mix.”

NOVEMBER

Miss Mapp closed early one Saturday in November. The town was already abuzz with anticipation.

"Can't believe it's Bonfire already", said Robert to Isobel. "Comes around with frightening speed."

"But lovely that Grace could come back for it."

"She wouldn't have missed it for the world, but God know what Nina will make of it. Her first taste of pagan England."

"It will certainly be something to write home about . . . or at the very least Instagram to death."

"Remember how appalled you were when we first experienced it for ourselves?"

Isobel smiled at the memory, "I thought we'd ended up in The Wicker Man. Dani thought my London squeamishness absolutely hilarious."

The shock of that first Bonfire was etched forever in her mind. In London, they'd gathered at the local park once a year for a firework display organised by the council. Families stood around chattering, children huddled close, a few 'oohs' and 'aahs' as the rockets and Catherine Wheels pierced the air with sound and light. Sparklers for the children old enough to grasp them; mothers anxiously hovering should they burn too close to small, gloved fingers. Then home for warm sausage rolls and a glass of red wine for the adults.

Neither of them had heard of Sussex Bonfire then, with its roots embedded not so much in Guy Fawkes and his gang, as eighteenth-century protest against authority and injustice. A time when civil disobedience was more likely to be tolerated on this one date each year, with Bonfire Boys blackening their faces to avoid identification and arrest. A time of mischief and mayhem.

That first Bonfire, Isobel had stood outside their house and seen the picturesque town transform from an Enid Blyton storybook into something dark, mysterious and magical.

"It's somewhere between a riot and Mardi Gras," Dani had said. "Or maybe a war zone would be more accurate."

Nothing could have prepared her for it: the hundreds of processing, elaborately costumed figures, many of them pushing terrifying, flaming barrels of tar down the road; others carrying huge, burning torches and crosses that had been soaked in petrol, which filled the air with sulphurous smoke and fire and singed throat and lungs. Then there was the diabolical noise: the thunder-clap of fire-crackers and the ear-splitting beat of drums; the cacophony of bagpipes and brass bands; the approving and thunderous roar of the crowd as effigies of current, political hate figures were carried to their 'deaths'. Onlookers were crammed three deep on the narrow pavements, at times perilously close to the leaping flames of torches and barrels. At the rear, a fine wooden boat was carried with pride to the Saltings where it was burned to ashes to the delight of the well-oiled crowd. There was nothing cosy or twee about Bonfire; it was a spectacle certainly, but one with a direct lineage to sacrifice and the burning of human flesh. Isobel had felt nothing but relief when it was over.

Robert of course had loved it all. "Must have its roots in the Celtic Fire Festival of Samain", he said. "Nothing to do with Guy Fawkes at all." He had not been so enthusiastic when he found Miss Mapp's windows smashed the next day. From then on, he was careful to board them up in advance of the annual madness.

Now, fifteen years later, they were old hands of Bonfire. Isobel loved it because it was part of the warp and weft of Grace's childhood. Bonfire in Sussex was not just one night in November, but an entire month of festival and fire. Local towns held the opportunity to join other bonfire spectacles, with Battle and Robertsbridge being particular favourites. Until they moved to Sussex, Isobel had hated the damp, darkening days of November, but now she felt re-energised by the ritual of Bonfire. Maybe they were all pagans at heart.

Grace was never going to miss out on Bonfire, so Robert and Isobel had made sure to book her Eurostar well in advance. The fact she was bringing Nina was a welcome surprise. At the back of her mind, Isobel wondered what George would have made of Bonfire. Her mind often drifted towards George these days.

"Penny for them, Bel?"

"What?"

"Your thoughts. You were miles away."

"Sorry. Just remembering past Bonfires."

"And?"

"Nothing. Just that."

"Oh."

An uncomfortable silence hovered over them. Since Paris, a miasma had begun to permeate home and shop. It was nothing she could put her finger on, but she was aware that she and Robert circled each other cautiously. She knew he was trying hard not to irritate her, but she was irritated by his efforts. Determined to give Grace and Nina a wonderful weekend, she was keeping conversation to safe and neutral parameters. It was probably as exhausting for him as it was for her, as if they were constantly rehearsing lines without actually saying anything.

She was aware of him looking at her.

"Know what I think of when I think of Bonfire, Bel?"

She was determined to be pleasant, "No, What?"

"Your face by torchlight. Entranced. Beautiful."

"Robert . . . ."

"I know it's not what you want to hear. Not from me at any rate."

"Compliments are always welcome."

"Depends who's giving them."

"What's that supposed to mean?" A flash of anger. A fire-cracker about to explode.

"I'm just telling you how I feel."

"Then why does it sound like a criticism?"

He sighed, a hand pushing his hair back distractedly. "I can't say anything right, can I?"

There was no answer to that.

"I can't even tell my wife she's beautiful it seems."

"Not right now."

"Not now. Not ever."

If she said nothing, he would surely change the subject. It worked.

He stood up, "Where are they anyway?"

"Grace wanted to show Nina the town before the crowds arrive. I think they were walking towards the Church."

"Ok. I'll walk up and meet them."

"Robert . . . ."

"What?"

" . . . . Nothing. It doesn't matter."

"This is Harry Potter England", said Nina. "I can't believe what I'm looking at – it's absolutely amazing."

Grace smiled, "Like it?"

"Like it! You bet!"

They were standing on St Mary's Church tower, looking over the rooftops of Rye, Grace pointing out her own house among the red tiled roofs. Behind them was the view to the estuary and beyond that the sea.

"Worth the climb?"

Nina laughed, "Definitely worth that – although I thought you were joking when I saw those ladders."

"Dad says it's amazing Health and Safety haven't banned it yet."

"How old did you say it was?"

"About nine hundred years."

"No way!"

Grace nodded, feeling a surge of pride for the church and the quiet little town where she grew up.

"What's the name of the river?"

"That's the Rother, but you can actually see three rivers from up here – look, that's the Brede – and that's the Tillingham."

"What's all this Cinque Port stuff we keep seeing?"

"Oh leave that to Dad – he'll love filling you in on all the history later."

A cold wind whipped round their hair, "Shall we go down now? Seen enough?"

"It's certainly a bit on the fresh side. Anyway, hadn't we go back and see your parents? They must be excited to have you home."

"Sure." It didn't come out with much enthusiasm.

"What is it?"

"I just wish . . . ."

"What?"

"Oh, you know." How to find the words? "I wish things felt normal. Between Mum and Dad."

"They don't?"

Grace shook her head, "I can't put my finger on it, but it's not how I thought coming home would be. How I hoped it would be."

"Your parents seem fine to me."

"But not to me."

Nina shivered in the wind, "I still think we should go back."

"Come on then. Just go carefully – getting down is even worse than getting up!"

That evening, the four of them headed for Grace's favourite bonfire night spot along Tower Street. They could hear the procession long before they could see it.

"What's that smell?" said Nina, her voice

tinged with alarm.

"You're about to find out," said Grace.

A moment later, she saw her friend's face go from utter disbelief to child-like wonder to naked amazement. It didn't matter how much anyone tried to explain what Bonfire is, it was only by experiencing it that a newcomer could understand. It's a time machine, her father had once said, transporting us to the dragon's breath of pre-history. What Grace most loved was the feeling all her senses had been turned to max. It wasn't possible to be an onlooker at Bonfire; everyone was part of the ritual just by being there. The one thing Bonfire wouldn't let her do was dwell on the future. It freed her mind.

"Are you OK?" mouthed Isobel to Nina, who was wide-eyed at the pearly king and queen now processing past, followed by what appeared to be a troupe of Vikings and behind them, a gaggle of skeletons in black cloaks and feathered hats.

Nina said something back but she couldn't hear.

"What did she say?"

Grace laughed, "She says, this is the most ripshit bonkers thing she's ever seen."

About a week after Grace and Nina returned to Paris, Isobel announced that she was popping over to see how everything was going.

"But why?" asked Robert. "She's only just been home and we were there less than a month ago."

Isobel had prepared the ground for this particular conversation, "She looks a bit thin, Robert. Just want to make sure she's as OK as she says she is."

"Thin? You mean thinner?"

"Well no doubt you didn't notice . . ."

"I didn't say I hadn't noticed."

"So had you?"

Their eyes met in stony silence.

"Thought not." Point scored.

"When you say 'thinner', enough for you to be concerned?"

"Yes."

"What exactly are you saying, Bel?"

"What do you mean?"

"Are you saying you think our daughter has an eating disorder?"

"No of course not."

"Of course not? But you're going to drop everything and rush to Paris on the grounds that she may – *may* - have lost a couple of pounds. You're not really making sense."

"The fact you don't notice anything about your own daughter is not my fault." Another point.

He sighed, taking off his reading specs to rub his eyes, "Can we actually afford all these

Eurostars – Grace coming back, you going there – and which hotel are you planning to stay in? It's not like Miss Mapp's booming at the moment."

Spiteful she bit back, "Typical to put money ahead of your daughter's well-being."

Really she had no idea where the money would come from; she'd filed another credit card application online that morning.

Robert could be accused of many things, but miserliness was not one of them. He stared her right in the eye and spoke very quietly, "Fuck off, Bel."

As she slammed the door with meaning behind her, she couldn't really tell whether that was a point to her or to him.

When she told Grace she was coming over for a long weekend, her daughter sounded even less enthusiastic about the idea than Robert.

"Any reason in particular, mum?"

"No, just to see you, sweetie."

"Well you did just see me – last weekend?"

"I know, but we didn't get much mum-and-Grace time with everything going on."

The briefest of pauses.

"The thing is I'm pretty busy right now with the course and everything."

"Not at the weekend, surely?"

"We do have homework, you know, and I'm pretty far behind with French compared with everyone else."

"Honestly, Grace, I won't get in your way. You can work in the afternoons and I'll just take you out for a couple of nice dinners. Perhaps Nina would like to come too?"

"No." Another pause. "Nina will be with her dad."

"Is George planning another visit too?"

She tried to keep her tone as neutral as she possibly could. The fact is she knew George was visiting that particular weekend, because she'd heard Nina telling Grace when they were getting ready to go out to Bonfire. Over the last week, she'd thought of very little else.

"Apparently he is", said Grace. "And now you are too. So much for my gap year!"

"What's that supposed to mean?"

She was more shocked by Grace's hostility than by Robert telling her to fuck off.

"Mum, you can't keep micro-managing me: the whole idea of a year away is that it *is* a year away."

"Are you telling me I can't come to Paris?" Isobel couldn't keep the edge of anger and resentment from her tone. How dare Grace act like this?

"No, of course not. I can't stop you going anywhere can I?"

She played the hurt card, "I thought you'd

be pleased to see me." She was turning into her mother, Passive Aggressive Pam.

Grace was silent. Intractable.

She tried again, "Look, you're right. I shouldn't have assumed you'd be thrilled to see me, but it will be the last time for a while and we could even do a bit of Christmas shopping together. What do you think?"

Grace's tone was flat, "OK Mum, but I really will have to do some work as well."

For a moment, Isobel thought about suggesting the four of them had dinner, but something told her this would not go down well. Did Grace already suspect there was an ulterior motive at foot? Impossible.

Later that day, in a tone she tried to keep as unprovocative as possible, she told Robert everything was settled with Grace and she would catch the Eurostar that Friday afternoon.

"So was she pleased?" he asked.

"She was absolutely delighted."

Grace came to the hotel to meet her, rather than inviting her to the apartment. They hugged, but for Isobel it was like hugging a board. Clearly, Grace was still angry, but why?

Over dinner and a bottle of house white,

she was relieved to see Grace's mood improve. She shared college tittle-tattle, mentioned a few friends – someone called Carlos seemed to crop up a few times – made them both laugh with her impersonations of Madame Chirol and Antoinette conducting very polite but barbed arguments. That reminded Isobel of something else, "Have you learned anything else about Katja?"

The shutters dropped again, "Learned? What do you mean?"

"Well, it seems a bit extraordinary that Madame Chirol agreed to renting her a room."

Grace shrugged, "Why?"

"Oh come on, Grace, you only have to look at her to see she's a fish out of water in that sense."

Grace looked sullen, avoided eye contact. There was something she wasn't telling. "Oh forget it. Now who's this Carlos you keep mentioning?"

"Just a friend, mum, don't get any ideas."

"Beautiful girl. You'll leave a trail of broken hearts behind you at the college."

At this Grace laughed, "Honestly, you are ridiculous."

One thing Isobel was careful not to do was mention George. She felt as if she were walking on egg-shells with Grace; sensed some intangible distance between them that had not existed before.

Over coffee, Grace's phone buzzed loudly. She

frowned as she read the message, fingers flying as she replied.

"Everything OK?"

"Yes, fine. Only Nina."

Best keep the tone careful and neutral tone, "Send her my love."

"Will do."

The distance grew a little bit greater.

Grace looked uncomfortable, "She actually wondered whether we'd like to meet her and George for a night-cap."

"Great idea." Just what she'd been hoping.

"I said you'd be too tired."

"Why did you say that? I feel fine – you're an hour ahead here, remember?"

Grace stared intently at her coffee.

"Wouldn't you like to meet them, Grace? Could be fun."

"I said I might pop by later."

"Later?"

"When you're back at the hotel."

She was so shocked she felt her breath catch. "I don't understand. Why on earth can't we all have a drink?"

Grace wouldn't meet her eye.

"George and I got on fine last time."

"Yes, mum, we all noticed."

A pierce to the heart.

"What's that supposed to mean? Grace?"

"It means what I said. It was embarrassing, mum."

She could feel anger rising, tried to beat it down, "What are you talking about? Did you think we should sit in stony silence all evening?"

"No of course not, but . . ."

"But what?"

"I don't want to see you flirting with Nina's dad. OK?"

For a moment she felt white-hot rage threatening to erupt, "We weren't flirting!" No response other than the raising of an eyebrow.

Her hands were shaking, but she managed to retain her calm, "You'd better go and meet them then. I'll get the bill and tuck myself up in bed like a good little mummy."

"Mum . . ."

"Go on. Please. I'd prefer to walk to the hotel on my own anyway. Give George and Nina my regards."

Grace nodded, picked up her bag and was gone. Isobel managed to pay the bill and slip quietly out of the restaurant before tears began coursing down her face. This was not how the weekend was supposed to be. Was she crying because of Grace? Or because of George? Really she had no idea. In her mind's eye she could see Robert pushing his hair back as he quietly told her to fuck off. At least someone would have enjoyed that little episode.

She slept badly that night and woke feeling something was wrong. Then the scene in the restaurant flashed through her head, sending a leaden weight deep into her stomach. She lay on her back watching the grey light seep under the curtains, thinking of the planned shopping day ahead and wondering whether to simply tell Grace she was ill and head straight for the Eurostar. When had her daughter become such a cow? She was acting as if she were Isobel's mother, not the other way round.

Automatically, she reached for her phone to check the time and saw the screen flashing with three messages. The first was from Robert, "How's Grace?" No greeting. No endearment. No kisses. Sod him then.

The second was from Grace – one word, "Sorry". Again no kisses. She gazed at the screen for a long time, running through all the possible sub-texts to that particular 'Sorry'. For causing hurt? For speaking frankly? For unbelievable ingratitude? The fact there was no greeting and no kisses implied she wasn't sorry at all, just going through the motions. Sod her too.

The third was from an unknown number with a 001 code. She sat bolt upright when she realised who it was, "Sleep well? Fancy brunch? 10am? Gxx". Brunch? How long ago had he sent that? It was now 8.43am and the message had pinged in at 8.10am. How did he even have her number? He must have asked Nina for it when she came to Rye for Bonfire. Presumably Nina didn't have the same misgivings as Grace then.

Dammit, she still had to get up and shower – but she could meet at 10.15am if she got a move on. Fingers hovering over the phone, she forced herself to calm down and think clearly. What on earth would she say to Grace? It wasn't as though Nina wouldn't mention it: George was bound to tell her. Cross that bridge when she got to it. She clicked on the box to reply, "Feel much better! 10.15am Papillon?" Best not add any kisses.

Then she scrolled up to Grace's message and replied, "No prob. Shopping this afternoon? Xx". She would tell her when they met. If she threw another mighty strop, she would say that George just wanted to have a heart-to-heart about Nina. Finally, she clicked on Robert's message and after much consideration wrote, "Fine. Chat later". No kisses for you, sunshine.

As she pressed Send, her phone pinged twice. From George, "Perfect xx".

From Grace, "OK. Meet me here 2?".

A one word reply to that, "Yes".

Looking anxiously at the time, she figured she still had an hour in which to get ready. She must calm down. It wasn't as though this was a *date*. But it is brunch at Le Papillon with a very handsome man, an inner voice countered – so, as her mother would say, best foot forward.

◆ ◆ ◆

As she stepped through the door into the restaurant, she felt dazzled by crystal, gilt, mirror and marble. Nina was right. This was like eating in Versailles. Resisting the urge to scan the tables, she smiled at the *maître d'* who asked politely, "Are you here to meet someone, Madame?" Why did they never greet her in French? Was it that obvious? She nodded and was about to give the name when she realised she had no idea what it was. Her mind had gone completely blank. She stared at the *maître d'* while she raced to find the answer. She could only think of Nina as Nina and George as George. Dammit. The *maître d'* was looking at her quizzically, "Madame? May I take the name?" It sounded lame even to her that she was here to meet a man whose name she didn't apparently know.

No alternative but to scan the tables while trying to look as if she frequently met men for a late breakfast amongst all this wedding-cake finery. At the far end, she saw George already on his feet – his right hand raised in greeting. Thank goodness for American punctuality. The *maître d'* followed her gaze, "Ah you are a guest of Monsieur Miller? This way, Madame." Nina

Miller. Of course.

In the forty seconds it took for them to walk from one end of the room to the other, Isobel kept her smile fixed to her face while beating down a host of unwanted and unhelpful anxieties. Too much make-up for this time of day? Would her lipstick stay in place? Had she overdone the perfume? Would she sweat with anxiety into the underarms of her cream, silk shirt? Too late now.

"Isobel, you look wonderful!" said George, as they exchanged the obligatory double kiss. "Here take my seat so you can enjoy the view of the room. Ladies always prefer their back to the wall, no?"

God, was he flirting with her already. Pricks of sweat under her arms.

A waiter hovered, "What would Madame like to drink?"

Treble gin-and-tonic. On second thoughts, forget the tonic. "*Thé de Chine, s'il vous plait*", she answered. "*Avec une tranche de citron.*"

It was basic French, but she was determined to make the effort. It went unrewarded, "We serve Marco Polo here, Madame. Is that acceptable?"

Really she had no idea. "*Oui c'est bien,merci.*"

At least George seemed impressed. "Another coffee for me", he said to the waiter. Then turning to her, "You fluent?"

"Sadly no. Far from it."

"Well you do a good impression."

"Thanks." In more ways than one.

When the menu came, she searched for something that she could eat without fear of dropping it down her shirt from nerves or leaving a tell-tale morsel between her teeth. The choice was bewildering, but she lasered through the options before settling on classic omelette. A safe bet. George was having none of that, "Come on, Isobel, I'm about to embark on eggs Benedict with all the trimmings they can throw at it. You have to do better than that. At least order some truffle on the side – it's very good here."

Money was always tight at Miss Mapp, so she found it hard to ignore the fact that one omelette was about to cost the same as her usual weekly shop. "Lovely", she said, turning to George with her warmest smile. "That would be a treat indeed."

And it was. In fact, breakfast with George was a shining, shimmering moment of absolute happiness. It was as if she had been beamed into a parallel universe, where Robert, Grace, her parents and Miss Mapp were barred from entry. A universe where another Isobel, so long forgotten, could wake and dazzle the world. As if, during that breakfast of omelette with truffle – so simple and yet so luxurious - she tasted a different sort of future.

George was so easy to get along with, as funny and charming over coffee and eggs as he was with a glass of champagne in his hand. He *got* her. He got her in a way that Robert never would.

Once the plates had been cleared away, he fixed her with his steady gaze. Melting brown eyes. Devastating with such dark hair.

"There was a particular reason I was hoping to see you, Isobel."

"Oh?" More pricks of sweat. She held her arms tight to her body.

"Something I particularly wanted to say."

"Go on." For the first time, George dropped his gaze – but only for a moment.

"I feel we already know each other well, Isobel. It's odd, but I felt that the first time we met. Do you feel that too?"

"Yes. I know what you mean." Now she felt it difficult to hold his eye. Why had she worn a silk shirt of all things? Stupid.

"I feel I can trust you." She nodded, but it wasn't what she had expected to hear. Trust to do what exactly?

Again that warm, brown-eyed gaze, "It's Nina."

"Nina?" What was he talking about? How did Nina come into this?

"Has Grace said anything?" About what? About them flirting? About Isobel's embarrassing behaviour? For one moment, she had a vision of her daughter bursting through the mirror-panelled doors and bearing down on them angrily.

She shook her head, "No George. What are you trying to say?"

He looked down at his coffee cup, played with the teaspoon, "Would you say Nina and I are close, Isobel?"

"Yes. Of course you are." She had no idea come to think of it.

"Then why won't she tell me?"

"Tell you what?"

"She didn't say anything when she visited you in England?"

"Say anything about what?"

"Did you notice anything?"

"Notice what?"

The parallel universe was dissolving away. It had started to rain, grey light taking the brilliance out of the gilt décor. They were the only guests left in the restaurant now. Waiters were clearing the tables with ruthless efficiency. They wanted them to leave, no doubt. It must be time to set the tables for lunch.

George's body language had changed – usually so outward, it was as if he had contracted and diminished. Something was paining him. Why hadn't she seen that before? Selfish cow that she was.

"Would you mind coming up to my room?"

"What?" Isobel pinned her arms close to her side. Were there stains?

"More private. For what I want to discuss."

"Oh." Had he asked her half an hour ago, the anticipation would have been unbearable.

"Please. Or are you in rush to meet Grace?"

"Well . . ."

"I really need to talk about this with someone. And you're not just 'someone' given how highly Nina thinks of you. As do I, of course."

It wasn't her fate to dazzle, so back in the box with that other version of herself. Good, sensible, mumsy Isobel would make everything all right.

"I'm not sure I can be much help, George, but I'm happy to listen."

The room was elegant and opulent – a suite in fact with separate sitting room and a balcony with views to the Tuileries. She could see the bed through the open door. She had imagined he would be tidy and she was right. No socks or underpants on the floor. No shirts thrown carelessly on chairs.

"Drink?"

She raised her eyebrows in mock alarm.

He laughed, "Well it is two minutes after midday. Gin? Wine? Champagne? Vodka?" He opened a full-length door to reveal shelves crammed with bottles, glasses and what Pam always referred to as ‘nibbles’, plus a full-sized fridge. “As you can see, this is a hotel that takes the mini out of mini-bar.”

In the end, they both opted for Chablis. The rain had stopped and the sun was sneaking through the clouds above the leafless tress beyond.

“George, please, what is it? What are you so worried about?”

A deep breath, “I think Nina’s gay.”

Gay? Was that all? “Being gay’s not so bad. My best friend is gay as it happens.”

Why did that sound so fake? Like something people say at moments like this?

She tried again, “How do you know anyway? If she hasn’t said?”

“Would you know if Grace were gay?”

A good question. Would she?

“Well as I said my best friend is gay and they’re very close. She would probably tell her first to be honest.”

“Unfortunately, I don’t have the convenience of a gay best friend.”

There was no edge to this statement, but still Isobel felt chastened, “Sorry.”

“What for?”

What indeed? For coming to this breakfast hoping for flirtation and possible seduction? For having Nina to stay without noticing anything? For having no idea what to say? For being impossibly, selfishly, idiotically disappointed?

"George, why do you think Nina is gay?"

He shrugged, "A hunch I suppose. She's never had a boyfriend. Never mentioned any boys. And now . . . "

"Now what?"

He met her straight in the eye, "And now I think she's in love with Grace."

For a moment, Isobel thought he must be joking. In love with Grace? The girls were close for sure, but no – not that. He must be mistaken.

"You're shocked."

"Surprised, not shocked."

"I didn't say it was reciprocated."

"Why don't you talk me through it?"

"I noticed when we met here for a drink this evening. I noticed how Nina looked at Grace. How she tried to stay physically close to her. How she hung on every word. I looked at my baby girl and thought, that's how you behave when you're in love."

"But you don't think Grace returns the same feelings?"

"I doubt Grace has even noticed."

Deep down, it struck her as odd that George could make this assertion with such quiet confidence. It wasn't as though he knew Grace very well. Robert would have regarded it as downright impertinent. She wiped Robert from her mind – it was George she was trying to listen to, "And you want to know if I have seen or heard anything to back up your 'hunch'? When Nina stayed with us in Rye?"

He nodded.

"To be honest, No. I just thought it was a great thing that the girls were such good friends – lovely for both of them."

Another pause, "I could ask Dani of course."

"Dani?"

"My best friend. The gay one. Maybe she would have noticed more than I did?"

George shook his head, "No don't do that. It seems disloyal of me to be talking to you about this – never mind your friends."

"Friend. I wouldn't talk to anyone else."

"Even so."

They looked away from each other, out towards the Tuileries trees.

"George?"

"Mmmmm . . . . ?"

"Are you upset that Nina might be gay. Or that she hasn't told you?"

Another silence.

"The latter. She would have told her mum, you see. It would have been different if Maria were here. Maria would have known what to do, what to say . . . I try to be a good dad, but I can't be a good mum too."

"How long ago did she die? Was it cancer?"

"Eight years. Breast cancer. Nina was twelve."

"A tough age to lose a mother."

"Yes."

"Tough for anyone at any age. Tough for you

too."

"Yes."

A silence descended. George no longer met her eyes.

"Are you telling me this because you want me to speak to her, George?" Please say no.

"No."

"OK". Such a relief.

"But I would love it if you could talk to Grace."

Please no.

"About Nina?"

A nod.

"And ask her if she thinks she's gay? And whether she's noticed Nina might be in love with her?"

That was not a conversation she was prepared to have.

"The former – not the latter."

"Ah."

"Please, Isobel, I really need your help. If Nina needs me, I want to be there for her."

Madame Chirol was nowhere in sight when she arrived at the apartment that afternoon. Grace must have been listening out for the bell, because Isobel heard her call out to Antoinette, "*Ne vous inquiétez pas - j'y vais.*"

She opened the door and gave her mother a

huge hug before ushering her into the deserted salon. It was as though last night had been nothing but a bad dream. Grace was clearly intent on making amends.

"How are you, mum? Nice morning drifting around Paris?"

She should tell her now – straight away – but that would get them off to yet another bad start.

"Lovely thanks. Paris is always beautiful no matter what the weather. How did your course work go today?"

"Good thanks – felt I made some progress for once. So where did you go?"

How on earth was she going to phrase this?

"Hi Isobel! How are you? Feeling better?" Nina was dressed in coat and scarf, presumably off to meet George. Grace dropped her eyes to the polished parquet floor, whether from irritation or embarrassment Isobel couldn't tell.

"I'm fine, Nina. Lovely to see you – how are things?" Please don't let her say anything.

"Great thanks. Dad and I were so sorry you weren't able to meet us last night, but he said he was going to message you and get you over for brunch. Did he do that?"

Grace was looking straight at her.

It was now or never. Any delay would only make matters worse.

"Yes, he did." She smiled at Nina trying to ignore Grace's gaze drilling into the side of her head. "I've just come over from Le Papillon actually. It was lovely to see him again."

"Oh great! Isn't it amazing? What did you have?"

"Omelette. With truffle. Delicious."

"I'm a sucker for the eggs Florentine personally." Then, turning to Grace, "I'll make sure he invites both of us next time. You'll love it."

A heavy silence descended when she left the room. Isobel waited until she heard the bang of the front door and the whirr of the lift, "Grace, please don't be upset."

Her daughter's tone was neutral, "Upset?"

"About me having brunch with George."

"Why should I be upset?"

"Because of everything you said last night."

"I said I was sorry."

"I know, but . . . it would have looked rude not to go. You must see that?"

"I'm not your mother."

Her exact phrase to herself that morning.

"The fact is he wanted to talk to me. About Nina."

"Nina?"

Were they going to replicate the exact same conversation she had with George? This time with Grace playing her role?

"Look, I think it would be better if we talk about this somewhere private." Christ, they actually were.

"It's OK – everyone's out or away this

weekend, even Madame Chirol. There's just Antoinette and us here right now."

"Could we have a cup of coffee then?"

"Sure. Usual?"

"Thanks."

Isobel tried to get her thoughts in order while Grace disappeared to put the kettle on. The afternoon had got off to a bad start, but there was no choice but to steam ahead now. Damn you George Miller.

When she came back with a tray of coffee and biscuits, Grace had noticeably relaxed. She even smiled as she offered Isobel a plain Digestive, "For lodgers only. We're only allowed the good biscuits when parents visit."

"Thanks. Just the one."

"So what were you and George actually talking about?"

"He wanted to quiz me about Nina. About how she is."

"Nina's fine. What's the problem?"

Better just plough straight in there. "It's something that's worrying him. It's a bit personal."

"Which is?"

Deep breath. "He thinks Nina might be gay."

Did she imagine it or did Grace ever so slightly flinch at that?

Her daughter's tone was defensive, "Why does he think that?"

"Long story."

"So what if she is?"

"So . . . he's worried that she hasn't actually told him. He feels guilty, I think, that she doesn't have her mum around to confide in. He wants to know if she's OK."

"Oh."

"He asked me to talk to you about it."

"Why?"

"Because you're her friend obviously. He just wants to know she's all right."

Grace sipped her coffee. Her whole manner told Isobel she had nothing to say.

"Grace, I don't think he's asking you to break confidences exactly."

A roll of the eyes.

"He just thought you could help."

Grace shook her head, "There's really nothing to tell you, Mum."

The last thing she was going to do was risk another scene. "OK. Let's leave it. I can tell him I tried and you didn't want to talk about it. End of story."

"Is that all?"

"All?"

"All that you and George talked about?"

"Well, yes . . . mainly."

"Mainly?"

A flash of anger, "We weren't flirting if that's what you are driving at. Specifically, *I* was not flirting, OK?"

For a moment, Grace put her head back and

closed her eyes as if she had a migraine brewing. Isobel tried again, "OK?"

"Yes, Mum. I heard you."

"Can we please stop all this weirdness, Grace? I don't know why you're so upset me with all the time, but I really would like to just take you shopping and out for dinner. I'm on the 11.28am Eurostar tomorrow . . . and then I won't see you until Christmas."

"I'm not upset with you. It's not that."

"So what is it?"

"Honestly, nothing."

Grace had always been a bad liar, but Isobel knew better than to push.

"Better get wrapped up then", she said as cheerfully as she could manage. "It's cold outside."

Grace had met Carlos a few times for a drink after college and had enjoyed hanging out with him and his friends. Things were reaching an awkward point though. On a few occasions, he'd tried to put his arms around her and kiss her, but she always gently pushed him away. It just wasn't what she wanted. She had other things on her mind.

One evening, soon after Isobel's visit, it happened again. They were sitting in a bar close to the CCFS, just the two of them sharing a bottle of wine. One moment, they were chatting normally. The next, Carlos moved in close, got his arm around her waist and pulled her towards him with intent.

Laughing, she tried to pull back with her usual, "Stop that, Carlos!"

He didn't. His breath was very close to hers, "Come here, *menina linda*. No more teasing."

The bar was crowded. She knew they looked like any other college couple on a night out, but now he had his tongue in her mouth probing urgently at hers. One hand was round her waist gripping her to him. The other was feeling under her shirt.

She came up for air, "Stop!"

It was no good. He had found a way to shut her up.

She began to push at him, kicking at his legs, but he simply gripped her tighter and became more ferocious in his demands. His hand was travelling downwards pulling at the buttons on her jeans.

She had to try something else. She forced her body to become relaxed, compliant, answering his mouth with hers.

It worked. His grip loosened as he interpreted her lack of resistance as desire. She seized on the moment and leapt to her feet, shouting at him to fuck off. The people at the tables closest to them stopped talking. She saw one of the women whisper something to her friend.

"*Graça*! Where are you going?" He was trying to smile as if they were lovers who'd just had a tiff, but his eyes were furious.

"As far away from you as possible!"

"It's just kissing. Why are English girls so frigid?" His English was certainly improving, even if his French was dire.

"We're *friends*, Carlos. I don't kiss my friends! Certainly not like that."

"Come and sit down if we're friends."

"We *were* friends. Not now!"

She threw some euros on the table, grabbed her jacket and ran towards the door. There was a taxi rank nearby and she decided to splash out on a cab, rather than risk Carlos coming after her. Once she was in the safety of the taxi, she realised she was shaking. She could still feel how easily he had pinned her to the bench; how defenceless she'd been even in such a public place. How could she have been so stupid, so naïve, so pathetic? She thanked her lucky stars, it hadn't happened somewhere where it had just been the two of them. They had often walked together along the river or in the park. How often had he thought he might do what he'd done that night? Simply push her to the ground and overpower her? The word 'rape' hovered on the perimeter of her mind. Would he have gone that far? She had no intention of finding out: this was as close as Carlos would ever get.

"You're back early," Nina was sitting in the kitchen, looking through the latest edition of French Vogue.

"Not soon enough."

"What do you mean? What's wrong?" She must have looked as shaken as she felt.

"Carlos."

"What about him?"

"We were in a bar and he . . . sort of leapt on me . . . "

Nina didn't seem as scandalised by this as she was, "That's men for you. One-track minds. Hope you hit him where it hurts."

"It was horrible, Nina. I couldn't fight him off."

"But you were in a bar, right? Nothing was going to actually happen."

"Supposing we hadn't been in a bar? Supposing we were alone and that had happened?"

"Every woman has her rape, honey." She said this in such a matter-of-fact manner that Grace doubted she had heard right.

"What are you talking about, 'Every woman has her rape' . . . you mean we all have to expect it?"

"I guess so."

"Has it happened to you?"

"Sex when I didn't want it? Yeah, more than once. I doubt the boys involved thought of it as rape, but it sure as hell wasn't consensual.

Sometimes you just have to grit your teeth and get through it."

"That's shocking!"

"Is it? Ask any of my girlfriends back home and they'd tell you the same."

"That non-consensual sex is the norm?"

"Sure. Must happen in Rye too! They take you out, act charming, make you laugh, ply you with drink – and then the next thing you know you're in the back of a car or up against a wall. Happens all the time."

"You seem very calm about it all."

"It's just life."

"Are you on Carlos's side?"

"'Course not. Boys like him aren't in the right, but they think they are. You're very pretty, Grace. He was never in it for friendship."

"Did you know this would happen?"

"How could I? I've never met Carlos. I'm just not as surprised by it as you are."

"I feel such an idiot."

"It's not your fault. Don't blame yourself. You just have to remember one simple truth."

"Go on."

"Women are physically weaker than men. All the equality laws in the world won't rectify that. Rape is an irregular verb."

"I've never thought if it as one of those."

"I said No. You said Yes. She said Stop. He said Go. Get it?"

It was certainly one way of looking at it.

◆ ◆ ◆

Isobel was just back from another depressing visit to her parents. She'd tried again to raise the question of some sort of care package being arranged, which had made Pam furious, "Are you suggesting we involve social services?"

"It's not what you think. Just someone from the council popping in to make an assessment and recommend some extra care or support."

"A social worker, you mean?"

"Maybe. Or they might send an occupational therapist."

"I'm not having a social worker in my house. What would the neighbours think?"

About bloody time probably.

"It's not a criticism, Mum."

"It's an insult though."

"I'm sorry you feel that way, but all I'm trying to do is get you and Dad a bit of extra help."

"We don't need help. And we definitely don't need a social worker."

It was no good trying to persuade her when she was this bristly, "OK, Mum, let's leave it for now."

"If you want to help, you can do one thing."

"What's that?"

"Take me Christmas shopping soon. Proper shops. Not the computer."

"OK, Mum. We'll sort it out."

She was just walking through the front door at home, when her phone pinged: George. Since coming back from Paris, she hadn't been in touch. She knew he would be anxious for news.

She read the message, "How are things? Did you get a chance to talk to Grace? G Xx".

Once she'd taken her coat off and poured herself a large glass of red wine, she sent a reply, "Hi there. All fine thanks. I tried but she didn't want to talk about it. Sorry".

Another ping. "Do you think Nina's OK?"

"Grace said she's fine. No need to worry".

Ping. "Can I call you?"

A month ago, that four-word question would have elicited huge excitement. Today, with her mum's intransigence souring her mood, it was plain irritating. She took a huge gulp of wine.

"Busy right now. Sorry. Soon?"

"Understood. Another time".

"Lovely. Take care".

"And you".

She was still sitting at the table, glass in hand, when Robert walked in fifteen minutes' later.

"You, OK, Bel? Thought you were still out. The house is in virtual darkness."

It was true. She'd switched on the kitchen light, but hadn't yet summoned the energy to do anything else.

"Just got in."

“Really?” Her glass was less than a quarter full. She knew he would have noticed.

“Bit depressed actually.”

“Why’s that? Your mum and dad?”

“Worse than that.”

“What?”

“Bloody Christmas. I can’t believe it’s only four weeks ‘til stupid, bloody Christmas.”

DECEMBER

The moment Grace walked into the apartment, she knew something was wrong. The door from the salon to the tenants' wing was usually kept closed, but today it was wide open and she could hear voices raised in anger. Antoinette was standing in the middle of the salon, looking anxiously towards the open door, seemingly reluctant to intervene. Of Madame Chirol there was no sign.

"*J'espère tout va bien, Antoinette*?" asked Grace.

The older woman shrugged, "*Ilya vraiment un affreux argument, Mademoiselle Peters*."

"*C'est qui*?"

"*Mademoiselle Miller et cette salope, Katja*."

Grace was shocked. She had no idea Antoinette disliked Katja to that extent. She moved towards the door.

"*Soyez prudent*!" called Antoinette.

"*Ne vous inquiétez pas*."

She walked down the corridor past her bedroom towards the kitchenette. She could hear what was being said clearly now.

"I won't do it, Katja! You can threaten all you want but it's not going to happen." Nina sounded both furious and close to tears.

"You promised me!"

"I never promised anything. And if I did, I've changed my mind."

"I won't let you back out. You owe me, you bitch!"

"You're a fucking mad-woman!"

Grace plucked up courage and pushed open the kitchen door, "Nina? Everything OK?"

By the look on her friend's face, she could see she was far from all right. "Go back to your room, Grace", she murmured. "I don't want you involved with this."

"Yes, get out of here, frigid little English girl" sneered Katja. "This is none of your fucking business."

Grace ignored her, "I'm staying right here, Nina. Why don't you tell me what all this is about? Antoinette's completely terrified by all the noise."

"I said it's none of your fucking business, English girl!"

Something snapped in Grace's usually cool head, "Fuck off yourself, Katja! You know my name so why not use it? What have I ever done to you anyway?"

"What, apart from *exist*, you mean?"

Nina turned to her, "Leave it, Grace. It won't help."

"Won't help what?"

Instead of answering, Nina shrugged and turned away. Katja laughed, "See! Nobody wants you here, English girl. Now for the third time – and before I *really* lose my temper – fuck off out of here!"

Grace ducked just in time. Katja had picked up a wine glass from the draining-board and flung it at her head. As glass shattered all around them, Nina grabbed Grace's wrist, "Are you OK?"

"Katja!" The tiny figure of Madame Chirol stood in the doorway, perfectly poised. There was absolute silence. Katja dropped her eyes to the floor, saying nothing.

Madame Chirol turned to Grace and Nina, "Please leave us, girls. We will talk about this later. But first Katja and I need to have a private conversation – once she has cleaned up this mess of course." With that, she shooed them away and shut the door firmly behind her.

"Do you think Madame will be OK?" whispered Grace.

Nina smiled for the first time, "Not sure, but she certainly knows how to make an entrance."

"I think you need to tell me what's going on."

Nina hesitated, "I'm not sure that's a good idea."

"What do you mean?"

"Like I said, I don't want to involve you."

"I'm involved now, don't you think? That glass could have hit my skull. She certainly meant it to."

"No."

"No?"

"If Katja had meant to hit you, believe me she would have done."

◆ ◆ ◆

Antoinette tapped on Grace's door ten minutes later with a tray of coffee and biscuits. "From Madame," she said.

"I think she's trying to keep us out of the scene of the crime," said Nina. "She never gives us the good cookies."

"Then Katja's done us a favour," smiled Grace.

Once they were settled on the bed, cups of coffee in hand, Grace tried again, "Please tell me what's going on, Nina."

"OK – but you won't like it."

"Try me."

"Katja and I . . . we have a bit of history."

"In what way?"

"Oh, you know . . ."

"You sleep together?"

"We did. For a while. Nothing serious – just sex."

Grace was annoyed to find she was inwardly shocked. So her mum had been right. But Katja? Why had Nina chosen Katja of all people?

"I said you wouldn't like it."

"It's not that. I'm just a bit surprised . . . not that you're gay, but how you and Katja ended up together."

"I'm not."

"You're not what?"

"Gay."

" . . . OK."

"It was an experiment. You know, come to Paris . . . new life . . . lose some inhibitions . . . try some stuff out . . . party . . ."

"Is that what pissed Katja off – that she was part of the experiment?"

"Not really. Katja enjoys sex with straight girls – it's more of a challenge from her point of view. But we never had any 'feelings' if that's what you mean."

"So what went wrong?"

"Nothing in that sense. We went to bed three times in total – quite fun, not really my thing – but then she tried to recruit me."

"Recruit you? Into what? A cult?"

Nina started to laugh, "Honestly, Grace, your face! Not a cult exactly – not in the sense you mean. It's called Femen. Heard of it?"

Grace shook her head.

"It's a radical feminist group – founded in the Ukraine, but based here in Paris."

"So is that where Katja comes from? Ukraine?"

Nina nodded.

"And that's why she's here - in Paris?"

"So far as I can gather, yes."

"And she wanted you to join her group?"

"A bit more than that."

"What do you mean?"

"All political groups need money. Katja wants me to give her money."

"Which you don't have?"

"I don't – but she's not stupid. She wants me to get it from George."

"Why would George give Katja money."

"To shut her up."

"What do you mean?"

"She has photos, you see. Her and me – not the sort of thing a father wants to see spread over the internet."

"Oh Nina!" For a moment, Grace pictured Robert's appalled face should that happen to her. "What are you going to do?"

"Absolutely nothing. She's not going to publish yet and lose her bargaining collateral, is she? So right now I'm playing for time."

Later that evening, Grace and Nina were invited to the salon to speak with Madame Chirol. Grace was convinced that Katja would be given notice to quit the apartment immediately, but Nina wasn't so sure, "You never know which side the old cat will jump."

It turned out Nina's instincts were right.

Madame Chirol poured them each a small glass of calvados from the crystal decanter on the buffet and invited them to sit.

"It is regrettable that Katja's temper got the better of her today," she began. "I apologise on her behalf to both of you, but in particular to you, Grace, for the incident with the glass. She will of course apologise to you herself in due course."

There was a silence. It seemed they were not expected to comment.

"You may wonder why I do not ask Katja to leave," Madame Chirol continued. "My own view is this is not necessary. She is a young woman of spirit and passion, but means no harm. I feel that she is better here, under this civilizing roof. Do you not agree?"

Grace very much did not agree, but she had no idea what to say. She looked over to Nina, but her friend was staring fixedly ahead.

Madame Chirol spoke again, "If you have nothing to add, I will invite Katja to join us, so that we can all be good friends - as before."

She rang a bell and Antoinette appeared. "*S'il vous plaît trouvez Mademoiselle Katja et emmener la ici.*"

Katja must have been primed to be ready and waiting for she walked in, scowling darkly, a moment later.

Madame Chirol poured another glass of calvados for Katja and invited her to sit next to her on the sofa, "You have something to say, I believe, Katja?"

Katja's black eyes were fixed to the carpet, "Sorry."

Madame Chirol tried again, "When apologising, always look at those to whom you are talking, Katja."

Black eyes bored into Grace. "Sorry, Grace. Sorry, Nina," she spat out.

"No worries," said Nina in markedly neutral tones. Grace was impressed at her composure.

"And you, Grace?" said Madame Chirol. "Are you happy to accept Katja's apology?"

What could she do but nod?

"Katja wishes you to understand that nothing like this will happen again. That is correct, isn't it, Katja?"

Katja's eyes were fixed on the carpet again, but she gave the briefest of nods.

"Isn't it, Katja?" said Madame Chirol again, this time in a tone edged with ice.

Katja straightened and looked at them, "Yes that is correct."

"*Très bien*. I am so pleased we have cleared the air", said Madame Chirol sweetly. "It would be a shame to break up our cosy little family over a simple misunderstanding, would it not?"

◆ ◆ ◆

Two weeks before Christmas, Isobel took Pam to Tunbridge Wells to do her few bits of Christmas shopping. Her mum had a list on which she had carefully written the names of those for whom she was buying presents:

Jack
Me (from Jack)
Isobel
Grace
Robert
Marianne

"Who's Marianne, Mum?"

"W.I. – I'm her Secret Santa for our Christmas lunch."

Other than Marianne, the names were unchanged from last year. It tugged at Isobel's heart to see how few people were on the list. Pam had been an only child, but Jack had had three brothers, all married, all three couples now dead. The last year had also seen the death of Pam's best friend, Carrie. "And now there is nobody who remembers me as a child," she had said sadly when Isobel drove her to Maidstone for the funeral.

Her parents' address book bulged with names and addresses going back many years, but most of them were now crossed through with a neat diagonal line recording their demise. Isobel imagined Pam sitting with ruler and pen carefully drawing these lines, as each message was delivered by phone, post or the death notices in the Telegraph. It struck her for the first time that old age required enormous courage.

Determined to give her mum a nice day out – Dani had offered to stay with Jack – she suggested they go to the department store first for a coffee. The plan was to do the shopping, have a light lunch and then get Pam home by mid-afternoon. Her mum had other ideas, "We could have a cheese scone each with coffee."

"If we have scone now, you won't want lunch. It's already coming up to eleven-fifteen."

"I'm not bothered about lunch, dear. A scone would be lovely."

"But I wanted to buy you lunch – give you a treat. We don't get out together very much."

"Yes but Jack will worry if I'm back late."

"Dad will be fine. He likes Dani visiting."

"Even so, Isobel. I don't like to impose."

"You're not imposing. I'm your daughter."

"On Dani."

"Dani really doesn't mind, Mum."

Pam looked out the window and for an awful moment, Isobel thought she may be trying not to cry. Why was she arguing? Wasn't she the one imposing by insisting on a lunch her mother would clearly not enjoy. "I'm sorry, You're right. Let's have scone and coffee and an hour at the shops – then I'll take you home."

Her mum looked relieved, "Thank you, dear. We'll do lunch another day."

And pigs might fly.

◆ ◆ ◆

The list was short, but patience was needed. Pam moved so slowly that it seemed like a five-mile hike from one end of the mall to the other. She chose socks for Jack and Robert and gloves for Isobel (careful to get her approval first). She chose a scarf for herself – her own gift from Jack. Part of the Christmas ritual was that Isobel would later wrap and label this ready for Christmas morning when Jack would present it to his wife with all the solemnity of one who has scoured London for the perfect tribute. But what was she to buy Grace?

"How about these?" said Pam, holding up a pair of pink, fake-fur ear mufflers that a twelve-year old might covet.

"I don't think they're quite her, Mum."

"Oh dear. Some nice bath salts?"

"Not sure. Good for Marianne perhaps?"

"We only spend five pounds on Secret Santa."

"OK, we'll find something in the food hall on the way out – a nice tin of biscuits."

"But what about Grace?"

Isobel looked around. What would Grace buy if she were here? "Tights!"

"Tights? Are you sure?"

"Yes she loves those thick, black ones in

winter. They go with everything."

Pam looked doubtful, "It seems an awfully boring thing to buy our only grand-daughter. Particularly when she's been living away all this time."

"Why not buy her two pairs – very practical – and give her a little bit of money too?"

Pam brightened, "Yes young people always need a bit of extra, don't they?"

"Absolutely. Look they're just over there."

But as she turned towards the tights, she saw Pam lurch to one side, "Mum!"

She dropped the wire basket and caught her by the arm, shocked by how grey her mother's face was. "You need to sit down."

Breathless, Pam struggled to get her words out, "I'm OK, dear. So silly of me."

"Not silly at all. Don't talk. Let me help you to that chair by the changing rooms."

Pam felt like a dead weight as they struggled a few feet to the chair.

A sales assistant ran over, "Is everything OK? Do you need a doctor?"

Pam shook her head, but no words came out.

"Could you get us a glass of water, please?" asked Isobel. "I think she just needs to sit down a moment."

She waited a few moments, holding her mum's hand and noting the colour slowly seeping back into her cheeks.

"Are you OK now?"

Pam was still gasping for breath.

"Are you in pain? Chest? Arms?"

A shake of the head.

"OK, don't try to talk. Just sit there quietly and try not to worry."

Within a few minutes, the sales assistant was back with the glass of water, "Someone from First Aid is on their way."

"Thank you. She's looking a little better."

Pam was struggling to stand. "Mum, you must sit down."

"But . . . Jack . . . ."

"Mum! Really. You must sit down. If you don't do what you're told, I'll ring for an ambulance."

Defeated, Pam sat and slowly sipped some water.

A woman of about Isobel's age appeared, "I'm Maggie. First Aider. Can you tell me what's wrong, Madam? Whether we need to ring for medical assistance?"

Pam shook her head vigorously. She was breathless, but managed to speak, "I'm fine. Just a silly turn."

Maggie caught Isobel's eye, a quizzical look.

"I think she just needs to sit here for a moment," said Isobel. "She says she's in no pain of any kind, but maybe we've done a little too much today."

"Christmas shopping were you?"

"That's right."

"Always busy in the run-up to Christmas."

"Yes, always."

"Well if you tell me what's on the list, I can send an assistant to help you."

"That's kind of you, but we were nearly finished. If Mum stays here, I can pick up the last few things for her."

"No problem at all. If your mum's well enough to speak, I have some questions I need to ask her anyway, for our own records."

She knelt down next to Pam, "Are you feeling a bit better, Madam?"

Pam nodded slowly.

"OK to speak?"

"Yes I think so. What a silly thing to happen. I don't know what came over me."

"Don't you worry. Your daughter . . . ?"

"Isobel."

"Isobel's just going to pick up the last of your bits and pieces and I'll stay here with you until she gets back."

Isobel squeezed her mum's hand, "OK, Mum?"

"Yes dear. I'm sorry."

"Don't be silly."

"But I am silly. What a thing to do."

And then her eyes welled with tears. Maggie patted her hand, "You've just had a bit of a shock, that's all. I'll ask one of the girls to bring you down a nice cup of tea."

Isobel retrieved the basket from where she'd dropped it and quickly scooted to the tights rack and into the food hall for Marianne's biscuits.

She headed back to where Pam and Maggie sat, her mum now sipping a cup of tea. "Was there anything else, Mum? Shall I pay and you pay me back?"

"No, dear, I've got notes in my purse. Take what you need."

"OK."

Maggie stood up, "Stay here, Pam, and I'll take Isobel to the till myself – that way I can jump her to the front of the queue. Please don't move." So they were on first-name terms now? What else had Maggie discovered?

As it turned out, quite a bit.

"Apparently, this isn't the first time your mum has felt dizzy."

"Oh?"

"She gets very tired and breathless at times, but she doesn't want to worry anyone."

"Did she say how long this has been going on for?"

"About six months."

"That long? Really? And she's never mentioned it to anyone but you before now!"

Maggie glanced at her, "Sometimes it's easier to talk to a stranger."

"I'm sorry, I didn't mean to sound rude."

"If I'm honest, I would have preferred to call an ambulance, but that would mean your mum being hours in A&E, all the time worrying about your dad by the sounds of it."

"Exactly."

"She must see a doctor though. As soon as possible. I suspect you might be looking at something wrong with her heart."

Isobel felt her own heart pounding with worry and shock. So much for giving her mum a treat in Tunbridge Wells. She paid for the shopping and Maggie walked back with her to say good-bye to Pam and check she was well enough to walk to the car park.

Once they were in the car, Isobel turned to her mum, "Are you feeling OK now?"

"Yes, dear, all fine. Nothing to worry about."

"I think there is."

"What do you mean?"

"Maggie told me this wasn't the first time . . . that you've felt dizzy?"

"I shouldn't have said anything."

"Yes. You should have. Before now in fact."

"I don't like to be a worry."

Isobel wanted to shout, "But you are a worry!" Aloud, she said, "If you don't want to be a worry, promise me that you'll see Dr Barnes next week."

"There's no need."

"Yes there is!"

Her mum looked at her slyly, "On one condition, Isobel."

"Which is?"

"You are absolutely not to tell your father about this."

"You promise to see the doctor if I promise

not to tell dad?"

"Yes."

"Deal! With one extra condition – that I come with you to see the doctor."

"You don't need to do that. Such a waste of your time."

"If you won't even tell dad about this, you need to take me with you."

"Very well. But I'm sure there's nothing wrong at all."

Isobel smiled, "You're probably right, Mum."

But deep down, a new fear had taken root.

When they arrived back, they found Jack and Dani playing backgammon in the sitting room. "You're home early," said Jack. "We've only just started this game." Isobel sensed disappointment. Dani was a particular favourite of his.

"Don't worry, Dad. I won't take Dani away from you yet. I'll make you another cup of tea if you like."

Pam kissed him on his cheek, "Have you been OK, dear?"

"Of course I have. No need for you to rush back."

From the kitchen, Isobel could hear the conversation. "Did you get everything you wanted, Pam?" asked Dani.

"Yes, dear. Thanks so much for today."

"No problem at all. I love a game of backgammon, even if Jack always wins."

"She gammoned me last time," he laughed.

Driving back to Rye, Isobel told her friend about the incident at the shops.

"Poor you," said Dani. "That sounds pretty stressful. Make sure she sees a doctor soon though."

"I will."

"I'm not exactly surprised though."

"No?"

"They're going downhill, aren't they? There was a big change today from last time I saw them."

"Is there?" Isobel was worried. "When was that?"

"October, I think."

"And what had changed?"

"Both of them seem far more frail. And . . . ."

"And?"

Dani looked embarrassed, "The house is grubbier."

"Smellier?"

"I suppose so, yes."

If things had got worse since October, what would Mrs Dawkins and the other neighbours now be saying behind her back?

"What am I going to do, Dani?"

"I wish I knew. It must be hard."

"To be honest, it's about as shit as it gets."

In fact it was about to get a whole lot worse. That evening Grace rang. She was catching the Eurostar back in a few days' time and wanted to check that Robert or Isobel could collect her from Ebbsfleet, but that wasn't the only reason she was phoning.

"I've got some news," she said brightly. Too brightly. Why did Isobel feel her chest constricting?

"Go on."

"I'm going to Miami."

"Amazing! When?" Isobel tried to smile down the phone, but her head was spinning.

"New Year."

"When in the new year?"

"No. I'm going for New Year."

There was a silence. "But we always spend New Year with Dani and Saskia. They're looking forward to seeing you so much."

"And I can't wait to see them either. It's just I won't be there for New Year."

Isobel could feel bitterness and disappointment rising like bile. "It seems a very sudden decision."

"Not exactly. Nina asked me a while ago, but I

only just said yes."

"Why?"

"Why what?"

"Why did you decide to say yes now? At this late stage? We've all been looking forward to seeing you so much for Christmas."

"Mum! You are seeing me for Christmas. I'll be there next week."

"But not for long."

"Long enough. I'll have nine days at home before I fly out."

Isobel's mind was racing, "Nine? So you fly out before the New Year?"

"Yes obviously. I'm going *for* New Year, not just after it"

"So the thirtieth?"

"The twenty-eighth actually."

"I see."

Isobel had the urge to throw the phone across the room. She was furious that George and Nina were taking Grace away from her family at such a special time of year. She was bitterly hurt that Grace had chosen to go. In fact, right then she didn't know who to be more angry with – Nina, George or Grace.

"Mum?"

"Yes."

"I know you're annoyed, but couldn't you be the tiniest bit excited for me. Palm trees in January!"

"Who's paying for this?"

"What?"

"How much are Dad and I going to have to fork out?"

Grace's tone was cold. "Nothing. George is paying."

"We can't allow him to do that."

"It's fine. Nina says it's all Air Miles – from the Amsterdam project."

"Oh." She knew she was handling this badly, but it was the end of a terrible day.

"Thanks for the update. I'll get Dad for you."

Just before she handed the receiver to Robert, she managed to say, "Bye. Love you."

Grace's voice sounded small and hurt, "Love you too."

Did she? How could she do this then?

She walked in the kitchen, picked up a plate and smashed it to the floor. Robert couldn't have failed to hear it. "Sorry!" she called out. "Slipped right through my fingers!"

Lying in the bath that night, she brooded on Grace's decision to go to Miami. Why did it hurt so much? Who exactly was she jealous of – George or Grace? Was she being pathetic reacting in this way? From the bedroom, she heard her phone ping. She tried to ignore it, but when it pinged for the second time, she grumpily climbed out the bath and wrapped a towel around herself.

Sitting on the bed, dripping into the duvet, she was irritated beyond belief by the message on her screen.

"Grace told you good news?"

Since when was losing your daughter to strangers good news? Typing into the bubble, she wrote, "Yes. Lovely. Thank you".

Two blue ticks. He'd been waiting for her reply then.

"Nina super excited".

Spoilt cow.

"Grace too".

"Hope you and R don't mind".

Did they even get a choice? "Course not. Great opportunity".

"Told her that's what you would say".

Since when had they had that conversation? "We'll pay for flight".

"No need. Air Miles!"

Smug bastard. "Does she need VISA?"

"ESTA. Nina will help her. Online".

Isobel felt as if she had been erased entirely. "I'm sure she'll have an amazing time".

"She will. I'll make sure of that!"

She was shivering in her towel and she wanted to cry. "Better go. Lots to do!"

"OK. Will email arrangements soon".

Suddenly she hated George. Really hated him. "Great. Thanks!"

"Ciao for now".
"Bye". Go fuck yourself.

On Christmas morning, Grace woke to the sound of St Mary's bells ringing for early Communion. She lay in bed, snug and happy, thinking of all the childhood Christmases she had spent in this cosy house, with its twisted stairs and wonky rooms. On Christmas morning, her father would light the open fires in both the sitting room and dining room, as well as the stove in the snug. Paradoxically, this often meant having to turn the central heating off as Christmas in Sussex was rarely cold. It was an extravagant gesture, part of the theatrical production her parents had long ago created that followed the same script year on year. Right now, they would be in the kitchen together, Isobel basting the turkey and Robert on hand to heave it into the Aga. Grace liked the fact she could visualise this so exactly.

Sitting up in bed, she saw a bulging Christmas stocking propped against her door. She thought last year's would have been the last given she'd now turned eighteen, but was delighted to see Father Christmas had apparently not given up on her yet. How many more years would she wake on Christmas morning in this house – in this bed – and find a stocking to open? Until she was married with her own children? Unimaginable.

She called down the stairs, "Happy Christmas! Guess what! Father Christmas has been!"

Robert appeared at the foot of the stairs, grinning, "Happy Christmas, darling! You must have been a good girl then!"

"Of course I have! Where's Mum?"

"I'm just coming!" called Isobel from the kitchen. "Happy Christmas, sweetie!"

It was part of the script that her parents would sit on the bed and watch her open her stocking. Robert brought up a tray of hot chocolate and perched on the end of her bed while Isobel climbed in next to her. Part of the magic of the stocking ritual was some things were unchanged year on year – always chocolate coins, a tangerine, some nuts, a diary and at least two or three books – while others were wonderful surprises. Grace was touched that there was a Miami theme in evidence – expensive fake tan, a nail varnish called Cuban Orange, an inflatable neck rest for the aeroplane and some very blingy sun-glasses. She made suitable squeals of excitement, while Isobel and Robert made comments such as, "How did Father Christmas know to get you that?" and "Haven't the elves been busy?" Once the stocking had been emptied and the chocolate drunk, Grace gave them both a big hug. "You really are the best parents ever! Thank you! I never thought Father Christmas would come this year!"

Isobel smiled, "You're welcome, darling. It's so lovely to have you home."

Robert nodded, "I second that. Now I'd better get going – have to pick Pam and Jack up by ten-thirty – see you both later."

Once she was showered and dressed, Grace went down to the kitchen where her mum was busy peeling Brussels sprouts. Complicated breakfasts were not part of the Christmas routine, so Grace edged round Isobel to make tea and toast.

"When are Dani and Saskia coming round?"

"Midday."

"Shame they can't stay for lunch."

"I know, but Saskia's brother is keen for them to go there. At least we can have a glass of champagne with them."

"And nibbles!"

"I don't think 'nibbles' really covers it this year, do you?"

They smiled at each other. In the corner of the kitchen was an enormous Fortnum & Mason hamper that George had sent them for Christmas. It had arrived two days previously and they'd emptied its lavish contents into cupboards and fridge with much excitement. "George has definitely raised the bar on Christmas this year," her father had said. "I can feel my cholesterol rising just looking at this lot."

Grace was relieved that her mum and dad seemed to be behaving normally together. On her previous visit at Bonfire, she'd been aware of tension exuding from both sides. It had made her feel as if she were the only glue holding them together; that in her absence, they had started to fray and tear. She was eager to embark on her own life, but she wanted Robert and Isobel to stay just as they had always been. She certainly didn't want to see any signs that her mother had been – or, worse, still was – independent and sexual. The thought of any attraction between Isobel and George made her feel physically anxious.

"Can I do anything?" She knew what the answer would be.

"Not right now, thanks. I'll just prep the vegetables before Granny and Grandad get here and then we can relax for a bit."

"How about some music?"

"Great idea. Just make sure it's Grandad friendly, please!"

"That leaves us with Doris Day or Frank Sinatra?"

"Doris."

"OK."

Grace wandered into the sitting room to rummage through the CD collection, loading Doris Day's Christmas Album into her parents' ancient sound system. She and Isobel had dressed the tree a couple of days ago, and Robert had looped vintage paper chains around the walls. She walked over to the tree, admiring its effect, lovingly caressing her favourite decorations. She was touched to see the *papier-mache* snowman she'd made at nursery school, which Isobel tenderly wrapped with tissue paper and brought out every Christmas. How had it survived so long? Doris was singing, 'I'll Be Home For Christmas' and suddenly Grace very much wanted to cry. Why had she never realised before how sad Christmas was? How fleeting?

As if on cue, she heard Pam's voice and the tap of Jack's stick on the wooden floor in the hall. "Granny! Grandad!" she flew out the door to welcome them and give them both a big Christmas hug.

"Grace! How lovely to see you. Hasn't she grown, Jack?"

"I'm pretty sure I'm the same size as when you saw me last, Granny!"

"You're different though. A proper young woman."

"Just dressed up for Christmas, that's all."

"Well, it's lovely to see you, dear," said Jack. "We've missed you."

"We have indeed."

"And I've missed you too."

Robert hovered behind, holding Pam's bag of presents. "Can you put these under the tree please, Grace?"

Isobel called from the kitchen, "Be with you in a moment. Just checking the turkey."

Grace led her grandparents into the sitting room, where they admired the tree and chuckled over the little snowman, before sitting down to enjoy the fire. While she chattered about her life in Paris, she took in how changed they were. Her grandad looked even thinner than when she'd last seen him, while her granny looked unusually tired, dark rings etched on her usually pretty face.

Robert popped his head round the door, "What would you all like to drink? Tea, coffee or something stronger? We'll open the champagne when Dani and Saskia are here."

"Sherry, please," said Jack.

"Same for me please, Robert."

"Grace?"

"Nothing for now, thanks, Dad. I've just had tea."

"OK. Two sherries coming up."

Isobel appeared a moment later, kissing her parents and wishing them a Happy Christmas. When Robert came in with the sherries, Grace noticed Isobel catching her granny's eye and giving a slight shake of her head. Why would she do that? Sherry on Christmas morning was perfectly normal.

Whatever message had passed between them, Pam chose to ignore it, raising her glass to wish them all a very happy Christmas. But Grace noticed she took only the smallest of sips before setting her glass on the table and not touching it again. What on earth was going on? Her granny wasn't a big drinker by any means, but she could certainly handle a glass of sherry.

By the time, Dani and Saskia knocked on the door, Jack was two sherries in and Pam's was still virtually untouched. The exact same thing happened with the champagne – one small sip and then ignored. Grace was so puzzled by this that she found it hard to concentrate on what was being said, but soon she was busy handing out smoked salmon blinis and miniature quiches.

"You're looking exceptionally beautiful," smiled Dani. "What's your secret? Milk of unicorn?"

"Flatterer! I guess I may have inherited some good genes."

"Very true – both your mother and your granny have wonderful complexions."

"Lucky me!"

"Absolutely. Although there may be another reason, I suspect."

"What's that?"

"Pheromones."

"What are they?"

"Hormones - they induce sexual arousal."

"Where's this going?"

"Are you by any chance in love?"

"Dani!"

"Shhh. Nobody else heard me."

Grace had no idea how to react, "What makes you think that?"

"Godmothers have magic powers."

"How annoying of them!"

"So I'm right?"

"Absolutely not. Why would you think that?"

"People in love look different to their usual selves."

"I can't believe they do!"

"What are you two talking about?" said Robert. "Or is it private?"

"I'm just catching up with my beautiful goddaughter," said Dani. "Now what have you done with Saskia?"

"She's in the kitchen with Isobel."

"Could you go and find her then? We're due at Brandon's at two."

When Robert was safely out the room, she turned to give Grace a good-bye hug and whispered in her ear, "I won't pry. But if you do want to talk about it, I'm always here for you."

"Thanks Dani, but there's really nothing to say. Godmothers just have vivid imaginations."

"Message understood. Happy Christmas, Grace." And then she was on her feet, calling for Saskia, saying her good-byes and wishing all of them a happy Christmas. Grace watched her go with a heavy heart. There was a lot she would have liked to tell her, but the time wasn't right.

◆ ◆ ◆

It was ridiculously beautiful. She had expected Miami to be many things – exciting, exotic, dangerous even – but she hadn't thought it would be heart-stoppingly spectacular. The only other city on the sea she'd ever visited was Brighton. Driving over Biscayne Bay towards Miami Beach was a revelation. Brighton it was not.

Nina sat beside her in the back of George's convertible, as excited to share Grace's first impressions of her home city as Grace had been to show her Rye. George drove with one hand, taking the role of tour guide, "This is route 195. We're going to go the long way round, head towards North Beach and then cruise down Collins Avenue towards Mid Beach and then South Beach's Art Deco district, to give you a sense of it all. Then we'll double back towards the Sunsets. Unless you want to go straight to ours if you're tired from the flight?"

"I'm wide awake, thanks!"

"Great. You can catch up on sleep later!"

George was a knowledgeable and entertaining guide, particularly when it came to the iconic art deco buildings along Ocean Drive. Grace had never seen anything like it: buildings in delicious ice-cream shades, some with ornate friezes, others lit by neon. A few were curved like boats, but most were strictly symmetrical. Her favourite was a pretty hotel in pink and turquoise.

"This district is why my dad became an architect, isn't that right, George"?

"Certainly is. A lot of inspiration here."

"I can see that," said Grace. "Very different to Rye!"

Nina laughed, "But both wonderful in their ways."

George and Nina lived on the improbably named Sunset Island Two. By the time they pulled into their elegant, waterfront home, Grace was flagging. Nina showed her the guest suite and left her to shower and nap, "Drinks on the terrace in three hours. That OK?"

"Amazing, thank you."

She was desperately tired, but her head was spinning with excitement. Just as Miami was the polar opposite to Rye, so George's cool, contemporary home was diametrically opposed to her parents' period house. The family bathroom in Rye would have fitted into her guest bathroom four times over. It had never occurred to her that George was wealthy, but now she was here, it was obvious. The Sunset Islands offered exclusive homes for the fortunate elite - all pools, palm trees and panoramic views. It was a different world.

Nina came to wake her up, "Sorry to do this,

but you'll recover quicker from jet lag if you try to get into our time zone."

"What time is it?" It was dark outside.

"About seven-thirty – getting on for midnight in Rye, but best not think about that."

She felt groggy and discombobulated, "OK."

"Grace, you have to wake up." Had she fallen straight to sleep again?

"OK."

Nina laughed, "Look at you, poor Sleeping Beauty. Jump in the shower – it'll help. Turn the water to cold."

She nodded and this time managed to sit up and then stumble towards the bathroom. Nina was right. The cold water was almost painful combined with the power of the shower, but it did the trick. Half an hour later, she joined them on the terrace, where George was already mixing cocktails.

"How are you feeling, Grace? What can I get you?" She had no idea. Rarely drank cocktails.

"Something not too strong, please, or I won't make it past nine o'clock."

Nina laughed, "None of them are strong, Grace. He means non-alcoholic."

For a moment she thought Nina must be joking. George looked embarrassed, "Drinking laws here aren't like Europe, I'm afraid. Zero tolerance in Florida for the under-twenty-ones."

"Crazy isn't it?" said Nina. "Probably should have warned you we'll be seeing in 2013 stone cold sober."

"Probably just as well given how sleepy I am. What do you recommend?"

"Non-alcoholic Miami Mule? Ginger beer, soda, lime and mint. That's what I'm having."

"Sounds delicious!"

The view from the terrace was beautiful, with the lights from the houses sparkling in the water and the warm night breeze in her hair. George sent out for Mexican and before too long was busy in the huge, open-plan kitchen unpacking a feast of *enchiladas, burrito, fajitas, filete de pollo* and two types of salad.

"He always orders too much," said Nina, as she laid the table on the terrace with brightly coloured ceramic dishes and turquoise blue water glasses. "Tomorrow you'll meet our housekeeper, Frieda. She's a wonderful cook."

"Does she come in most days?"

"Four times a week. Her husband, Juan, comes with her – he helps with the garden.

"Is she as gossipy as Antoinette?"

Nina laughed, "Nothing like Antoinette, which is a good thing if you ask me."

To Grace, it was all perfect. She was happy to sit back and let Nina and George do most of the talking, while she soaked in the view, the house and the balmy December air. She couldn't quite believe she was there.

When she started yawning at about ten, George suggested she went to bed, "With luck, you'll sleep through and wake up in the right time zone."

She wasn't going to argue. Nina fussed around her, making sure she had water by her bed and a charger for her phone, "I'm only opposite, so wake me if you need anything."

"I'll be fine. Thanks."

"OK. 'Night, Grace."

"'Night, Nina."

"It's lovely to have you here."

"It's lovely to be here."

She slept for a full twelve hours. The first thing she heard was George's voice and Nina answering with a laugh. She smiled and rolled onto her side. It was going to be a wonderful two weeks.

Two days later, the three of them drove down to Ocean Drive and found a good place on South Beach from which to watch the firework display that marked the start of 2013. It was a far cry from the pagan undertones of Sussex Bonfire, but to Grace it was just as sensational. The bay was full of boats, from big to large, sending out lights like nautical glow-worms. She was mesmerised by the scale and audacity of the beautifully choreographed pyrotechnics. Every time, it looked like a dizzying finale had been reached, on came another wave of exploding light.

Back at the house, George opened a bottle of champagne and poured them each a glass, "Just this once. Don't tell anyone. I really don't want to start the new year in jail."

"Orange suits you at least," laughed Nina.

He smiled at that and raised his glass to the two of them, "Happy New Year, beautiful girls!"

"Happy new year, George!" they chorused.

Nina and Grace hugged, and Nina gave her father a kiss.

Grace hesitated. She had caught George's look.

"Go on, you guys!" laughed Nina. "Wish each other a proper Happy New Year, for chrissake!"

She put her glass down and put her arms around George's neck, kissing him softly on one cheek, "Happy New Year, George."

The next day, George drove them down the Florida Keys towards Marathon. Grace was as excited as a four year-old when she saw a sign warning of Crocodiles Crossing. She was fascinated by the names of the individual Keys, such as Little Torch, No Name and Little Duck. However, her favourite part of the trip was crossing the Seven Mile Bridge towards Grassy Key, where they stopped for lunch.

"Happy?" said Nina.

"You bet. This is the best New Year's Day ever!"

They were sitting in a café on the waterfront, eating lobster and fries. George was on his phone outside checking whether the local dolphinarium was open.

"Made any new year resolutions, Grace?" She had, but this wasn't the time to share them.

"Not really. You?"

"Same one every year. Learn to draw like Drian."

"Sorry, no idea who that is."

"Etienne Drian. Fashion illustrator. Goes right back to before the First World War."

"I thought you wanted to be a fashion designer, not an illustrator."

"I do. But I want to be able to draw properly first."

"You can already!" This was no false compliment. Grace was in awe of Nina's artistic talents.

"Thanks, but I need to be a lot better . . . oh hi George . . ."

"We're in business. Fancy seeing the dolphins, Grace?"

"That would be magical."

Walking back to the car, Nina squeezed her hand, "You like my dad, don't you?"

"Of course I do, Nina." Why was she asking?

Nina smiled, "He likes you too. Very much. We always love the same things in life."

"You're very close. Hope I'm not in the way. Three's a crowd, after all."

"The exact opposite! Having you here completes the circle for us. Know what I mean?

"I think so." Not really.

"When mum was alive, we were such a tight three. Having you here reminds me of then . . . . in a good way."

"Only one thing for it then."

"What's that?"

"Your dad will have let me live here for ever!"

"Better marry him!"

They were still laughing as they climbed into the back of the car.

"What are you two up to?" He smiled at them in the rear view mirror.

"Just making plans," grinned Nina. "This is going to be a helluva year."

JANUARY

She knew there was a chance of snow, but nothing prepared her for the blizzard that had spread icing sugar over every corner and crevice of the Parisian cityscape. Isobel stood at the window of the little hotel bedroom in Montmartre, looking down at the blanketed square, bare branches etched against the grey sky. Snow was still falling. She left the curtains open and went back to bed. The light seeping into the room was tinged with blue.

She wasn't due to meet Grace until lunch-time, but she couldn't settle back to sleep. Instead, she sat half upright mesmerised by the snow-flakes drifting past the window. Snow stilled her mind. For the first time in a long time, she felt at peace. At home, she dreaded snow, associating it with icy roads, treacherous cobbles and a downturn in sales at Miss Mapp. But here she had a childish desire to get out into the snowy landscape and explore this new, pristine white version of Paris. It came to her suddenly what she would do: visit the church of Saint-Sulpice, where long ago she and Robert

had enjoyed an organ recital on their first visit to Paris together. His idea of course. She could remember very little about the church other than the powerful presence of The Great Organ. It was one of the first jokes that she and Robert had shared: welcome to my Great Organ. There was one other fact that Robert had told her on their visit; that Saint-Sulpice was where the Marquis de Sade was baptised.
She suddenly wished that Robert was with her now and that caught her by surprise. When was the last time she had really missed her husband?

It was Friday, so hopefully her visit would not clash with a service. She sent Grace a text message, confirming she would pick her up at lunch-time and then dressed. Thank goodness she had bought sensible flat-heeled boots and thick gloves. This would be a real adventure.

It proved to be more of an adventure than she'd bargained for. The walk downhill to Abbesses was perilous enough, but Isobel took her time, nodding to the dog walkers who greeted her – the only other people to have braved the snow it seemed. It was about ten by the time she arrived at Saint-Sulpice, but the church was open and she enjoyed browsing around for an hour or so, admiring the enormous shells that doubled as holy water fonts and the handsome Baroque interior.

Isobel wasn't religious, but Pam always lit a candle in any church she visited, and she felt the need to do the same. Was this allowed? She wasn't Roman Catholic after all. She rooted around her purse for a couple of euros and chose a long tapering candle from the stand, carefully lighting it with the flame from another. She closed her eyes and tried to say a prayer, but was lost for words. In the end she mumbled "God bless Grace, Robert, mum and dad." It all sounded very hollow. She sat down at the end of a pew and closed her eyes and tried again. It was a stream-of-consciousness type prayer, an amateur attempt. But as she tried to send her thoughts to a god in whom she didn't believe, she realised she was really praying for herself. It wasn't what she'd intended. She had started with an intention to do a good thing; to send out blessings on those she loved, even those she was no longer sure she fully loved. Instead, all she seemed capable of beaming into the universe was me, me me.

Irritated with herself, she decided to give up on candles and prayers and go to find a coffee. Stepping out of the church, the snow was blinding and brilliant. It had stopped falling, but lay thick as an eiderdown on the square. She began walking back towards the Metro where she had passed a few cafés, all in a line. It happened so suddenly, she was confused as to why she was now lying on her back looking up at a blue-flecked sky. Dammit. Please God don't let her have broken anything. How ironic: two prayers in the space of minutes.

Someone was helping her to her feet, asking her something in French.

"So sorry. Fine now." Passers-by were looking towards her with concern, relieved to see her on her feet. She realised she was wet through.

"English?"

She nodded. Apologised again.

"You need to sit down. Give me your arm, Madame."

She shook her head. Tried to say she was perfectly OK. Was mortified to find she was crying.

"Please, Madame. This way. Are you sure you can walk all right?"

She nodded and took his arm. They went into the nearest café where he ordered them both a coffee, and a Cognac for her, "For the shock."

She felt such a fool. How babyish to cry just because she'd had a fall. She suddenly had a vision of her mother after the incident at the shops and felt terrible. So this is what it felt like to be old.

She wiped her eyes and managed a smile, "You must think me such an idiot. I was trying to be so careful too."

He smiled back. For the first time, she noticed how elegantly he was dressed. He was what her mum would have called "a dish", with indigo eyes and curly hair tinged with grey. Hard to put an age on him. She realised she may have been staring a little too intently.

He held out his hand, "Jean-Luc. Pleased to meet you."

She shook his hand, "Isobel. Thank you so much, Jean-Luc. I'm sorry to have caused you such trouble."

"No trouble at all. Are you feeling better?"

"Much. Thank you. Please don't let me hold you up – you look as though you're going somewhere important."

"Nothing that can't wait, I assure you. Are you here on your own? Should I call someone?"

"No. Thank you. I'm visiting my daughter – she's studying here - we're not meeting til this afternoon though."

By the time she had finished her Cognac – "I insist, Isobel, it will warm you up" – she had learned quite a bit about Jean-Luc. He was a film director, mainly television series, who lived not far away near the Jardin du Luxembourg. He had been on his way to his office where he had a client visiting from New York.

"Then you must go! Please don't be late on my account."

"It is fine, Isobel. He is not due until

afternoon. I was going to check something before his arrival, but there is plenty of time."

He asked her about Grace and she told him how she hadn't seen her daughter since Christmas, as Grace had only just returned from a vacation in Miami.

"Are you staying with her?"

"No she rents a tiny room with a single bed. I'm actually staying at a small hotel in Montmartre. Lovely rooftop views though."

"Which one is that?"

She answered automatically, but was distracted by having to check her phone. What time was it? Oh no – already midday.

"I'm so sorry, Jean-Luc. I have to go. I'll be late for my daughter. Please let me get the bill."

"Not at all. I insist. But are you sure you will be OK? Your clothes are still very wet."

This was true. For the last half hour, she had been gently dripping onto the seat and floor. When she stood, she felt her coat heavy with water.

He hesitated slightly, "Could you let your daughter know you will be a little late?"

"What do you mean?"

"My apartment is not far from here. I could lend you something dry to wear."

She laughed, "I couldn't possibly borrow your clothes. And I really can't make you any later than you are already."

"Not my clothes."

Ah.

"Your wife's?"

"She is away right now. You are a similar size, I think. Truly she would not mind."

Doubtful. She would mind if Robert took a strange woman back to our house and offered her the pick of her wardrobe.

"No. Truly. But thank you all the same. Grace will have something I can borrow until I get back to the hotel."

"Then at least let me find you a taxi. You will catch a chill if you don't change your clothes soon."

She was shivering with cold even after the Cognac, so she accepted his offer with thanks. As she was about to step into the taxi, he held out his hand to say good-bye, then lent forward and kissed her gently on both cheeks. He smelled wonderful.

"Good-bye, Jean-Luc, and thank you again."

"*Au revoir*, Isobel. My pleasure."

◆ ◆ ◆

"Goodness, Mum, what on earth happened?"

"I slipped. Snow. Stupid thing to do."

"You're soaked. Better come straight to my room and find something to borrow. Leave your boots by the door though. Better take your coat off there too."

It seemed their roles were reversed. She followed Grace through the Chirol drawing room to the lodgings beyond.

Grace had made her little bedroom very cosy, covering the walls with art postcards and cramming her one shelf with photos and fairy lights. Isobel looked around with approval. "Where did that come from?"

It was a new throw on the bed. Mexican perhaps? Hot colours and bold patterns.

"Miami."

Of course. Deep breath. "Can't wait to hear all about it."

"Let's find you something to wear first."

She was nowhere close to Grace's slim figure, but in the end they found her a baggy jumper and some tracksuit bottoms she could just about squeeze into. Grace hung the wet clothes over the little radiator. "Coffee?"

"Yes please. And then we should go and find some lunch."

"No need. I bought cheese and bread yesterday."

"That sounds perfect. Seems very quiet here. No Nina?"

"She stayed on with George for a few days. Everyone else is out."

"Surprised the weather didn't put them off!"

Grace smiled, "Nothing would prevent Madame Chirol from getting to her Bridge."

Over lunch, Isobel heard all about the Miami visit.

"What did you say the place where George and Nina live is called again?"

"Sunset Island Two."

"I still think it sounds like a made-up name. Is there a Sunset Island One?"

"Yep. Four in total."

"Photos please!" Grace had sent a few while away, but Isobel was curious to see more of George's house.

"I'll get my phone. Prepare to be amazed."

She had to admit, it was pretty amazing. "I had no idea Miami was so beautiful. All this water."

"I know. Driving to Miami Beach from the city is pretty spectacular. Feels like you're driving over the Bay for miles."

"George's house looks incredible."

"Actually it's not as palatial as some homes I saw on the Islands, but even so . . . "

It was Spanish in style, on the waterfront, with palm trees punctuating the lawn and the ubiquitous turquoise blue of the pool.

"Lovely."

"It is. Worth squillions too."

"I bet. Pretty different to our house!"

"Chalk and cheese."

"And you, Grace? Any more I can see of you?"

Grace scrolled through quickly. "Here."

She held out the phone. Grace on a lounger

by the pool, cocktail in hand. Very beautiful. Very happy.

"You look great, darling. Any others?"

Again the hasty scrolling. Grace and Nina in the garden with the Bay behind them. Bare legs, short skirts, huge smiles.

"Gorgeous girls. Did you go out much at night?"

"Not so much in the evening."

"Why was that?"

Grace laughed, "I told you. Too young to drink in America, Mum."

She stayed with Grace most of the afternoon, but by four o'clock they noticed it had begun to snow heavily again. They could hear voices elsewhere in the apartment. Madame Chirol must be back from her Bridge. Presumably that was Antoinette she was talking to, but it was too indistinct for Isobel to make out what was being said.

Grace went to make more coffee. When she came back, she was holding a plate of the 'parent' biscuits. "I think you should go back to the hotel, Mum. Antoinette said the snow might cause problems on the Metro. Montmartre's a long walk from here."

"You're right, sweetie. How are my clothes doing?"

"Not bad. Do you want to change back into yours or keep those for now?"

"I'll change. Let's have that coffee first."

"You can stay here if you like."

"Think I need my own warm clothes. How about you coming back with me?"

"Is there room?"

"It's tiny but we could manage. Cosy! At least then we can have the evening together."

"Great plan. Don't want you falling over again."

"I'm not that decrepit, Grace!"

Grace laughed, "So you say."

If walking down to Abbesses had been a challenge that morning, the walk up to the hotel was even more so. Snow whirled all around them, settling on their eye-lashes and eye-brows, so they could barely see where they were going. At one point, Grace skidded, nearly crashing into a stationary car. Isobel began to think she would happily exchange this frosted, urban beauty for ease of getting around.

However, it was one of the happiest evenings they had spent together for a long time. They ate omelette and frites at the bistro opposite the hotel, then curled up in Isobel's bed and watched television. English-speaking channels were few, but they found an American one showing old episodes of *Will & Grace*.

"How old *is* this?" said Grace.

"Nineties I guess."

"Did you and Dad watch it?"

"Now and then."

"What on earth did Dani make of it?"

"No idea. Don't think we ever discussed it. Why?"

"It's so . . . last-century!"

Isobel laughed, "Well it would be, wouldn't it? At least they got one thing right."

"What's that?"

"The name. Very tasteful."

Later that night, when they had turned off the light and curled up spoon-like, with Isobel's arms around her daughter, Grace said something she rarely voiced, "Love you, Mum."

Isobel squeezed her, "Love you too, sweetheart."

Later still, Isobel was woken by a noise. It was Grace talking in her sleep. Most of it was an incoherent mumble, but one word was uttered with perfect clarity. "George."

◆ ◆ ◆

The next morning, they walked arm-in-arm up to Sacré-Cœur, enjoying the satisfying crunch of fresh snow under their feet. The Basilica rose slowly out of the narrow streets. White on white. The view over Paris was literally dazzling, not a cloud in the azure blue of the sky.

There was no more snow forecast and the bitter cold of the previous day had gone. The snow wouldn't last long. Things would soon be back to normal.

After croissant and coffee in the square, they agreed that Grace should head back to do her homework for the week. Isobel would pick her up after lunch and they would go shopping together. If this was going to be a bad winter, Grace would need a better coat.

"Have you talked to Dad?" asked Grace.

"Not yet." A twinge of guilt.

"OK. I'll give him a call later."

"He'd like that,"

"You should do the same."

"Will do. Promise."

Watching Grace head off down the hill, Isobel brooded on how to fill her morning.

The snow looked so beautiful she decided to pass the time by walking to the Montmartre cemetery. She knew Zola was buried here somewhere, but the snow was thick on the burial plots, so she had no hope of finding him without someone to guide her. It was so perfectly still and peaceful that she felt as if she were far from the city. She walked around the little houses of the dead, admiring the statuary and mentally selecting the one she would choose. Occasionally Grace would spring to her mind. Or George. But after a while, she realised there was another name bubbling up from deep within her sub-conscious: Jean-Luc. What would have happened if she'd accepted his offer to go back to the apartment and change her clothes? What had he intended to happen? Why was she even bothering to contemplate it?

Back at the hotel, the concierge called her over. "Madame Peters, a moment."

Were they going to get ratty that Grace had stayed with her? Fine. She would just have to pay the extra.

"These came for you, Madame."

Twelve creamy roses.

"For me?"

"Yes Madame."

"I think there's been a mistake."

"No, Madame." A shy smile. "Your name is Isobel, yes?"

Why was he asking her? "Yes."

"That is what it says on the card."

He pointed to the address on the envelope, 'Isobel' and then the name of the hotel. No Madame Peters.

She took the bouquet and made her way to her room. She knew who they were from before she opened the card. There was only one possibility. She remembered him asking where she was staying, but had no recollection of telling him.

'Dear Isobel, I very much hope you have recovered from your fall. Please say we can meet again. I enjoyed our coffee very much. Warmest Regards, Jean-Luc.' There was a telephone number at the bottom.

The extraordinary nerve of it. The wonderful, miraculous nerve of it. She looked at the roses and then back to the card. The ball was in her court. What was she going to do?

She phoned the concierge. What time had the flowers been delivered? While she had been choosing the dream home for her dead body apparently.

She sat on the edge of her bed, immobile with indecision. She still had three hours before she was due to meet Grace. She could make up an excuse and push that to four hours. She looked in the mirror. Not great, but a hundred times better than yesterday when she was soaked in snow and crying. Was this all a misunderstanding? Maybe Jean-Luc was a serial killer or a con man. Maybe he made a habit of literally picking up women off the streets. She thought back to breakfast at the Ritz with George. That didn't end so well. Only one way to find out. She reached for her phone and dialled the number.

Grace could not work out what was wrong with her mother. For one thing, she'd messaged her to say she would be an hour late, but with no reason given. For another, she had actually been nearly two hours late, but had arrived with a huge smile on her face and no apology or explanation. She had just lost track of time she said. Had been exploring the area around the Jardin du

Luxembourg for a change. She didn't explain why they couldn't have done that together

"Isn't that close to where you were yesterday?" asked Grace. "Where you fell over?"

"I suppose it is."

"So what did you find?"

"Find?"

"Around the Jardin du Luxembourg? Any shops we should look at?"

"I didn't really notice."

"Didn't notice?"

"No."

"But I left you before ten and it's nearly three now – five hours is quite a long time. What were you doing if you weren't shopping?"

"Just wandering in the snow. Time sort of drifted past."

That was the other thing annoying Grace. Isobel was all smiles and a spring in her step. She looked different somehow to the way she had looked last night or even that very morning.

"Well you could have rung. I thought you were here to see me and we've barely seen each other at all."

"Nonsense. We were together all yesterday afternoon and last night. Anyway I thought you had course work to do."

"Yes but I finished it ages ago."

"You sound cross, Grace. What's the matter?"

"I just think you should have let me know." She sounded petulant and she knew it.

Isobel simply smiled again. Maddening.

"Come on then. Let's head up to Boulevard Haussmann. We've plenty of time to find you a coat."

Even when they arrived at Galeries Lafayette, Isobel wasn't her usual self. Usually she would be by Grace's side, pulling things out, regaling her with cries of "This one!" or "That's so you!" Instead, she left Grace to look on her own and seemed lost in thought much of the time. She also checked her phone a great deal, smiling as she did so.

"Is it Dad?"

"What?"

"The messages you keep looking at?"

"Oh I see. No."

"Dani then?"

"Dani? No."

"Well who then?"

"What do you mean?"

"Who keeps messaging you?"

"No-one, sweetheart. I'm just checking my train hasn't been cancelled by the snow."

"Why would that make you smile?"

Isobel stopped smiling, looked annoyed, "I have no idea what you're talking about, Grace. If I'm smiling, it's because I'm here in Paris with you."

An air of coolness descended.

"Sorry," said Grace. "What do you think of this?" She held up a long cream coat with fake fur collar.

"It's nice," said Isobel, a shade uncertainly.

"You don't like it?"

"I do actually."

"Well?"

"It just seems a little old for you, Grace. Not very studenty."

And that," said Grace, 'is exactly why I like it."

Isobel lay on her hotel bed, too disorientated by the last thirty-six hours to take her clothes off and actually get into bed. What an idiot she'd been. Not so much because of Jean-Luc, but because of Grace. Of course she must suspect something. Isobel knew she'd been walking around with a huge Cheshire Cat grin on her face most of the afternoon. Dani would have seen through it straight away: any woman would. Why hadn't she thought to get her cover story up to speed first? She was never late for anything, as Grace well knew. Surely she could have come up with something better than "wandering in the snow"? When Grace had asked her what she had "found", her mind had gone completely blank. Then she had wanted to laugh out loud. She had "found" an extraordinarily handsome man who had led her by the hand to his beautiful apartment, where he had kissed her, undressed her and made love to her for what seemed like hours. She hadn't a clue what the Jardin du Luxembourg looked like. All she could bring to mind was the curve of Jean-Luc's buttocks.

She was euphoric with excitement. She knew guilt and regret would come knocking on her door eventually, but right now she was saturated with happiness. It occurred to her that it wasn't just she hadn't been *this* happy for a long time, she wasn't sure she had *ever* been quite so happy. When she met Robert? Not quite like this. When she had given birth to Grace? Different again. She wanted to skip around naked in the Place Emile Goudeau below. She wanted to relive the morning over and over in her head. In fact she had done precious little else all day.

She looked at her phone. Midnight. She had to be up early to catch the Eurostar home, but she wasn't sure how she would ever get to sleep. She checked her messages again and re-read the last one from Jean-Luc sent just under an hour ago, "Goodnight, sweet Isobel. I wish you safe travels and very much hope you will return to Paris before too long." Two kisses. It was a restrained message given the afternoon they had spent together, but she was in no doubt he was as anxious as she was to be . . . re-acquainted. How the hell would she make that happen? It was Robert's turn to visit Grace next, but even that wouldn't be for at least a month. Money was tight and there was no way he would agree to any more visits by her until March at the earliest. Even then he would probably argue that it was so close to Easter, it would be better if Grace came to them. What on earth was she to do?

She was under no illusions. They weren't teenagers; they were two consenting adults who had found an affinity and an attraction that had led from one thing to another. She was married and not unhappily enough to do anything about it. Jean-Luc was married and happily so by his own account. His wife may have been absent physically, but her presence was everywhere in their apartment. She – they – had impeccable taste. In photographs, they looked like the golden couple they undoubtedly were.

"Where is she?" Isobel had asked, sitting up in bed as Jean-Luc brought her a post-coital espresso.

"Rome."

"Doing what?"

"Working."

She had wanted to ask, which sort of work was that? But it was obvious he didn't want to talk about his wife. Neither did he make any reference to Grace or Robert. It occurred to her he would consider it bad manners to do so. For the same reason, she couldn't ask whether he did this a lot? Took women he hardly knew to bed whenever his wife was away? Or was it an open relationship and right now she was bedding her lover in Rome? With horror, she realised she might well have picked up an infection. Too old to fall pregnant at least? Surely that was true?

All the time her mind turned over the events of the day, there was one thought she tried again and again to bury. Yet up it would come, from deep in the ocean bed of her mind. A giant squid of a thought, ugly and threatening. *Robert.* What was she going to tell Robert? Nothing or everything? Did she secretly want him to know or did the idea terrify her? For the love of her, she couldn't work it out. Robert wasn't just her husband; he was her best friend. For all their ups and downs, that was still true. Did she owe him the truth or did she owe him her silence? She had never been unfaithful before and yet she had needed worryingly little persuasion. Twelve creamy roses – she was looking at them now – was all it had taken. Yet she knew even that wasn't the truth. Jean-Luc could have saved his money; the roses were superfluous. The fact was she had gone to bed with Jean-Luc because *he* had wanted so badly to go to bed with *her*.

"Why me?' she had asked.

They had made love a second time and she lay on her side while he gently stroked her back.

"Mmmmmm?"

"Why choose me?"

He had pulled her over so she faced him. He looked very serious.

"Is that a serious question? Why am I making

love to you?"

"Yes."

"Because I wanted to make love to you from the moment I helped you up from the ground. You were so wet, so upset, so helpless - yet so lovely."

"I looked terrible."

"No, Isobel. This where you are wrong. You looked *in need*. I wanted to take you home there and then, run you a hot bath, kiss you all over."

"In need? Not sure that is the biggest compliment of my life, Jean-Luc."

He laughed. "Then you don't understand men, Isobel. A women in need – *of us* – is very sexy and desirable. Why would I not want you? You're beautiful. Look how you make me feel."

She looked. Which is how she had come to be an hour late for Grace. She couldn't help smiling at the memory, although her eyes were dropping with tiredness. And that is how she came to fall asleep, fully-clothed on her bed, waking to the insistent ring of her phone just before five.

At first she thought it was the alarm, but when she reached to turn it off, she saw the word Home on the screen.

"Robert?" She knew she sounded half asleep, could barely make her mouth work.

"Bel. Sorry if I've woken you." For a moment, she thought he was crying. Struggled to pull herself awake.

"What is it?"

He seemed to be struggling to form his words too. "It's Pam."

"Mum? What is it?"

"You need to come home, Bel."

She was wide awake now, "I am coming home. You know I am. What is it?"

"I'm at the hospital. With Jack."

"Hospital? What's happened? Has she had another fall?"

He was crying. Couldn't hide it any longer, "She's dead, Bel. I'm so sorry. She died about half an hour ago."

When they finished talking, she sat on the edge of the hotel bed, dry-eyed. Robert had been crying so much by the end of the call that she'd struggled to take in the details. Why wasn't she crying? What sort of daughter didn't cry at the news of her mother's death? It was impossible that was why. Her mum wasn't dead at all. Robert had made a stupid mistake. She would go home, go to the hospital and find Pam sitting up in bed, charming the nurses and persuading the doctors to allow her straight home to cook Jack's tea. She had looked fine a few days ago when Isobel had seen her last. Paler and more breathless perhaps, but fine. She was booked in to see a cardiologist in a couple of weeks' time, but the GP had been clear she was not an urgent case. It must have been someone else that had died and the hospital had stupidly given Robert the wrong name. There was simply no way her mum had died.

But even as she tried to persuade herself that the hospital had got it wrong, she knew there was no mistake. Robert who never cried had sobbed like a little child. Automatically, she began to pack; the Eurostar left at eleven. She needed to call them as soon as possible and try to get Grace a seat on the same train. Robert and she had agreed it would be better if Isobel gave her the news. The very thought made her feel sick.

Her phone pinged. Robert?

It was Jean-Luc, "Good morning, sweet Isobel. I am enjoying honey on toast. It reminds me of you." Three kisses this time.

She looked at the phone and felt like throwing it out the window. How could she have done that? What a gold-plated, egotistical, selfish bitch. Quickly she tapped a command: block this number. She certainly did not owe Jean-Luc any sort of explanation.

It wasn't until Thursday, five days later, that Isobel cried. She had got up to make breakfast and was stirring porridge on the Aga when, for no obvious reason, she began to cry noisily and snottily. Tears splashed into the pan. Robert heard and came to put his arms around her, saying "Please, Bel, don't cry."

"I can cry if I bloody well like!" she shouted. "You did. Leave me alone!"

And then, throwing the wooden porridge spoon at his head, she rushed from the kitchen upstairs to her bedroom where she sobbed and sobbed. She heard Robert's footsteps outside the bedroom and knew he was wondering whether to knock on the door. After a moment, she heard him walking slowly downstairs. She buried her face in the pillow and shouted loudly in her head for her Mum to come back *now*. She pleaded with her, cajoled her, bargained with her, but mainly she said sorry. There was so much to be sorry for she realised, from the big things "I should have given you more grandchildren" to the small things "I should have taken you shopping more often". Interspersed with specific regrets was a continuing mantra like an ear-worm in her head, "I'm so sorry, Mum, I'm so sorry, please come back. Please let me try again." After an hour of crying, praying and pleading, she was exhausted and fell into a deep, dreamless sleep.

When she woke up, Dani was sitting on the edge of her bed. She had checked up on Isobel every day, bringing round Saskia's home-made pies and stews. Far too much of it. The freezer was now bulging.

"Tea," she said, pointing to the mug on the

bedside table. "Lots of sugar."

"I don't take sugar."

"I know. Good for you though. Helps in times of shock."

"I'm not in shock, Dani. I'm just sad."

"Not going to argue with you. Just drink the tea."

Isobel pulled herself up into a sitting position.

"I must look like shit."

"You have looked better."

She sipped the tea miserably, "I never thought I would miss her so much."

"We never know until they've gone."

Isobel began to well up again, "Wish I'd known that. Made more effort while I had her."

"It's not how it works, sadly," said Dani. "How's Jack doing?"

"Not great. Far too quiet. Grace insisted that she would stay with him until we sorted something out, but she looks terrible. Mum's death has shocked her to the core. We all took it for granted that she would out-live Dad."

"Seems very cruel."

"It is. And now . . . . "

"Now?"

"And now Robert and I are faced with what to do – about Dad. This house isn't suitable – far too many winding stairs up to the bedrooms. Do we find him a live-in carer, which he will hate, or do we bite the bullet and find a nursing home?"

"What does Robert think?"

"He thinks given Dad's frailty, a good care home is the answer. But Mum was so adamant that it would never happen . . ."

Tears began to roll down her face once more. Dani took the mug from her hands and put her arms round her, "What will be will be, Bel. Jack will adjust given time. Maybe you should start looking. Grace can't hold the fort forever."

Isobel nodded, "I know. The funeral isn't for nearly three weeks and there's no point her missing out on her course for all that time. We think she should go back this weekend and come back the day before the service. Robert and I will take turns staying with Dad."

"Saskia and I can help too. Add us to the rota."

"Would you really? Seems a big ask."

"I wouldn't offer if we hadn't discussed it."

"Thanks Dani. You're an absolute rock."

"No problem. With everything that's happened, I never had the chance to ask how Paris was last weekend? Robert says you had bad snow – he was panicking you might get delayed coming home. Thank goodness you didn't."

Last weekend. Just one week ago she was here in Rye packing for her trip to Paris. It seemed a life-time ago. "It was eventful, to be honest."

"The snow you mean?"

"Yes. Beautiful of course, but a bit of an adventure." She couldn't say anything more. Not right now.

"And Grace?"

"Fine. Had an amazing time in Miami by the looks of her photos. Then this happened. It's what Robert would call Compensation Theory."

"Meaning?"

"The pendulum swings. Something brilliant is followed by something terrible."

"Never the other way round?"

"Not in my experience, no." She blew her nose loudly.

"Then we need to do something about that. More tea?"

She nodded, "I'll wash my face and come down. Is Robert OK? I threw something at him."

"He told me. Apart from having porridge stuck in his hair, he's absolutely fine."

◆ ◆ ◆

"Tea, Grandad?"

He looked up, barely seemed to register who she was for a moment. "No, Grace love, I'm fine."

Her Grandad was sitting in the chair he always sat in, next to the fireplace where Grace had lit the electric fire. She had already turned the central heating up because the wind outside was icy. She was terrified her Grandad would fall ill next, so the house was far warmer than usual. She half expected her Granny to walk in at any moment, tutting as she turned the thermostat down.

There was no flue in the tiled fireplace; it was for show only. Her Granny had loved it, because it had niches where she could arrange knick-knacks and a mantel that was perfect for photos. Her Grandad seemed to be staring at these, but Grace could tell he wasn't really seeing anything. He had been like this since Sunday. Staring fixedly ahead, lost in his own world, eyes red although she had not caught him crying openly.

"Mum will be here soon?"

"Isobel? That's nice."

"She'll be staying with you tonight, remember?"

He looked surprised, "Where will you sleep, duckie?" There was only one single guest bed.

"I'm going home to pack, Grandad. Have to go back to Paris tomorrow – we talked about it yesterday? Then I'll be home again for Granny's . . . . you know . . ."

He looked blank. "Granny's?"

"Her funeral, Grandad. I'll be back for that."

He nodded sadly. "Should have been me, Gracie. Me that went first."

"Don't say that, Grandad. Please."

"True though. And now I'm nothing but a bloody nuisance."

Grace had tried hard not to cry in front of him, but she felt tears pricking her eyes, "No you're not. You're not a nuisance at all. We never think that."

The doorbell rang. Grace hurried to the door, relieved to have something to do. Mrs Dawkins stood on the doorstep, holding a plate of limp-looking shortbreads.

"Hello Grace dear. Just thought I would pop by to find out how Jack's doing?"

Did she want to be invited in? Grace wasn't sure her Grandad would appreciate the call.

At that point, he called from the sitting room, "Who is it, Grace?"

"Mrs Dawkins, Grandad. Just asking how you are. She's baked you some biscuits."

"Tell her I'm doing as well as can be expected. And thank her for asking. I don't want any bloody biscuits though. Diabetes."

"OK, Grandad."

Mrs Dawkins shifted uncomfortably, tried to smile. "Let me know if there's anything I can do to help. Poor Pam. Of course it had been on the cards for a while, but a shock nonetheless."

Why couldn't Mrs Dawkins just sod off with her horrible biscuits? Grace knew her mother loathed her and she could understand why. Prying busy-body.

She wasn't going to give up that easily though. "Where's your mother? Surely she hasn't left you to look after poor Jack?"

What a cheek. Didn't she think Grace capable?

"She's on her way. We're on a rota."

"A rota? Would you like to include me on

that? I could easily stay over once or twice a week."

"Thank you, Mrs Dawkins, but I think we're fine. I'll tell Mum you called."

"Don't worry. I'll drop back later for a nice chat with your dear mother. I need to ask her about the flowers anyway. For the church, you know. Pam always had very definite ideas about flowers, so we want to get it right."

It was no use. The tears were starting again.

"Oh my dear, I'm so sorry. Is there anything at all I can do?"

Unable to speak, Grace shook her head and gently closed the door. She could see the shape of Mrs Dawkins through the crinkled glass of the door. Surely she wasn't going to ring the doorbell again? Slowly the shape receded down the path.

"Grace?"

She made a monumental effort, "Yes, Grandad?"

"Let's have a nice cup of tea after all, duckie."

The vicar came round to see Jack to talk about the funeral. Isobel sat next to her father, holding his hand, wishing she could wave a wand and make it all go away.

"Did you have any readings in mind? Anything Pam particularly liked?"

"She liked Psalm 23." Jack spoke with such confidence that Isobel was embarrassed she didn't know which one Psalm 23 was.

"And who would you like to read that?"

"Isobel here could do that, couldn't you, love?" She nodded. Wished she could say No.

"Anything else? What about hymns?"

"She always loved '*Jerusalem*'."

She had anticipated this. "Let's not have that one, Dad."

"Why not?"

"I've never heard it sung well, to be honest. Gets very screechy."

She could see the vicar trying not to smile. At least he was on her side.

Jack looked annoyed, "What do you suggest then?"

"How about '*Lord of All Hopefulness*'? She always loved the words to that."

"Ideally, we need two at least," said the vicar "Any others come to mind?"

"'*The Day Thou Gavest Lord Has Ended*'," said Jack. Then turning to Isobel, "I want that one too."

"Well, let's deal with mum for now," she said cheerfully. "One at a time."

"Is there a family member who will give an address?" asked the vicar. "Or do you want me to do it?"

He was relatively new to the parish. Had met Pam, but not in her heyday.

"I'm not up to it, Isobel," said Jack sadly. "I know I'm letting her down, but I just can't do it."

"You're not letting her down, Dad. Robert won't mind doing it." He wasn't there to disagree.

"Is that your brother?" asked the vicar.

"My husband. I'm an only child."

"That just about covers the service then. Will you be having an order of service printed?"

Isobel nodded.

"Leave it with me then and I'll work out it out. The order that is." He smiled and stood up to leave.

"More tea, vicar?" Had she actually said that? It sounded like a line from the local am dram society.

"No, thank you, Isabella. I'll be on my way."

"Isobel."

"Sorry?"

"I'm Isobel, not Isabella. Not that it matters." He looked at her blankly. His mind must be on a higher plane.

When he'd gone, she went off to the kitchen and made another tray of tea for herself and Jack. It was her turn to stay that night.

"We need to have a chat, Dad."

"Do we?" He looked sly; she guessed he knew what was coming.

"We do. There are decisions to be made."

"I'm not going into a home." He was right as it happened. She'd spent the last week searching for a home, but the only ones remotely suitable had a waiting list. As the waiting list depended on residents dying, it was impossible to predict how long it might take to find him a place.

"I know you don't want to go into a home, but you will have to have a live-in carer."

"Your mum never wanted someone else living here."

"I know she didn't, Dad, but there isn't a choice."

"I might not like them. The carer."

"You'll get the chance to meet her in advance."

"A woman then?"

"Do you prefer a man?" That would be typical. Live-in male carers were in scant supply as every agency had told her.

"I don't prefer either. Strange people in my house. I don't like it."

"I know, but they – she - won't be a stranger for long."

"Why can't you move in?" Surely he wasn't serious?

"Dad! I can't leave Robert to live here." Even if there were no Robert, that would be out of the question.

"You could see him at weekends. It's not as though you have much to do with Grace away."

"No, Dad!" His selfishness was comic in its monstrosity.

Jack looked sulky, "Have you found someone then?"

"I think so, yes. I haven't met her yet, but the agency sent me her CV and she looks great."

"Can I afford her?"

Jack had retired on a generous pension, "You won't be out on the streets, if that's what you mean."

"I won't like her."

She had anticipated this reaction too, "You are not to be difficult about this, Dad. No unpleasantness or awkwardness. If this carer doesn't work out because of your attitude, you will have to go into a home. End of story. Final."

It was a bluff she had to try.

There was a long silence. "When's she moving in then?" Christ! Had she actually won the battle?

"Just after the funeral. We'll keep our rota system going until then."

"Doesn't sound as though I have a choice."

"No. You don't." Guilt washed over her. "Sorry."

"Can I meet her at least?"

"Of course you can. I need to meet her too. We'll get her over here as soon as possible."

"What if I don't like her? Really don't like here."

"If you don't like her – and *I don't like her* – we'll keep looking. But you can't just take a dislike to her for any old reason."

"Well, there'll be one good thing, I hope."

"What's that?"

"She might make better tea than you. Not this bitter slop."

She wasn't going to rise to the bait, "Shall I tip it down the sink?"

He shook his head, "No, I'll put up with it."

"We all have our crosses to bear, Dad." The Jack-shaped one on her back was proving very heavy indeed.

FEBRUARY

Isobel sat in the front pew between her father and Grace, staring fixedly ahead. Out of the corner of her eye she could see the edge of the pine coffin, topped by the floral tribute that she had chosen from the undertaker's catalogue. Pam had been insistent on pine in the letter of wishes she left with her Will. She always did hate money to be spent unnecessarily.

Robert gave the tribute they had written together, weaving an affectionate picture of her mother: Pam the good wife, the loving mother, the devoted grandmother, active member of the local community, arranger of flowers at this very church. Beside her, Grace wept quietly into a crumpled handkerchief Pam had embroidered for her, while Jack surreptitiously wiped a tear from his eye. Isobel herself was dry-eyed, unmoved. She floated above the congregation that had gathered to say their farewells, determined to focus her attention elsewhere. She was relieved to hear the distant hum of a lorry, latching onto the noise as it rumbled towards the village until its vibrations could be felt down the ancient pews, following its progress down the street as it became more distant and then was lost from earshot.

Robert was coming to the end now. He had rehearsed at home with her and she recognised the cues of the winding-up paragraph, mentally willing it to be over. She could not wait for this day to come to an end. But then he said something for which she had not prepared. "I have talked about Pam as wife, mother, grandmother, friend and neighbour, but I have not said what she meant to me, as her son-in-law."

His voice choked. Isobel looked straight at him, appalled that he might start to cry. Grace was sobbing uncontrollably now and she could hear the ripple of handbags opening as women felt for dry tissues. Men blew their noses loudly.

Robert took a deep breath and pushed on, "When Isobel and I first met and she took me to meet her parents, I knew I was not what Pam was hoping for." Where was this going? Why was he not sticking to the script?

He smiled, "Isobel was, after all, an only child, a precious prize – beautiful and clever. I was a penniless book dealer, punching far above my weight.

"But when Pam realised how much I loved her, she took me aside and said she had absolute confidence that I would never do anything to harm or hurt her daughter and that she gave me her blessing in full." Had her mother said that? It was news to her.

"As our own only daughter enters adulthood, I can now fully recognise what generosity of spirit that took. What faith she laid in me. I never told Pam I loved her," here his voice cracked, "but I did. For without Pam there would be no Isobel and no Grace. She gave me everything I hold most dear."

As he took his seat at the other side of Jack, she saw her father squeeze his hand. Grace lent her head on her mother's shoulder, splashing tears down her sleeves while Isobel gently patted her arm. Robert looked over at her; he knew she hated surprises. She managed to smile and mouth, "thank you" but inwardly she thought how embarrassed Pam would have been to hear such a public display of affection. Not her mother's style at all.

Her parents had bought a double funeral plot in the church graveyard some years ago, so Robert supported Jack at the head of the funeral procession as they followed the coffin down the aisle. Isobel tried not to focus on anyone in the congregation, but she vaguely took in Saskia's blotchy face and Mrs Dawkins' horrible hat.

Was a burial preferable to immolation?

Certainly it made a change from the grim impersonality of a crematorium, but seeing the coffin lowered deep into the ground was shocking even so. Pam had got her way on the cheapness of the coffin, but Isobel had insisted on ordering her mother new black trousers and a cream silk blouse as her going-away outfit. She had taken these to the funeral parlour along with a few pieces of Pam's costume jewellery and her favourite lipstick. The girl on reception seemed used to dealing with such requests, but how did Isobel know that she had not simply taken them home and tried them on for size? What a horrible person she must be to even think such a thing.

Pam would have been shocked by such a waste of money, that much she did know. Now looking down at the coffin lying on the mud, with rain threatening to fall, she knew how pointless such gestures were. Apparently, it took over a decade for a body to decompose. That was ten years of not trying to imagine what was going on deep in that grave. For the first time, she thought how very selfish her parents had been. Why couldn't they have chosen the crem like everyone else? The scattering of ashes would have marked the final chapter. This burial felt like a beginning not an end.

"Are you OK?' whispered Robert. "You've gone a bit pale." She nodded, miserably. The vicar finished his blessing and the undertaker handed her and Jack a cream rose each. She heard her father whisper, "good-bye, love", as he let his rose fall down onto the coffin. She closed her eyes and tried to pray, but nothing came, so she mouthed "bye, Mum" and let her own rose fall.

The rain was falling heavier now, so one of the undertakers took Jack's arm and escorted him carefully down the brick church path to the community hall where Mrs Dawkins' 'ladies' had organised tea and sandwiches. Robert held an umbrella over her and Grace as best he could; none of them spoke. Grace had stopped crying but was pink-eyed and pale. Behind them, the funeral congregation followed with lowered voices.

It had been a beautiful funeral. Everyone said so. Isobel stood with cup of tea in hands, while people she barely knew told her how like her mother she was, how much they would miss Pam, how unexpected her loss had been. Then they would look over at Jack, sitting with Grace at the side of the hall, and whisper, "What about your father? How is he doing?" Isobel found herself repeating the same mantra, "Do I? Thank you. It was a shock for all of us. Dad's bearing up well, all things considered." The tea grew cold, untouched, unnoticed.

Robert was praised for his tribute, "Pam would have been so moved." Isobel nodded her appreciation, while wondering if people secretly shared her own reservations. What Pam had hated more than anything was "a fuss", a description so vague it could cover almost any social situation, including her own funeral. After about an hour, people began to hover around her in a sort of nebulous queue, saying their good-byes and thanking her for the hospitality. She realised her feet were killing her.

It had been agreed that Robert would stay with Jack that night. Her father was looking grey with exhaustion, but was determined to stay to the bitter end. "Can't let Pam down", she heard him say crossly when Mrs Dawkins suggested he might want to go home "and put his feet up".

Mrs Dawkins was having none of it. "You be careful, Jack Wilson" she said archly, "or you'll be following Pam down that hole quicker than you think."

Isobel was furious. Such insensitivity. But Jack laughed for the first time since Pam's death, "You're probably right, Mavis. I do feel a bit done in." Mavis? Since when had those two been on first-name terms?

Robert helped Jack into his coat and she walked over to kiss her dad good-bye. "I'll see you tomorrow," she said. "I'll be there when Lauren arrives and help to settle her in."

"Don't want a strange woman in my house. And I don't think it's necessary." Robert shot her a look and gestured he was going to say good-bye to Dani and Saskia. Coward.

"Dad, we've been through this. You can't be on your own."

“Your mother wouldn’t have liked it. A stranger in the house.”

“She wouldn’t have liked the idea of you being on your own. You know that.”

“I can manage.”

“No, Dad, you can’t. Come on, we’ve agreed this is for the best.”

They had been through it many times over the past two weeks.

“Grace could stay a bit longer.” Not so much a statement as a question.

“No she can’t, Dad. She has to go back to Paris this week. You know that. Please let’s not start this again. Not now.”

Robert reappeared, “Ready, Jack?”

“Where’s Grace?”

“Here I am, Grandad.” Telepathy. Isobel saw how carefully she put her arms around him, so as not to throw him off balance.

“Will I see you tomorrow, duckie?”

“Of course. I’m coming over with Mum to meet the . . . the . . . .”

“Lauren,” said Isobel.

“Lauren,” repeated Grace.

He was beaten and he knew it, but who could blame him for putting up one last fight? “Don’t like the name Lauren.”

Sitting on the Eurostar, going back to Paris, Grace couldn't work out how she felt about anything. Was she pleased to be going back or did she dread it? Was she a terrible person for feeling immense relief to be getting away from her parents and her sad, lonely grandfather? Would "going home" ever feel the same now her granny was gone? How would she cope back at Madame Chirol's feeling as she did? She felt as if she were a small boat that had lost its anchor and was now drifting rudderless into the uncertain, open sea.

Her granny dying so soon after her return from Miami had felt like a punishment from the gods. The fact was that Dani had been right: she was desperately in love, but had absolutely no-one in whom she could confide. When Nina had made the joke at Grassy Key about her marrying George, it had twisted a knife in her gut. How would she ever be able to tell Nina that she was madly in love with her father? That he gave every sign of reciprocating that love?

Staring out of the window, she traced back all that had happened in the last four months, from when she and George had first met in the Tuileries Gardens when she was on the ridiculous carousel. When Nina had introduced them, he had given her such a direct look her legs actually trembled. Then they'd all met for a drink in Le Papillon that night, and she'd felt furious with her mother for taking all of his attention. In frustration, she'd knocked back the champagne so quickly, the room had swum.

The next day, a message had flashed onto her phone from a number she didn't know. "You looked so beautiful riding a white horse. George".

It turned out he'd asked Nina for her number, saying he wanted to stay in touch with Isobel and Robert and needed their contact details. From then on, they'd messaged each other three or four times a week, rising to three or four times a day. She knew it was hopeless and she knew it was wrong, but she couldn't resist. Deep down, she couldn't believe that someone so handsome, worldly and successful could have picked her out. Carlos had no chance after that.

Deceit didn't come naturally to Grace, so it troubled her keep her infatuation secret from Nina: particularly when she accompanied her to dinners with George, her friend ignorant of the fact that he and Grace had already exchanged messages that day, or even met on occasions beforehand. George had kissed her and held her, but never suggested they go to bed. When she had shyly made it clear she would like it if they did, he had remained resolute, "Not yet. We need to be sure."

She guessed the thing that held him back was the one person they never mentioned when they were together: Nina.

Staying with George in Miami over new year

was a kind of torture. He'd been friendly and attentive of course, but had been careful never to do or say the slightest thing that might alert Nina to what was going on. If Nina left the room, George would find a reason to do the same.

"George isn't neglecting you, is he?" Nina would exclaim on her return. "His manners are usually better than that." What she didn't know was that messages silently criss-crossed the elegant interiors of the Sunset Island Two house all day long, messages that were anything but neglectful.

"Does George have any girlfriends?" she had once asked Nina as they sun-bathed on the lawn.

"I think he has dates from time to time, but nothing serious. I'm the only lady in his life."

"What about when you're older?"

"Who knows? I think he shut down that side of himself when mom died. One thing's for certain."

"What's that?"

"They'd have to get the Nina seal of approval first."

What made it worse was that Nina and she were so close. She loved the friendship they shared, would have done anything for her, yet she knew she was living in a state of double-think, refusing to engage with the messy consequences that lay ahead. Somehow there had to be a way forward for her and George. Nina loved them both – no matter how shocked she might be at first, surely she would accept them as a couple in time?

Her father's words at the funeral had hit her hard, especially the bit about him recognising how generous Pam had been to welcome him into the family. About her mum being such an adored only child. She had put her head on her mum's shoulder and wept without control. It had felt as if she were crying for her own parents, her own confused and guilt-ridden life.

By the time she got back to the apartment, it was gone eight. Damn. That would mean that Madame Chirol would be in the drawing room. Even though she lived there, Grace hated walking in unannounced.

Madame Chirol was seated in her usual spot, glass of calvados in one hand, a book in another. She looked up, "Good evening, Grace."

"Good evening, Madame."

"I did not expect you back so soon. How did it go? Your poor grandmother's funeral?"

"It went well, thank you."

"And your parents? How is your mother coping?"

"As well as can be expected, Madame. Sad."

"Death is always a shock. And you are a close family, *non*?"

Grace nodded. The wretched tears she had blinked back on the Eurostar were springing up again. Madame Chirol tactfully chose not to notice, "You must be tired, child."

"I am rather."

"*Bonne nuit.*"

"*Bonne nuit*, Madame."

She went to her room, flung her bag on the floor and lay on the bed, willing the tears to stop. This morning, she could barely wait to leave Rye. Now she wished with all her heart, she was back in her old bedroom, listening to the bells of St Mary's.

There was a gentle knock at the door. Nina of course. The one person she did not want to see right now.

"Come in."

Her friend stood in the doorway, hesitant, "I can come back later."

"No really. I'm fine."

"You don't look it."

"I'll be OK in a minute."

"Shall I put the kettle on?"

"Coffee would be nice. Thanks."

"Coming right up."

By the time, she reappeared again, mugs in hand, Grace had recovered her composure and shoved George deep into the recesses of her mind. Nina sat on the edge of the bed, while Grace sat cross-legged on the pillow. For a while they didn't speak, just blew steam off the coffee and took tiny sips of scalding liquid.

"How did it go? The funeral?"

"OK. Better than I thought in some ways. Worse in others."

"Such as?"

"My mum held it together well. My grandad not so much."

"Must be hard. What's going to happen to him."

"A carer. She's called Lauren. Met her yesterday – she seemed nice."

Nina nodded, "Well that's good."

"Yes."

"I Skyped George earlier. He sends his love."

"Thanks. Send him mine too." She always said that. Tried to keep her tone as flat as possible.

Nina hesitated, "I'm so sorry, Grace, about your granny. I liked her very much."

"And she loved meeting you too."

"How's your mum coping?."

"I think she's still shocked it was so sudden."

"She probably didn't know much about it. At least that's what people always try and tell you . . . ."

"Were you with your mum, Nina? When it happened?"

"George took me in that morning. To say good-bye. They knew it was close."

"What happened?"

"Nothing." She took a deep breath, "In a way,

it was already too late. She was out of it on morphine. She had no idea I was there. Well that's what I thought."

"What do you mean?"

"George said I should talk to her, tell her what I was up to at school, try to act normally. To be honest, I just felt embarrassed trying to do that. I couldn't think of anything to say."

"So what did you do?"

"George asked the nurses to leave me alone just for a minute or two. I still couldn't believe she was actually going to die, but then I realised that what she might like to know was what I was going to do when I grew up. She couldn't be here, but I could share my secret with her."

"And?"

"So I lent in real close and I said, 'mommy, I'm going to go to Paris, France one day to study fashion.' I remember being very anxious she would understand I meant this Paris – there are loads of them in America."

"Did she react?"

"No, nothing. I patted her on the arm and kissed her forehead and then George came in and that was that. She died that night."

"Oh Nina, that is sad. To think she never knew – and yet here you are."

"That's the funny thing. She was in and out of consciousness that evening, but George was with her the whole time. She wasn't making much sense, but her last words took him by surprise.

Know what they were? 'Paris, France'."

She smiled, "Turns out that George was right. He said the last sense to go is hearing – that's why he wanted me to keep talking. Once I knew that, I had to get here. Motivation!"

"That's amazing. Why have you never told me that before?"

"I don't know – maybe the moment never felt right. One thing you're going to learn is that all deaths lead back to other deaths. Your granny dying has nothing to do with my mother dying and yet it rips the sticking-plaster off the wound."

"I'm sorry."

"Don't be. Sometimes I like to remember, even though it hurts. That's something else you're going to find."

On the Tuesday after the funeral, Isobel was back in Miss Mapp, covering for Robert. It was nearly a month since her mother had died, in which time the shop had been closed more than usual. Dani and Saskia had offered to help out, but as Robert said this was the winter dead zone, so a few extra days of closure wouldn't make much difference. It was now mid-afternoon and she had sold nothing but two cards and a half-price diary. Who waited for February to buy a diary?

Its theme was cats and looking at the customer – a big, untidy woman of a certain age – it struck her she might be buying it for the pictures. She suddenly imagined her cutting out the pages and sticking them to her kitchen walls. This thought made her sad. She tried to smile brightly as she took the money, but when the door closed, she put her head in her hands and wished she didn't feel so desolate.

Robert was yet to dismantle his display of poetry books from the window, a half-hearted attempt to rustle up custom around Valentine's Day, which had fallen the previous week. One of these was a volume of Robert Graves' Complete Poems and contained a personal favourite of Isobel's:

She tells her love while half asleep,
In the dark hours,
With half-words whispered low:
As Earth stirs in her winter sleep
And puts out grass and flowers
Despite the snow,
Despite the falling snow.

Again and again, she recited these words in her head, conjuring up Saint-Sulpice in the snow, Jean-Luc helping her to her feet, the creamy roses and the magical day they had shared together. Pam's death had been so sudden and shocking, it had flung Jean-Luc from her mind. Worse, it had marred the magic of what had happened, tarring it with something tacky and grimy. She felt as if the Universe had punished her, unequivocally and swiftly, for her betrayal of Robert and the life they shared together. She was numbed and neutered by her own treachery.

It was more than that: how could she keep pretending she loved Robert and was happy in her marriage when she had found it so easy to betray him? The ugly truth was that she was bored and miserable. What did she want to happen exactly? This was the question that murmured at the back of her mind, but which she drowned out with the mundane. What were they eating tonight? When was the MOT due? Had they paid the water bill? Did Jack need more winter vests? *What did she want to happen?* Really she had no idea.

If only she hadn't thrown in her own job all those years ago. Grace was already halfway through her gap year and with every month that passed, Isobel was aware her own discontent was burgeoning. What would she do when there were no more reasons to go to Paris? No excuses to get away from Robert and Jack? The truth was she was jealous of Grace and all the opportunities that lay before her. She hated herself for it, but was powerless to extinguish the canker of envy that had taken root deep inside. Her own parents would never have supported the idea of a gap year; never encouraged her to widen her horizons. They had shown little interest in her working life, seeing it – as it turned out correctly – as something that would end with marriage and motherhood. No wonder she had never valued the tangible success she'd enjoyed as a working woman.

In fairness to Robert, the decision to jack it all in and move from London to Rye was far more her idea than his. So preoccupied was she with Grace that she hadn't seen how empty her life would become. She had allowed herself to become subsumed into Robert's work, handmaiden to Miss Mapp. Why hadn't she fought for something to call her own?

She thought of confiding to Dani, but she felt too ashamed to even do that. Robert had behaved faultlessly since Pam's death – supportive, loving, kind, tender – Dani would rightly point all of that out. It was Robert who had taken the call from Jack in the middle of the night; Robert who had called the ambulance and followed it through the mist to the hospital with Jack beside him silent with fear; Robert who had sat by the stretcher stroking Pam's cold hand while the doctors broke the news to Jack that there was nothing they could do to bring his wife back to him. And if that wasn't enough, he had then had to call Isobel and tell her that while she had been trolloping around Paris, her mother had died. Although of course, he had used no such language. Trolloping was a verb she applied solely to herself.

Now that the funeral was over and she had so little on the horizon, she found her mind more and more drifting back towards Jean-Luc. She still had his number on her phone, but hadn't dared unblock it. What would he be thinking of her? She could have sent him some sort of explanation by now. Even if they were to never meet again, surely she owed him that?

It was no good. It had to be done. She pressed Unblock and then sat for ages trying to find the right words. In the end, the best she could manage: was "Sorry not to have been in touch. My mother died unexpectedly. I put a block on my phone because it seemed best at the time. I hope you understand. Isobel".

She didn't add any kisses. She didn't want him to interpret her message as in any way flirtatious. They would not meet again.

The rest of the day dragged onwards. She flicked through the fiction section, but couldn't settle to anything weighty. In the end, she chose a book of short stories by Elizabeth Taylor, one of her favourite authors. Now and again, she checked her phone, but there were no messages. There were no customers either. By four o'clock, sick of her own dreary company, she decided to close early. As she pulled down the shutters, she heard her phone ping. It was Robert: "On way back. ETA 6pm xx". He was going to be pretty unimpressed with total sales amounting to two cards and a half-price cat calendar. How on earth were they going to keep going on that?

Another ping. This time an 0033 number. Something to do with Grace? "I am so sorry for your loss, Isobel. Please let me know if you come to Paris again xxx".

He didn't hate her then? Wasn't angry? Of course she wouldn't contact him again, but she felt relieved to know he harboured no ill feelings towards her. It was a nice message – neutral, but nice. Three kisses. What was code for three kisses? How much would he like to see her again? It had taken him over two hours to reply, after all. Had he just seen the message? Had he tried to ignore it? Or had he struggled like her to find the right response? And why the fuck did she care? Nothing would ever happen again.

Nothing would ever happen again. How true. How bloody true. Not just the fact that nothing would ever happen again with Jean-Luc. Nothing. Would. Ever. Happen. Again. She could have that inscribed on her gravestone. 'Nothing Ever Happened Again.' The chances were she would stay with Robert, not quite miserable enough to leave, not quite happy enough to be content. Miss Mapp would totter along into her dotage, which judging by today was closer than Isobel had feared. Grace would finish her gap year and then flit straight to university at Durham, where she would probably meet an unsuitable man and rarely visit her dull parents in Rye. Jack would slide downhill, but possibly last for years, a 'creaking gate' kept alive by doctors and sheer bloody-mindedness. Nothing would ever happen again.

Depressed by her own company, she headed for home. She definitely would not reply to Jean-Luc. She would delete the message and quite possibly re-block his number. Their afternoon in bed had been like rubbing shoulders with the angels, but Pam's death coming hard on the heels of her adventure with Jean-Luc had been a sort of aversion therapy. It had killed all the joy of that unexpected event; had turned passion into ashes. It was impossible for her to think of being in bed with Jean-Luc without Pam's disappointed face hovering over them. Did the dead see our shame?

The key turned in the lock and Robert appeared in the kitchen doorway, "Hi, Bel."

"Hi, Robert. Good day?" He had been at a local auction where he'd planned to bid for a couple of random lots. Sight unseen.

"Not brilliant to be honest. Mostly tat, but I did find this in one of the job lots." He held out a small red book.

"What is it? Can't read the title from here."

"Dickens. 'A Tale of Two Cities."

"Not a first edition surely?"

"It's dated 1859, which would fit. Need to do some research though – there's lots of fakes around. How was the shop?"

"Quiet."

"Oh dear. How quiet?"

"Two greetings cards and a half-price calendar."

"That good, huh?"

"That good."

"Boring day for you then. Sorry."

"Very. Anyway it's cold chicken for supper when you're ready."

"Great. Be there in a minute."

As she fried the potatoes from yesterday's supper to serve with the chicken, she mulled over the fact it had turned out not to be such a boring day after all. One message from Jean-Luc. Three kisses. She wouldn't be sharing details of that with Robert.

Grace had been almost relieved when Nina told her the Amsterdam project was finished and George wouldn't be visiting so often. She knew already of course: he'd messaged her the day before, expressing heartfelt misery at the prospect of not seeing her for a while. She missed him desperately and fantasised about him constantly, but the fact was she'd slipped behind with her course work since her granny had died and knew that the excitement of seeing George would have made it even harder to catch up. Without George around, it was easier for her to be with Nina, although the secret she carried felt like an unexploded bomb.

Since the terrible row between Nina and Katja before Christmas, things seemed to have calmed down in the lodgers' wing. Grace had seen very little of Katja, partly because of being back in Rye and partly because Katja was keeping even more anti-social hours than usual. One morning she walked into the kitchen and found Katja slumped on a chair, head on the table, seemingly dead to the world. It was obvious by the look of her that she hadn't yet been to bed.

Grace tried to tip-toe around her, scared to rouse the sleeping tiger, but Katja opened one eye, "Time?"

"About seven-thirty, I think. Would you like a coffee ?"

She waited for the abuse to start, but incredibly Katja had lifted her head, nodded, and then slumped once more.

Grace put the mug in front of her, "Be careful. It's hot."

"Thanks."

Wonders would never cease. There's a word she never thought Katja would say. Not without the menacing Madame Chirol standing over her at least.

After a couple of minutes, Katja sat up and looked her straight in the eye, "Your *babushka* died?"

Babushka?

"My Granny? Yes."

"I'm sorry. That's shit for you."

Grace nodded. It was shit, but right now she was more taken aback by the fact that Katja was acting like a real human-being.

"I would hate my *babushka* to die. I would fucking hate it."

She sounded so angry – so Katjaesque – that Grace almost felt relieved. She couldn't imagine Katja having parents – or siblings – certainly not a granny.

"Do you see much of her? Your *babushka*?"

Katja narrowed her eyes as if she thought Grace were being provocative, "You taking the piss, English girl?"

"No! I just wondered. Sorry."

Katja sighed and put her head back on the table, "'Course I fucking see her," she said. "All the fucking time."

Later, Grace relayed this conversation to Nina who burst out laughing, "Grace, you must have worked it out by now."

"What?"

"Madame Chirol and Katja. She's Katja's *babushka*! Didn't you know?"

"What!" And yet it made perfect sense. Why else would Madame Chirol tolerate Katja living there? Why else would she pull her up on her manners? Refuse to give her notice?

She felt a total fool, "When did you find out?

Why didn't you tell me?"

"I thought you knew! It's obvious that Madame Chirol would have kicked her out before now if they didn't have blood ties. She hardly fits in!"

"Do you know for certain?"

"Yes I asked Antoinette. She hates Katja, but she knows there's nothing she can do about her. She called her '*vipère au sein*' – the viper in the bosom."

"What else do you know about her?"

"Nothing much."

"But she comes from the Ukraine. I don't understand."

"I think that's her mother's side. Madame Chirol must be her paternal grandmother."

"Why do you say that?"

"I'm pretty sure I've only ever heard her mention sons. Never a daughter."

"Where are Katja's parents then? Are they divorced?"

"Absolutely no idea. Fancy asking her yourself?"

They looked at each other and started to laugh, "No thanks! I'm not *that* curious."

"Thought not", said Nina. "Me neither."

The fact was that Grace was curious, not just about Katja but about Madame Chirol. She realised she'd been living under the Chirol roof for nearly six months now and yet knew very little about her elegant landlady. One thing that was obvious was that she was top dog so far as the family went. Various Chirol relatives were dispersed through the courtyard buildings – cousins, nieces, nephews – and they took it in turns to pay homage to her on Sunday afternoons. Grace tried to keep out of the way at these family teas, but sometimes it wasn't possible to avoid the drawing room entirely. Madame Chirol would insist on presenting her formally to each family member and she would shake each hand and try to answer in French what they enquired of her in English. How was she finding Paris? How were her studies progressing? Had she made friends here? Was she home-sick?

Madame Chirol would always invite her to join them, but when she politely refused, she never pressed her to do so. It was all part of the ritual. Now she came to think about it she had never once seen Katja sitting at the Sunday tea. Was she not invited?

One day she was sitting in the kitchen when Antoinette came in to refill the fridge with milk and butter. Grace's French had improved considerably since starting her studies at the CCFS, so she made an effort to engage her in more conversation than the usual 'hello and how are you'. She knew Antoinette liked her – probably because she made far less mess than the other two. The older woman was happy to sit and chat, laughed at her questions, but answered them with ease. Did Grace not know the history of Monsieur and Madame Chirol? That Monsieur had been a great figure in the La Résistance? Many medals? That he and Madame had met and married soon after the War when Madame was just eighteen? Madame had been a great beauty in her day - a personal friend of Monsieur Dior. Four sons the couple had, but one was dead, "*C'est vraiment triste.*"

"*Il est mort comment,* Antoinette?"

This was the only point at which Antoinette hesitated, "*Suicide, Mademoiselle.*"

At the sight of Grace's shocked face, she clearly felt she had said enough. But Grace could not let her go without one more question, "*C'etait le père de Katja*?"

A nod. Then Antoinette bade her good-day and headed back to her kitchen at the other end of the apartment.

Grace sat alone in the little kitchen, thinking over what she had heard. She would tell Nina about Madame Chirol and Dior – Nina would love that connection given her obsession with fashion – but she decided not to share the fact Katja's father had committed suicide. She felt bad for asking Antoinette about it so directly. It wasn't the sort of thing anyone would want to have as a source of gossip, least of all someone like Katja. What about Katja's mother? Why wasn't Katja with her? It struck her that she was the only lodger with a full quota of parents.

◆ ◆ ◆

Nina was thrilled by the Christian Dior news, "No way! The New Look!"

"I guess so."

"You know what I mean, right?"

"I think so."

"The post-War fashion he made his name with - tight-fitting jackets and A-line skirts? Look – like this!"

And she grabbed a piece of paper off her bedside table and drew an outline of a Dior silhouette for Grace.

"Wow, Nina! Your drawing gets better and better. I didn't know that style was Dior!"

"Yep. Iconic. Can't believe that Madame Chirol knew him."

"Good friends apparently."

"Incredible! So how old was she in 1947? The year he launched the New Look."

"I'm guessing about twenty by what Antoinette said."

"So she would have been wearing those very same clothes? I cannot believe it!"

"Why don't you ask her?"

"Wouldn't dare!"

"She might be glad to tell you. You never know."

"Come with me."

"What?"

"I came in about ten minutes ago. She's sitting in the drawing room reading a magazine."

"Really? Now?"

"While I feel brave enough!"

"OK. Come on."

Madame Chirol was her usual inscrutable self when they walked into the drawing room, "Is there a problem, young ladies?"

"No, Madame, " said Nina. "Just wanted to ask you something."

"*Oui*. Go ahead."

Nina took a deep breath, "Is it true you knew Christian Dior, Madame?"

Madame Chirol smiled, "Yes. We were intimate friends. Why do you ask?"

"Did you ever wear The New Look?"

"I did. Why? Is this for your fashion course, Nina?"

"Not exactly. It's just Dior is my hero and I had no idea you knew him!"

"And how did you discover this?"

"It was me, Madame," said Grace. "Antoinette told me."

"Indeed. And what was the context of that conversation may I ask?"

Grace didn't know how to answer this. Madame Chirol clearly thought she had been snooping and so she had, "We were just chatting, Madame. It came up."

"Really?" Her tone was cool, but not angry.

She patted the sofa for Nina to sit next to her. Grace sat down opposite.

"It never occurred to me that someone studying fashion today would have any interest in the clothes I wore when I was a young woman. We are going back more than sixty years. I am an antique, you know."

Nina laughed, "You are far from that, Madame."

"So what do you want to know?"

"What was it like? To wear those incredible clothes?"

Madame Chirol gave her a piercing look, "Would you like to see?"

For a moment, they didn't understand what she meant. Then Nina spoke, "You have photographs?"

"I do. But I have something else too."

"Oh?"

"Follow me."

Neither Nina nor Grace had ever dared go through the drawing room to Madame Chirol's private quarters. Hearing footsteps, Antoinette appeared from a side room and looked startled to see the three of them walking down the corridor. Her eyes caught Grace's as if to say, what have you said?

Grace held her breath. Would Antoinette be in trouble? Apparently not. Madame Chirol teased her in French about her lack of discretion, but then asked her to accompany them to her bedroom. In the centre of the room was a four-poster bed hung with faded, golden silk drapes embroidered with pink roses. To the left and right of this were two enormous armoires. She instructed Antoinette to open the armoire on the left and lift down a box from the top shelf. Photo albums. She gestured for her to put them on the stool at the foot of the bed.

The real surprise was when she opened the doors of the other armoire, which was bulging with clothes. "Here, Nina," she said. "Come and look."

Grace saw Nina physically gasp, "Dior?"

"Yes, Dior. Also Schiaparelli, Chanel, Balenciaga, Vionnet . . . come on, pull some out and take a closer look. You too, Grace." She began to pull clothes out of the armoire and pile them on the bed.

Nina looked shell-shocked, "But Madame, these should be in a museum."

"Yes. I have had quite a few museums come to tell me that."

"But what if something were to happen?"

"What would happen? They are just clothes, you know. No burglar would look twice."

Nina did not seem so sure, "They're beautiful. I've never seen anything like this other than through plate-glass."

"Through plate-glass, you cannot feel them."

"Even so."

Madame Chirol looked at her, "Nina, you see

a collection of clothes that belongs in a museum. You are not wrong. But do you know what I see?"

"No, Madame."

"I see a diary of my life."

She began to pick out individual garments, "Here is the dress I wore for my going-away outfit. Here the jacket I wore when I left hospital with our first son. Here the suit my husband bought me on our first anniversary. He always liked to accompany me when I visited the fashion shows each season. He was proud of my figure always."

She opened one of the photo albums and Grace gasped. Antoinette had been right. Madame Chirol had been a great beauty. Page after page showed her immaculately and fashionably dressed. Here she was at the races in Deauville. On a yacht in Monte Carlo. At a black-tie dinner at Versailles. In New York, London, Rome, Buenos Aires . . .

There were press cuttings too, pages and pages of them. By her side always the same man, older than her, dark and handsome. Occasionally, a family shot of four young boys, dark like their father, beautiful like their mother – but these Madame Chirol never commented upon, swiftly turning the pages to show them an evening dress by Balmain or a coat by Givenchy.

Nina was virtually speechless with excitement, reduced to saying "I don't believe it!" and "Amazing!" over and over again. Grace longed to ask questions about Madame Chirol's life, but sensed she would learn more if the old lady were left to look through the photos and talk. Antoinette stood by silently, but Grace sensed this was a new event in her experience. As for Madame Chirol, she seemed to be enjoying herself hugely. Then suddenly her energy flagged. Grace had seen the same thing happen with her own grandparents – vibrant one moment and depleted the next. The colour drained from her face. Antoinette stepped forward, whispered something in Madame Chirol's ear, gestured that Nina and Grace should leave now.

Nina was still in raptures over what she had seen, but Grace took the hint, beckoning her friend to follow her back to their own wing.

"Would you like us to help put everything away?" asked Nina.

Madame Chirol shook her head wearily, "No. Antoinette, knows where everything goes."

"I can't thank you enough, Madame. This has been one of the best days of my life. Truly."

"No need. My pleasure. Good evening, girls."

"Thank you, Madame."

"Bye, Madame."

As they crossed the drawing room, Grace felt as though they had been in a time machine for the last hour. It was what her father would call discombobulating.

"Want a coffee?" she asked Nina.

"No, thanks."

Her friend looked nervy with excitement.

"What are you going to do now? It's still early."

"Draw, Grace. I'm going to stay up all night and draw."

And with that, she headed for her bedroom and shut her door gently but firmly. Grace could take a hint. She lay on her bed thinking of Madame Chirol's impossibly glamorous life and wondering what her own had in store.

At first, his messages had been cautious, but now - a week since she had unblocked his number – they texted back and forth regularly. He was more flirtatious with each passing day, slightly more risqué in his tone. It might not have been the same as the love letters Robert had sent her when they first met, but it felt like a courtship nevertheless.

She rarely made the first move, preferring to respond rather than initiate. Typically, the first message would arrive around eleven in the morning: she often envisaged him heading for an early lunch, ordering a glass of wine, thinking of her. This morning it was eleven-twelve exactly.

"Morning snow queen. What are you doing

today? xxx".

"In the shop. No customers! Xx".

"One day I will visit that shop of yours xxx". How lovely that would be.

"I would like that. What would you look for? Xx".

For a couple of minutes, no message came through. He clearly took the question seriously.

"The original Snow Queen xxx".

"The book? Xx".

"The person xxx".

"Cheat! Which book?"

"Love In A Cold Climate xxx".

"Very witty Xx".

"Have you read it? xxx".

"One of my favourites. Love the Mitfords Xx".

"I seem to remember the heroine is called Fanny? An interesting name Xxx". She laughed out loud at this.

"Naughty! The main heroine is actually Polly Xx".

"Not Linda? Xxx"

"That's Pursuit of Love Xx".

"I am in pursuit of love. Are you coming back to Paris? Please say yes xxx".

"If I can, I will Xx".

"I will that you can xxx".

She heard the shop bell and looked up smiling. It was Dani.

"You look happy. Am I interrupting?"

"Not at all. Give me a moment."

Quickly, she sent one more message, "Have to go. Customer. More later Xx".

An answering ping, "Kisses xxx".

"Is that Grace on the phone?"

"Yes. She's fine." It was so much easier to lie. She didn't want to share Jean-Luc with anyone, not even Dani. He was her private pastime. A little beam of warmth in her otherwise mundane life.

"I was just dropping by to invite you and Robert round to dinner on your birthday. Saskia reminded me it's coming up fast."

"Thanks, Dani – that's really kind of you both." It was her forty-ninth birthday the following month.

"Anything you particularly fancy, birthday girl?"

"A face lift? Hair dye? False teeth?"

"Stop it! You know what I mean."

"If Saskia could make her boeuf bourguignon, Robert and I would both be in heaven."

"Done."

"Shall we bring anything?"

"No. Our treat."

"Really? It's not like it's a very special birthday."

"All birthdays are special. Consider it the run-up to the big one next year."

"Thanks! Rather not think about that, to be honest."

"Nonsense. I'll be there before you, remember. I'll send a report from the other side." Dani was five months older, due to turn fifty in mid-October.

"Are you doing anything special for it? Your fiftieth?"

"Bloody hope so. Saskia wants a big party."

"Good for you!"

"But then we might be having an even bigger party next year."

"Why's that?"

"If Saskia and I are allowed to marry properly – which looks unbelievably likely, we're going for it!"

"Dani! How wonderful!"

"Thanks. We've waited a long time for it. We can wait another year."

Later that day, Isobel mulled over the fact that Dani and Saskia were so keen to be married even after being so long together, and even after the recognition of a civil partnership. What was it about marriage that attracted people? What was it that made marriage so different from the inside looking out, to the outside looking in?

"What's the best thing about marriage?" she asked Robert over dinner.

He looked taken aback by the question, "Ours or in general?"

"In general."

"Safety, stability, security, companionship."

"Not very romantic."

"What do you mean?"

"You're right, but it's not very romantic. Why does anyone want to get married based on that. Why did we?"

"So you do want to talk about our marriage in particular?" Did she?

"Is it any different to what you just said?"

"Yes and no. I think we have all of those things, plus we have Grace, plus we have fun."

"Do we?"

"Don't we?"

"I suppose so." What fun did he mean?

"Well, I have fun with you, Bel – even if it isn't reciprocated. You make me laugh a lot."

"I infuriate you most of the time."

"No you don't. It's me who infuriates you. Anyway, what sparked this off?"

"Dani and Saskia. If the government pass this bill, they can get married next year. Dani says they can't wait."

"And you're wondering why they would bother?"

"Not exactly." Yes, spot on.

"I guess they're just in love, Bel – and they want everyone to know it."

"And after that?"

"They'll be like the rest of us – and live happily ever after." Something in his tone made her look up.

"Are you being sarcastic?"

"Not at all. I'm still living happily ever after.

It's just you're not."

"I don't know whether I'm happy or not, to be honest. Wish I did." That much was true.

"I know, but I'm here for you regardless."

And that, she realised, was the definition for which she had possibly been searching.

MARCH

Isobel had to admit the bungalow looked and felt fresher. Jack was sleeping when she arrived, but Lauren led her into the familiar sitting room and offered to make her tea or coffee while she waited for him to wake. For the first time she felt like a guest in her parents' house. This made her irrationally irritable.

"I can make it myself. No need for you to wait on me, Lauren."

"It's no problem at all. Tea or coffee?"

Why pick a fight? "Tea, please."

"What sort do you like?"

Isobel looked at her as if she were mad. Which tea? Pam only ever had one sort, the type commonly referred to as 'builder's'.

Lauren smiled, "There's peppermint, camomile, green or breakfast. Oh and a new type I saw last week – turmeric?"

For a moment Isobel was sure she could hear Pam tut-tutting in her ear. Fancy teas. Well I never!

"Breakfast tea's fine, thank you. Milk no sugar."

"Coming right up. Of course Jack's very partial to camomile."

Was he? Since when exactly? It was only tea, but she felt it was treacherous of him to discover this liking for camomile now that her mother was dead.

Lauren brought in a tray on which she had carefully laid out a mug of tea, a little jug of milk and a saucer for the tea spoon. "Biscuit?"

"No, thank you. Not having one yourself?"

"I had a green tea not that long ago."

"Ah."

"I would sit down with you, but I think I heard Jack stirring. Better check."

"I can go . . ."

Too late. Lauren was already out of the door and halfway down the corridor. A moment later, Isobel heard voices and – double treachery – laughter. When had her dad ever laughed when Pam helped him out of bed?

She sat sipping her tea, wishing she did not feel so poisonous. The fact was that Lauren had everything under control: the house, the cooking, the routine and Jack. In the three weeks since she had moved in, she had made her mark in small but significant ways. She had persuaded Jack to the doctor's and had his medication assessed, which undoubtedly had improved both his stamina and mood. She was a more imaginative and talented cook than Pam, so for the first time in years, he was putting on weight rather than losing it. They did a circuit of the garden twice a day, something Jack loved doing now the bulbs were out in force. She had also insisted on a visit from the occupational therapist which had resulted in deliveries of all kinds of equipment, including a bath hoist in the bathroom and a commode by Jack's bed. Her father looked cleaner, smarter, happier and better nourished than Isobel had seen him look for years. Why couldn't she feel grateful instead of thoroughly pissed off?

A ring at the door-bell.

"I'll go!" Isobel shouted.

"OK. We'll be there in a tick. Just getting Jack's socks on!"

Mrs Dawkins stood on the doorstep, "Mrs Peters! How nice. I was expecting to see Lauren's cheery face."

"Do come in, Mrs Dawkins. Dad won't be a moment." She led her to the sitting room.

"Well if you don't mind? It's Lauren I came to see really. She has a recipe for me – Thai fish stew – she made it for Jack and me last week and it was delicious."

How jolly cosy! The three of them sat around the table eating Thai food. Pam's tuna pasta was about as cosmopolitan as things usually got around here. Isobel could feel her mood darkening further.

"Tea, Mrs Dawkins?" Her own was cooling in the mug. What she really wanted was an enormous vodka.

"Do call me Mavis. It's silly this Mrs Dawkins and Mrs Peters thing, isn't it? Lauren and I have been on first name terms from the moment we met."

Of course they had.

Isobel nodded, "Likewise. Isobel."

"I know that of course. Pam was always talking about you, 'Isobel this and Isobel that'. The apple of her eye you were."

She felt pin-pricks of tears behind her eyes, blinked them away rapidly as Jack shuffled into the room pushing a Zimmer frame. Another new and sensible Lauren initiative that her father would never have countenanced in her mother's day. Lauren hovered behind, ready to catch him should he stumble. They both greeted Mavis enthusiastically.

"And Isobel's here too, Jack," said Lauren. Why did she feel affronted at this stating of the bloody obvious?

"Yes I can see that. Hello, Isobel – were we expecting you?"

Expecting her?

"Just thought I'd drop by and see how you're doing, Dad." She gave him a peck on the cheek and sat down nursing her luke-warm mug.

"Very thoughtful of you, I'm sure."

Lauren and Mavis disappeared into the kitchen. More lively conversation and laughter. How could a Thai recipe be so hilarious?

Jack spoke first, "How's Grace doing? Coming home soon?"

"She should be back for Easter, Dad. Not before then."

He grunted, "I know it's only Paris, but she feels very far away."

"I know. Me too."

"How are her studies going?"

"OK I think. She doesn't tell us much to be honest."

"Well let's hope it's worth all the effort – and the money."

"I'm sure it will be, Dad. Expanding her horizons you know."

"Ha! She's too young to have them expanded in my book."

"We've been through this already. She's already halfway through, remember? Anyway seems like she's not the only one having her horizons expanded."

"What's that supposed to mean?"

She tried to sound light-hearted, "Thai food I hear?"

"And very nice it was too. Tasty."

"But not the sort of thing you used to eat."

"Not the sort of thing your mother used to cook."

"No."

A silence descended.

She hadn't come here for a fight, so she tried again, "You're looking well, Dad. Feeling OK?"

"Tired. Not too bad considering."

"That's good. Getting on well with Lauren here?"

"She's an absolute treasure. Very lucky to have found her."

It took all her self-control not to stand up and slam out the room. He'd been so objectionable when she had insisted on a live-in carer. Had put up every obstacle he could. Her mother had only been dead six weeks but now another woman was living here who was described as a 'treasure.' She should be pleased and relieved, but Pam had sacrificed so much in the last few years and Isobel didn't remember her ever being described as a 'treasure'.

Fury made her catty, "Apart from the name?"

"What?"

"Lauren. You don't like the name."

"What are you talking about, Isobel? Lauren is a lovely name."

Just as she was contemplating throwing the mug of tea at his head, Lauren popped her head round the door, "Did I hear my name? Do you need anything?"

"No, we're fine," said Isobel. "Lovely tea, thank you."

"You're very welcome. Mavis and I are just in the kitchen having a little catch-up. We thought you two should have some father-and-daughter time on your own. Would you like to stay for lunch? We're having home-made carrot and coriander soup. Jack's favourite."

Since when? Since he discovered that there were other soups other than oxtail and tomato?

Jack stared straight ahead, giving no indication he wished her to stay. He seemed to have drifted completely out of the room.

"Thanks, Lauren, but I'd better be getting back soon. It was just a quick visit to see how you were getting on."

"Oh we're fine. Aren't we, Jack?"

Not much response, even to the treasure.

Mavis bustled in and took his hand, "I'm off now, Jack, but Lauren has invited me over tomorrow. Apparently she's planning spiced meatballs with goat's cheese. Can't wait."

He nodded, but barely seemed to register where he was. "One of his little turns", Pam would have said.

Isobel noticed that Lauren and Mavis exchanged glances, a private language from which she was excluded. What did they know that she did not? She could hear them whispering as they left the room, a murmuring that continued for a few minutes at the front door.

"Dad?"

"Mmmmm?"

"You OK, Dad?"

A switch seemed to flick deep in his brain, "You still here, Isobel? Yes I'm fine. Where's Lauren?"

"I think she's warming up your soup."

"Ah. Lunch-time already?"

"Yes."

"You staying?"

"No, Dad. Think I'd better get back. I'll drop by soon."

"Ok, dear. Miss her do you?"

"Grace?"

"No, not Grace. Your mother."

"Mum? Yes of course I do. I miss her very much."

"So do I, love. So do I."

One thing Grace had yet to work out after nearly six months of living at Madame Chirol's was what Katja did with her time. Clearly, she didn't have a job, given the long disappearances and the anti-social hours she kept. Neither was there any indication she was at college. Nina had mentioned a feminist organisation she was involved with – Femen – but how exactly did that keep her busy? She hardly looked the type to be out leafletting or organising meetings. What did Femen actually do?

She tried asking Nina.

"You know, 'down with the patriarchy', 'reclaim the female body'. That sort of thing."

"But what do they actually do."

"Naked body activism."

"What?"

Nina looked at her with affection, "I always forget how young you are!"

"Don't patronise me!"

"Sorry."

"Naked body activism? They take their clothes off and call it a protest?"

"Sort of."

"Am I being stupid or do lots of men like women taking their clothes off?"

"Uh huh."

"So you defeat the patrimony by giving them what they like?"

Nina sighed, "You'll have to ask her, Grace."

"As if."

In the end curiosity got the better of her and she plucked up courage when she next encountered Katja in the kitchen.

"Nina told me about Femen," she said, trying to sound as nonchalant as possible.

Katja raised her eyebrows, "Told you what, English girl?"

"My name is Grace."

"Sure. I know."

It was no good. She would never win these battles with Katja.

"I was interested that's all."

"In Femen?"

"Yes."

"Why?"

"Could you tell me more – about what it does? About what you do?"

There was a long pause. Katja looked at her intently, "It's better you don't know."

"Why?"

"That was my question to you."

"I might want to get involved."

Katja burst out laughing, "You, English girl? No, I don't think so!"

"Why not?"

"You have no idea what you're talking about."

"How can I? You won't tell me."

Katja smiled, "Good joke though! You and Femen."

"Does Madame Chirol know? *Baboushka*?"

This hit the spot, "You leave *Baboushka* out of this! Get it, Grace? You don't say one word to *Baboushka*!"

It was the first time Katja had used her name. Progress of sorts.

"I won't! Sorry!"

For a moment, Katja glared at her and then seemed to soften slightly, "What do you want to know anyway?"

"What Femen does? Why the naked protests?"

"Because bare breasts are weapons."

"Are they?"

"Sure they are."

"But don't most men like bare breasts?"

"We don't bare them for men. We hate men."

It was no good. Grace was still confused, "So you want to defeat men – 'the patriarchy'?"

"Yes."

"By protesting topless?"

"We don't call it 'protesting topless'. It is Sextremism. 'My body is my weapon' – understand?"

Grace shook her head miserably. She suddenly felt very young. Nina was right.

Katja smiled at her for the first time, "Now you see the joke? You and Femen? How can you be involved with the battle when you don't understand the war, little English girl?"

There was something else bothering Grace.

"Have you told them yet?" asked Nina the next day. They were in the Musée Carnavalet where they had visited the cork-lined walls of Proust's bedroom, fully reconstructed from the original at 102, Boulevard Haussmann. Grace had been particularly moved by the fifteen pens carefully laid out on a series of occasional tables.

She shook her head.

"Shouldn't you do it soon? Easter's coming up fast."

"I know. It's my grandad I'm worried about."

"You could go and see him next month."

"I know."

The fact was that she'd been invited to go to Miami again at Easter and she had said yes without hesitation. George had only visited Paris once that year and while he flooded her with loving messages, she was desperate to feel his arms around her. Could think of very little else. She knew it was going to cause waves with her mum and dad, particularly coming so soon after her granny's death. And while she hated the idea of hurting her grandad's feelings, it would be intolerable to say no. As for Nina, she would worry about that later.

Her friend seemed more worried about her family than she did, "Maybe I could come to Rye again?"

"When?"

"Next month. You come to Miami for Easter and I could come with you to Rye after that? Might help to sweeten the pill?"

"Brilliant idea!"

Nina was right. Isobel had been frosty at the news when she phoned home that evening, but had thawed a little at the prospect of both girls visiting in a few weeks' time. In fact by the end of the conversation, she sounded positively enthusiastic.

"I'll come and see you before you jet off."

"With Dad?"

"Not sure. Rather depends on Miss Mapp."

"OK – when would you come?"

"I'll look at the calendar. Some time next week probably."

"Only I do have a lot of course work to get through by the end of the term."

"That's fine. I can occupy myself during the day."

"Well, that would be great!"

Later, she gave Nina the good news.

"Did she sound OK?"

"Yes. More than OK."

"What do you mean?"

"She sounded pleased. I could have sworn she was trying not to laugh at one point."

"Weird."

"Yes, that's what I thought."

"Good though – parental permission granted."

"Very good indeed!" She flung her arms around Nina with uncontained joy.

Robert took the wind out of Isobel's sails by announcing he would go with her to Paris.

"But what about Miss Mapp?"

"Saskia says she's happy to step in if we ever need her to – Dani and she would cope fine for a couple of days."

"Seems a bit of an imposition."

"Not really. One quick trip to see our

daughter. They'll understand."

"What about Dad?"

"What about him?"

"Is it fair for us both to leave the country given how frail he is?"

"He has the Incomparable Lauren. He'll be fine."

"But what if something happened?"

"Something did happen, remember? When you were in Paris last time?"

"Don't remind me! It proves my point. What would have happened if you hadn't been here?"

"Well maybe it's your turn."

"For what?"

"To stay at home on call for Jack while I flit off to Paris for a day or two?"

She looked at him appalled, not least because what he said made perfect sense. Robert hadn't visited Paris since they were there together in October. Since then, she'd been over twice without him.

"But I really want to go." She sounded like a spoilt teenager and she knew it.

"And so do I."

"Can we afford for both of us to go?"

"Bel, we can barely afford to put petrol in the car. You know that."

"Another credit card maxed out?"

"Almost certainly."

She used her last bartering chip, "Of course you'll have to go in June on your own. To bring

Grace back. It's only fair as I took her over."

"What are you suggesting?"

"How about I go for one last time next week? She and Nina come here next month. Then there's only May to get through and you go on your own in June."

He gave her a very steady look, "Wouldn't you like to go with me? Might be nice for Grace to have us both there."

Her plans for seeing Jean-Luc one last time were crumbling into dust. Disappointment bred fury.

"Why are you always so keen on playing happy families?"

"I could just as well ask, why are you not?" His tone was calm, but she could tell he was close to snapping.

Rather than ramp the tension up to a full-blown row, she conceded defeat, "OK. I'll check out the Eurostar for the best deal."

"Perfect."

As it turned out, one small, red book intervened.

"I can't come to Paris," said Robert the next day. "You haven't booked seats yet, have you?"

"No, not yet. Why can't you?"

"I forgot I made an appointment with the auction house in London. To get the Dickens authenticated."

Typical Robert. Never any idea what day of the week it was. She was irritated and delighted in equal measure.

The Dickens appeared to be a genuine first edition. Not only that, it was apparently inscribed by the author to someone called George. The writing was too faint to make out the surname. Neither Isobel nor Robert could believe their luck could turn in this manner, but the opinion of the auction house would seal their financial fate for the next few months one way or the other.

"Shame you can't come." She tried to sound sincere, but wanted to whoop with joy.

"Come off it. You're itching to make the trip without me as we both know."

"Not true."

"Really?"

"Really."

He put his arms around her and she tried not to shake them off. Since reigniting her relationship with Jean-Luc, she recoiled from any physical contact with Robert. It was as if her body could only answer to one man.

"If this book turns out to be what it says it is, I'll take you to Paris and we'll stay at Le Papillon. Like that?"

Not with him, she wouldn't. Now she knew she could go to Paris unchaperoned, her head was full of Jean-Luc.

"That would be amazing." She was shocked by her own duplicity.

He bent to kiss her, but that was too much.

"Not now, Robert. Think I heard Dani at the door."

◆ ◆ ◆

The cheapest Eurostar meant leaving on Tuesday and coming back on Thursday, meaning she could spend all day on Wednesday with Jean-Luc. His response was not quite what she'd been hoping for, given the excitement pounding through her own head.

"Belle Isobel! Wonderful news. Where shall we meet?"

Did she have to spell it out? "Your apartment perhaps?"

"Not possible. So sorry."

He gave no reason, but it was obvious. His wife must be back in town.

"Lunch then?"

"Perfect."

He sent her the name and address of a restaurant close to Rue Saint-Honoré. Clearly he did not want to risk an encounter too close to home. The table would be reserved under the name of Monsieur Valette.

She took Grace and Nina out to dinner on the first night, but noticed that Nina did most of the talking. Grace seemed preoccupied and distant, but not unhappy. Probably the demands of the course were taking their toll now that the final exams were looming in a couple of months.

She walked them back to the apartment, but refused their offers of hot chocolate, "Straight to bed for me. It's been a long day."

"'Night, Isobel, and thanks again for dinner."

"'Night, Nina. If I don't see you again this trip, look forward to seeing you back in Rye next month."

"'Night, Mum."

"'Night, Grace. See you tomorrow evening."

"Not before then?"

"No. You said yourself you're busy with the course. I'm fine to drift around Paris for a day."

"Sure?"

"Sure."

"Where shall we meet?"

"I'll text you."

Walking back to the hotel, she heard her own phone ping. Jean-Luc surely? It took all her willpower to wait until she reached her room to read the message.

In fact it was from Robert, "Hi Bel. Call me when you get this. X".

Oh god. Not again.

It was not yet ten at home, so she knew he would answer straight away. She expected anxiety in his tone, but he sounded jubilant.

"You're never going to believe it!"

"What?"

"Don't tell me you'd forgotten, Bel?"

"Forgotten what?" And then the penny dropped, "Not the Dickens?"

"Yes! The fucking fantastic Dickens!"

"Go on."

"Not only is one of the first thousand, Bel – and they are like the proverbial hen's teeth – but they've deciphered enough of the inscription to know who George is."

"Who?"

"George Eliot – Mary Ann Evans! He was an admirer of her work, apparently."

"Wow!"

"Wow indeed!"

"And that means . . . . ?"

"Are you sitting comfortably? That means the estimate will be six figures – they think a couple of the big American institutions may be interested in bidding."

"I can't believe it. Where's the catch?"

"No catch, Bel. We're soon going to be in the money!"

"When exactly?"

"June. They say they need a few months to build up interest from collectors across the world and that the June sale is one of the highlights of their year."

"I don't know what to say, Robert. That's

almost too good to believe."

"I know!"

"And nobody can come after you for a share?"

"Nope. It was part of one lot. Sight unseen. It was probably a house clearance and nobody thought to go through the book-shelves properly. It's not as though it looks that exciting."

"Robert, you're amazing!"

"First compliment in months!"

"Well you are. We can clear the credit cards!"

"We can do a lot more than that. I promised you a stay at Le Papillon for one thing!"

So he had. She wished she could feel more enthusiastic at the prospect.

"Shall I tell Grace?"

"Why don't we wait until it sells? Then we can give her the true figure. There will be commission to pay of course – even so, it will make a huge difference to us."

"OK. Makes sense. Our little secret until then?"

"Absolutely."

When they had said their good-byes and hung up, Isobel lay on her bed, trying to make sense of the direction her life was taking. She and Robert had been so worried about money for so long that she couldn't believe a windfall of this magnitude was about to land in their laps. Robert drove her mad and she was bored most of the time, but anyone listening in to their conversation just now would have thought they were a tight team. Was she in a happy marriage or an unhappy one? That should be such an easy question to answer, but she didn't honestly know. If only it were possible to take a marriage sabbatical once in a while to which all parties happily agreed.

After hearing Robert's voice, the planned lunch with Jean-Luc no longer looked romantic and glamorous, but seedy and pointless. It wasn't as if she really thought she had a future with Jean-Luc. It was all a fantasy and she knew it. Should she cancel? Block his number again? Pretend nothing ever happened?

She couldn't bring herself to do that. She would go to the lunch, but that would be it. No more jumping into bed with a man she barely knew. It had been a wrong turn, a lapse of judgement. She would see him once, but never again.

She arrived early, but he was there already. He stood up when he saw her and kissed her on both cheeks, "Isobel, you look wonderful."

It was true she had taken special care with her hair and make-up that morning, but she suspected he would have said these words regardless. A charmer, Pam would have said.

She was amazed to find she felt completely

calm. This was nothing like the quivering anticipation she had felt when George invited her to breakfast or the schoolgirl excitement when she had agreed to meet Jean-Luc previously. In fact it was he who appeared nervous and distracted, rearranging the cruet set as they waited for the waiter to bring the menus. Once the orders were taken and a bottle of perfectly chilled Sancerre had been delivered to their table, he took her hands in his and looked deep into her eyes. She held his look.

"I thought you would cancel," he said.

"Did you? Why?"

He laughed, "Well, you did block my number last time."

"I'm sorry, Jean-Luc. My mother's death threw me completely off kilter."

"Off kilter?"

"I couldn't think straight."

"I understand. I'm so sorry about your mother."

"Thank you."

"But I have missed you, you know."

"Have you?" She found this unlikely. It seemed to her that Jean-Luc had a very rich and satisfying life.

"You don't believe me?"

"I'm not sure what I think about anything these days."

"When I could not reach you, I was distrait. Here was this beautiful woman I had found in the snow, with whom I shared an afternoon of pure pleasure, only for her to disappear entirely as if she had never existed. I cannot tell you how happy I was to get your message, Isobel. You were real after all!"

She laughed, "Goodness Jean-Luc. I'm very flattered. I'd no idea I had made such an impression."

His tone changed from amusement to despondency, "Ah. I see."

"What?"

"You think I do this a lot. Pick up women from the street and take them to my bed."

The fact was she did think that. "Well I doubt I was the first."

He had not yet let go of her hands and now gripped them tighter, "You are wrong, Isobel. I may not always have been faithful to my wife – and would not expect her to always be faithful to me – but I do not like sex to be casual. It is too beautiful for that. Too profound."

He dropped her hands as the waiter appeared with their first courses, topping up their glasses before melting away once more.

Isobel was not feeling as calm as she had when she walked in. For one thing, she had forgotten how attractive Jean-Luc was: not just how he looked, but his smell, his voice, his touch. For another his evident desire for her was sparking equal desire in her. After another glass of this delicious wine, she would find it impossible to say no to anything. She reached for her glass.

It was a long and enchanting lunch. The last time they'd met, they hadn't really talked other than in the most cursory way. Desire had hastened them straight to bed for a conversation of a different type. Jean-Luc knew she was married to a book-seller in Sussex, had one daughter and that her mother was dead. For her part, she knew he was a film director and was married with no children. This felt more like a first date than a second, a chance to flesh out those details.

Just before the waiter served the second course, he asked her the question she most dreaded at parties.

"What do you, Isobel? For work I mean? I don't think you ever told me." She tried to sound upbeat, but the answer always embarrassed her.

"I don't really. I help Robert in the shop a bit, but I gave up my own job a long time ago when Grace was born."

"Why did you do that?" The starkness of his response took her by surprise.

"I suppose I wanted to be a good mum to Grace. We thought we would have more children, but it didn't happen. We left London to get a bigger house and a garden, but it was too far for me to commute. I suppose I just put myself to one side and . . ."

"You lost your confidence." How on earth did

he know that?

"You're very perceptive." She tried to keep her tone light, but inside she was dying.

He smiled at her, "It's not a criticism, Snow Queen. What did you do before you had your daughter?"

She told him a little about her boss and the responsibilities of her role. He recognised the name.

"He is a big shot, *non*? I met him once long ago at a dinner my first wife organised."

"I didn't know you'd been married before."

"It's not important. But you must have been very organised to do all that – not an easy man to work for I imagine?"

"That's true." What hurt her most was that she'd been good at her job. Had turned her back on something that had once made her so proud.

"Don't you get bored – now that your daughter is grown up?"

She nodded miserably.

"Go back! Get yourself another job!"

"It's not that easy, Jean-Luc." Nearly twenty years had passed. She wouldn't know where to start.

"How do you know if you don't even try?"

He was trying to help, but he was just another man with no idea how impossible being a woman could be.

She smiled brightly, "One day perhaps. Now tell me about you: what's your latest project about?"

Later, they ordered Cognac with their coffee and he lent forward, his hand under the table stroking her inner thigh with a gentle upwards motion. She knew she was falling into the abyss, powerless to resist.

"I booked us a room, Isobel. Not far from here. Will you come?"

"Where?"

"Just say you will come."

Bad man. There was no chance of not understanding what those words really meant.

"I shouldn't."

"But it was you who suggested we go to my apartment?"

That was true. It had been her suggestion.

"I want to, Jean-Luc. I do. It's just my husband . . ."

Jean-Luc's irritation was tangible. She felt as if she had made a terrible *faux pas* in this discreet restaurant made for lovers, like a Bateman character who didn't understand the etiquette of a society parlour game.

"Your husband . . . my wife . . . must we live every moment of our lives according to others? Your mother just died, Isobel. How much time do any of us ever have?"

He was right. What harm could an hour or two do in the big scheme of things? She would have her sabbatical.

◆ ◆ ◆

What she wasn't expecting was to be led through the imposing doors of Le Papillon.

"Here?"

He smiled, "Yes. Have you been here before?"

"I came here long ago – and for breakfast more recently."

"Breakfast?"

"Not what you think, Jean-Luc."

He kissed her hand, "Just wait one moment, *chérie*."

She wanted to laugh. *Chérie*! It was such a cliché: to be here in Paris, with a handsome man, who was about to check them into an impossibly glamorous hotel and take her to bed.

Just as well George wasn't in town. For a moment, the thought of George, Nina and Grace had a sobering effect, but then Jean-Luc was by her side and an inscrutable bell-boy was assigned to escort them to their room.

The last time had been wonderful, but this was a masterclass in love-making. Jean-Luc believed in taking his time to an agonising extent. She had once read an interview with a sex therapist, which included the advice, "It's women who should 'run' the fuck". This seemed good advice given how selfish most men were in bed, but right now Jean-Luc was running the fuck and she was more than happy for him to do so. Time and again he brought her to the point of ecstasy, until she was soaring high into the heavens. So dazed was she afterwards that for a moment she couldn't understand how they came to be in this sumptuous bedroom when they should be on some distant tropical shore. He rolled her into his arms and they lay quiet and breathless.

Time passed in which they said not one word. Then he rolled her onto her stomach and began stroking her from neck to feet. It was almost embarrassing how pliable she was.

"I adore you, Isobel. You do things to me. We are good at this, you know."

"We certainly are."

And then she fell into a blissful sleep.

Her phone was beeping when she surfaced. It was already getting dark outside.

She sat up sharply. What on earth was the time?

It was six-twelve. Could have been worse, but Grace must be wondering what had happened to her. Three missed calls. Two messages.

The first had been sent at four-twenty-nine, "Hi Mum, hope you're having a fun day. Where shall we meet tonight? xxx".

The second had been sent at five-thirty-four, "Mum – you ok? Worried xxx".

Quickly she replied, "Sorry - phone died – will pick you up at 7.15pm xxx".

A moment later, another ping, "Phew! OK! Xx".

Jean-Luc was still fast asleep. She tip-toed to the bathroom, ran a bath and tidied her hair as best she could. There was no time to luxuriate in the beautiful marble bath – she had given herself thirty minutes precisely to get dressed and freshen up. While she touched up her make-up, she ran through her cover story in as much detail as if she were working for MI6. She had visited the Musée d'Orsay that morning and seen the latest Impressionists exhibition; she had stopped for lunch there and then walked through the Tuileries to the Rue Saint-Honoré for a spot of window-shopping, including a look around Colette. That was when she had realised her phone had died. She had decided to walk back to her hotel and put it on charge. Then she had seen Grace's missed calls and messages.

She checked her phone again: six-forty-four. She would have to wake Jean-Luc up to say good-bye. Luckily, Grace's apartment was only a ten-minute taxi ride from here.

She shook him gently and he opened sleepy brown eyes, "Where are you going, Isobel? You are dressed already."

"It's nearly seven o'clock, Jean-Luc. I have to

go to meet my daughter."

"Really? That late already?"

"I know. We both slept well."

They looked at each other and smiled.

"When are you coming back to Paris?"

"I'm not sure I am."

He looked shocked and sat up in bed, "But of course you are. Your daughter is here."

"Only until June, Jean-Luc. She's coming home next month for a few days, so I won't have an excuse then. And I promised Robert I wouldn't come over in May either."

"But you must!"

"I don't see how I can."

"Please, Isobel, we must find a way. I thought this was the start, not the end."

"The start?"

"Of our *grand amour*!"

She smiled, "Is that what you call it?"

He looked hurt, "Don't you?"

He really did like her then. The knowledge of that took her by surprise. She was desperate to see him again too, but had no idea how.

"It probably wouldn't be until May. Can you wait until then?"

He cheered up immediately, "Two months is two months too long, but yes I can wait. I will miss you, *chérie*, but I will carry you here and here."

He pointed first at his chest and then at his cock. Isobel laughed out loud.

"Come here, Snow Queen."

She leant forwards and he wrapped her in his arms and kissed her long and hard, "Don't forget me. OK?"

There was little chance of that.

Back in Rye, the whole episode with Jean-Luc was so at odds with her usual, everyday life that at times she doubted it had ever happened. More than anything, she longed to tell Dani, but she didn't know how to start that particular conversation. Dani loved Grace and Robert, so it would put her friend in a compromising situation were she to offload about her two afternoons of fabulous, illicit sex in Paris. Also, Dani told Saskia everything. It would be doubly compromising to ask her not to on this occasion.

It was hard to feel enthusiastic about Easter with no Grace coming home. It was also the first such occasion with no Pam. Isobel rang her father to invite him to Easter lunch.

"With Lauren?" he said.

She hadn't considered Lauren until that moment, but tried to sound enthusiastic, "Yes of course. Robert can pick you both up that morning."

"Could Mavis come too?"

"Sorry?"

"Mavis Dawkins. Could she come too?"

How on earth had that come about? "Yes, but doesn't she have her own family to see at Easter?"

"Only got that useless son of hers. Be nice to include her."

Anything to keep him happy, "OK, Dad. Could you ask her for me? Check her 'dietary requirements'?"

"What are you talking about, Isobel?"

"It's a joke, Dad. Don't worry about it. I'll roast a leg of lamb."

"Lauren makes a lovely lamb dish. With something called rose harissa."

How bloody typical of her. "Mine will be a plain roast, Dad. Traditional for Easter."

"I'm sure it will be very nice. Kind of thing your mother loved."

When she put down the phone, she couldn't help thinking there was something barbed in that remark.

She told Dani about Lauren and Mavis over hot-cross buns on Good Friday. Dani roared with laughter at Isobel's description of the increasingly exotic menus that Lauren produced, with Mavis Dawkins as unofficial secretary of her personal fan club.

"Sounds like Jack's got a *ménage à trois* going on, Bel."

"Oh God. Don't say that!"

"Two women fussing around him. Must be in heaven."

"Poor Mum. What would she think?"

"She would be properly furious knowing Pam!"

"Quite."

"I'm sure women of a certain age would still find him quite a catch. Which one would you want as your step-mother?"

"Stop! Doesn't bear thinking about."

"By the sounds of it, I would go for Lauren myself. Decent grub at least." She paused, "Anything else on your mind?"

"What do you mean?"

"I can't put my finger on it, Bel. Just feel like you're keeping something from me."

"That's odd."

"Is it?"

She loved Dani, but she wished her antennae were not quite so firmly attuned at times.

"There is something."

"But 'it's complicated'."

"Well yes, it is."

"Robert?"

"Not exactly."

"It's a man!"

"God, Dani! OK, it's a man. I didn't want to tell you, because it doesn't seem fair on you. Makes you an accomplice to the crime."

"So there's already been a crime?"

"In a manner of speaking."

"Isobel Peters! You are a dark horse. What on earth is going on? Who is it?"

"I don't want you to tell Saskia."

"Saskia's my wife in all but name. She's completely trustworthy."

"Even so."

"OK. My lips are sealed. At least for now."

"I suppose I'll have to settle for that."

"I suppose you will."

"I don't know where to begin."

"Like all the best stories, I suggest at the beginning."

She had to hand it to Dani: she'd always been a good listener. She never interrupted once as the story of Jean-Luc unfolded from the encounter in the snow to the afternoon at Le Papillon. The only thing Isobel left out was what they actually did in bed. She would leave that to Dani's imagination.

"And now you don't know what to do?"

"Exactly."

"You know you don't have a future with him, but you can't resist the possibility of such a future."

She hadn't thought of it like that, but it was true. She spent a lot of time wondering whether there was a way in which she and Jean-Luc could ever make it work.

She nodded.

"And Robert?"

"What?"

"How do you feel about Robert?"

"To be honest, I don't know."

"You don't want to leave him?"

"Not right now, no."

"You want to have your cake and eat it?"

"I suppose I do. Is that shocking of me?"

"I suspect it is what most married people want, at least at some point in their lives."

"Even you?"

"Not me, no."

"I know I've behaved badly, Dani. Robert hasn't done anything wrong. Look how great he was when my mum died. What I did in Paris was despicable, I do know that."

"But you don't regret it."

"No, I can't. It was like a gift, you see."

"In what way?"

"Here I am, about to be forty-nine, a bookseller's wife in Rye, with an ailing father and a daughter about to leap the nest. The doors have been slamming shut for years. Jean-Luc kicked a few of those doors down and let in the light. I will be for ever grateful that he did."

"But it's not the real world."

"No. It's not."

"You're going to see him again, aren't you?"

"If I can, yes."

"Do you want me to help you?"

She hadn't expected this. Sympathy possibly, but not practical action, "Could you?"

"I think so. After all, I haven't visited Grace in Paris yet myself."

"So we could go together?"

"Exactly. Robert won't argue with that."

"And Saskia?"

"Leave Saskia to me."

"Wouldn't that put you in a really difficult position? I know how much you care for Grace and for Robert."

"I think when someone kicks your friend's doors down, it matters. Seems to me this is something you need to get out of your system, one way or the other."

A few days later, she and Robert arrived at Dani and Saskia's for her birthday dinner. As always, Saskia had made the table look beautiful, with bowls of bulbs from the garden carefully placed down the central table runner. As well as bringing a bottle of pink champagne, Robert brought Dani and Saskia a present from Miss Mapp: a lavishly illustrated hardback on planning the perfect party.

"For next year," he smiled.

"You told him, Bel!"

"Well, it wasn't a secret, was it?"

"No. We just don't want to jinx it getting through Parliament."

"Not much chance of that, I reckon."

Over champagne, they gave Isobel her present: a silk, kimono-style dressing-gown.

"It's beautiful!"

"I second that," smiled Robert. "Very you."

She'd thought her birthday would make her sad; the first one without Grace. In fact, it was one of the best she could remember. Robert had closed Miss Mapp for the day and driven her to Dymchurch stopping at some of the charming little churches scattered over Romney Marsh on the way, her favourite being St Thomas à Beckett at Fairfield, which stood all alone in a field surrounded by streams and sheep. They'd had fish and chips on Dymchurch beach, then weaved their way back past Camber Sands, stopping for a brief walk over the dunes. Isobel remembered driving back from Ebbsfleet after leaving Grace in Paris for the first time, and how she'd stopped at Camber to pull herself together. It seemed an eternity ago.

Grace had rung to wish her happy birthday when they got back to Rye. She'd sounded excited to be going back to Miami in a few days' time, chattering about the luxury that awaited her on Sunset Island Two. Her own nineteenth birthday had fallen the week before Isobel's, and not being there to celebrate it with her had also been a first: they would mark it belatedly when she came to Rye in a month's time.

Grace wasn't the only person to have been in touch that day. Jean-Luc had messaged her first thing.

"Joyeux Anniversaire Snow Queen. Don't

forget me xxxx". As if she could.

She was touched by how much effort Robert, Dani and Saskia had made to give her a memorable day. The food was delicious: Rye Bay scallops to start, washed down with more champagne; and a boeuf bourguignon to follow that was just as good as Isobel had anticipated. It was one of those evenings where she felt suffused with warmth and affection for family and friends. She vowed to make Dani and Saskia's wedding as happy an occasion as she could.

"Saskia's made you a stonking cake," said Dani, when the dishes had been cleared away. "But first I have a poem to read to you."

This was surprising. Dani wasn't big on poetry.

"It's by Rudyard Kipling." Even more surprising. Not 'If' surely? That would be a weird choice.

Dani pulled out a sheet of paper and began to read:

I go to concert, party, ball –
What profit is in these?
I sit alone against the wall
And strive to look at ease.
The incense that is mine by right
They burn before her shrine;
And that's because I'm seventeen
And She is forty-nine.

Isobel began to laugh, "What is this, Dani?" Dani ignored her.

I cannot check my girlish blush,
My colour comes and goes;
I redden to my finger-tips,
And sometimes to my nose.
But She is white where white should be,
And red where red should shine.
The blush that flies at seventeen
Is fixed at forty-nine.

Robert and Saskia were laughing too. Three more verses followed, then

She calls me "darling," "pet," and "dear,"
And "sweet retiring maid."
I'm always at the back, I know,
She puts me in the shade.
She introduces me to men,
"Cast" lovers, I opine,
For sixty takes to seventeen,
Nineteen to forty-nine.

They applauded when she finished.

"That's perfect," said Robert. "What is it?" Unusual for him not to know a literary reference.

"It's called 'My Rival'. Saskia read it to me on my forty-ninth and I loved it."

"I love it too," said Isobel. "Forty-nine isn't

over the hill then?"

"Far from it," said Dani. "Old Rudyard nails the sexiness of the older woman perfectly." She smiled, "The only thing Saskia didn't tell me when she read it is that it actually has one more verse."

"Oh?" said Isobel, "Why not read that too?"

"Let's just say it's best to end on a high!"

APRIL

Grace put the mug down on her bedside table. She took a deep breath and tried to sound normal, “You said we need to talk.”

Nina looked at her, eyes widening, “Well we do, don’t we?”

“I suppose so.”

“You suppose so?” Her tone was sharp.

“Nina, I don’t know what to say.”

“Start with sorry maybe?”

“I’ve said I’m sorry. I’ve said it over and over again. You know I have.”

“And yet I don’t believe you.”

It was no good. Grace’s resolve crumbled and she began to cry, “I know you hate me.”

“Snivelling won’t help.”

“Please, Nina. I’m still your friend.”

“Well I’m not your friend. How could we ever be friends?”

“I’m sorry, Nina.” She could barely speak. “I just don’t know what I’m supposed to do.”

“I don’t know what I’m supposed to do either.”

Grace’s nose was running. She wiped it on the

back of her hand, rather than get up from the bed. The atmosphere in the room grew heavy.

It was no good. She crept across the room to her bag and some clean tissues. Nina stared fixedly at her, "I feel such an idiot."

"Why?"

"Not seeing it coming."

"We didn't mean to hurt you."

At that Nina lost her temper, "Don't give me that cheap bullshit, Grace! All these months of George stopping off in Paris on his way to and from Amsterdam. All the time we've spent together, the three of us. His idea about inviting you over for new year. And then again at Easter. The way you took up the offers with such enthusiasm. None of it was about me, was it?"

She was starting to shout now, "None of it was about me! His daughter! Your so-called friend. It was all about the two of you. I was just a useful alibi so far as you were concerned. I liked you so much, Grace. How could you do that to me?"

Nina too was sobbing, but with rage not contrition. Grace worried that soon Madame Chirol would be knocking on the door. The problem was that everything Nina said was true. She had nothing to say in her own defence.

After a while, Nina managed to choke out some words, "Why didn't you tell me, Grace?"

"I didn't know how to."

"Why didn't you tell him you weren't

interested? Couldn't you have asked him to stop for my sake?"

There it was. The nub of the whole problem. The truth was she had wanted him just as much as he had wanted her. More possibly.

"How do you think all this makes me feel?"

There was no answer to that. She shook her head miserably.

"It makes me feel utterly betrayed if you must know, once by my father and once by you. Can you imagine how mad my mother would have been? About George taking up with some English slut barely out of kindergarten? What about her?"

"Your dad will always love Maria."

It was the wrong move. "What a fucking nerve! Have you and George actually discussed my mum? How dare he! And how dare you!"

"Please don't be angry with him, Nina. He loves you so much."

"Yep. He loves me so much he invited my best friend to Miami and then screwed her when I was sleeping just up the corridor."

Grace felt completely out of her depth. Whatever she said made things worse, but she was desperate to try to put things right, "I just hate the idea of coming between you and George."

"It's a bit late now! You should have thought about that before you ended up in bed with him! I've spent the last hour yelling at my dad and telling him how much I hate him. And now I'm here in Paris – with you. I don't know which of you I despise the most."

She took a deep breath, "The bottom line is either I move out or you do."

Deep down she knew it would come to this, "Better be me."

"Fine."

Grace was hunched up on her bed, wishing she could be left to cry on her own, but not daring to say so.

"I hope you got what you wanted. I hope screwing my dad was worth it for you."

"I love him, Nina." The tears started again, "I love him so much and I don't know what to do."

"Are you for real? You think you love him?"

Grace nodded.

"Then you're dumber than I thought. You need to get over that quick."

"I don't know how to; I can't think about anything else."

"It's not going anywhere, Grace. I'm sure you've stroked his ego big time, but there's no way George will be looking at a future with you. He's my dad. I know him."

"It wasn't just sex. I promise you it wasn't just that."

Nina stood up and walked over to the door, "If you think that makes me feel better, you don't understand the first thing about me. Do you know what I wish?"

"What?"

"I wish it was your mum that George had decided to fuck. That would have made so much more sense."

◆ ◆ ◆

She had known the moment she walked back into the beautiful house on Sunset Island Two that this time he would be unable to resist.

On the first visit at New Year, she'd slept in the bedroom next to Nina's, but at Easter George apologised that this room was out of action, "Some kind of plumbing issue with the shower. I've put you in the guest suite instead."

The guest suite was opposite his own master suite.

"Do you mind, Grace?" Nina had asked. "You can share my bed if you prefer."

"That's one option," smiled George, "On the other hand, the guest suite has its own Jacuzzi and balcony. You're not cooped up in Madame Chirol's sardine-can now."

He didn't come to her on the first night or on the second, but on the third night at around two in the morning, she heard a gentle tap on the door.

"Come in," she whispered.

The door opened and George was silhouetted against the dim of the corridor. He crept towards her, carefully shutting the door behind him. Two hours' later, he crept back into his own room. Grace had wanted to shout with happiness. She hadn't been able to fall asleep until the sun was rising at about seven, finally waking at midday.

"You're still jet lagged," said Nina.

All through the day her body yearned for George. Every time they passed each other, electricity fizzed and crackled. In their efforts to hide what was going on from Nina, she began to think they were hiding something else.

"What's going on?" she asked on the sixth night.

Grace looked stricken. "Going on?" said George. "What are you talking about, Nina?"

"You two," said Nina. "You've got a secret."

"What makes you say that?"

"Grace can't even meet your eye."

George laughed, "Looks like we've been outed, Grace. Shall we tell her?"

Grace thought she might be sick. Tell her?

"Grace is no good at keeping secrets, Nina. Least of all from you."

"So?"

"So we have a surprise for you. Only we weren't going to tell you just yet."

"Go on!"

"I've arranged for you to study in Milan after Paris. At the Ferrari Fashion School – if you fancy that?"

"George!" Nina flung her arms around his

neck. "That would be amazing!"

Grace was stunned, "How had he thought of that so fast?" Stupid of her. He must already have been planning it of course.

"Grace! You never let on!"

She shook her head, "George asked me not to; he wanted to be sure first."

His eyes met hers. They both knew what she really meant.

Lying in George's arms on the final night, she had asked him what would happen next? What were they going to do? Did they have a future?

He had grown still at her questioning, "Not sure, honey. What do you want to happen?"

"I want to be with you, George. Properly with you."

"I just don't see how we can."

"Because of Nina?"

"Because of everything."

"Because of Maria?" She had never mentioned Maria until now.

"Because of *everything*."

"I love you, George."

"I know. Me too." But he hadn't said the words back to her.

Grace had been quiet on the way to the airport. George too was subdued. Nina made jokes about them having one too many non-alcoholic Miami Mules the previous night and Grace had gone along with her friend's joshing. On the plane, she felt sick with despair at leaving

George again.

Nina sat by the window and Grace in the middle, but as nobody came to claim the outer seat, they loaded their bags into the middle and Grace moved to the aisle. It was a night flight, so once they'd eaten and the trays had been cleared, she pretended to fall asleep while Nina tuned into '*Moonrise Kingdom*'. Grace was still wide awake, with eyes firmly closed, when the movie ended. Nina soon fell into a snuffly sleep. It was a relief for Grace to open her eyes and stare at the dimly lit ceiling, on which she played out scenes with George as if it were a projector screen. When the pilot announced they were beginning their descent, she went to the loo and splashed her face.

She could see as she walked back to her seat that Nina was awake. She was holding Grace's phone in her hands. She wasn't smiling.

"You forgot to put your phone on Aeroplane mode. Here."

She handed Grace her phone. On the screen was the name George and the words, "The bed's too big without you xxx".

This couldn't be happening.

"When were you going to tell me?"

She had no idea what to say. Her mind was blank.

"I mean, you're not going to tell me this is a different George – right?"

Miserably, she shook her head.

"Bitch! When were you going to tell me? About you fucking my dad?"

Embarrassed, Grace turned round to see who was listening. With relief, she realised that the sound of the plane in descent was just about enough to drown out how angry Nina was, but the Englishness of her reaction was a red rag to a bull, "Don't turn away from me!."

"I'm sorry, but . . . ."

"Sorry!"

Grace put her head in her hands, "Please, Nina, Please can this wait until we're back?"

"You're goddam lucky, I need a pee so badly. Let me past."

Grace stood up to let her out, trying to ignore the pain as Nina stepped deliberately onto the top of her foot, crushing her weight down as hard as she could as she passed. Grace moved to the window seat desperate to avoid any confrontation, but when Nina came out the loo, she picked up her bags and walked to the back of the plane where there were some spare seats. At Charles de Gaulle, they disembarked separately. Grace saw her on the platform of the RER, but they avoided eye contact. It wasn't until the evening that Nina had stormed into her room and said they needed to talk. Now she was going to have to find somewhere new to live as soon as possible. How was she going to explain that to her parents? They were expecting her and Nina in Rye in a couple of weeks.

In some ways, she knew she had got off easily. Nina would have been well within her rights to have slapped her face. What hurt her the most was George's silence. Not one message since Nina had found that message on her phone that morning. He must have been shocked to have to his daughter on the phone, yelling abuse, but hadn't he thought of her at all? Did she mean nothing?

As Isobel opened the fridge to take out the salad that she and Robert were eating that night, she heard the ping of her phone. Her heart leapt. Jean-Luc? No. George. Apart from a 'Happy Easter' message, on which he had attached a photo of Grace and Nina by the pool, he hadn't been in direct contact for a couple of months. What on earth could he want now?

"Are you back in Paris soon?" No kisses.

Was she imagining it or was there a sense of urgency? Must be just busy at work. No mention of how she and Robert were, which she thought rude.

Her reply was equally curt. "Maybe next month".

"OK. Let me know. Would be good to meet".

What did that mean? Why would it be good

to meet? What was going on?

Before she decided how best to reply, her phone began to ring. The name George flashed on the screen.

"Hello George. Is everything OK? I was just about to reply to you."

"Hi Isobel. Yes fine. I just felt really bad."

"Bad?"

"I wasn't thinking. Sending you that message and not asking how you are. How things are since your mom . . ."

Something told her this wasn't the reason for the call, but at least he'd remembered, "Thanks for asking. We're all coping as well as can be expected. You know what it's like."

She hadn't meant it to come out like that. How crass of her. Losing a thirty-something wife surely counted for more points than losing an elderly mother in the game of bereavement poker.

Before he could reply, she leapt in again, "I feel bad too, George. With everything going on, I never rang to thank you for having Grace to stay again. I'm sure she had a wonderful time. Lucky girl!"

Grace and Nina had arrived back in Paris that evening; they were due to visit Rye in a fortnight's time.

"Have you spoken to her?"

"Not yet. I'll probably try her tomorrow."

There was a silence, as if he wanted to say

something else but couldn't.

"Sure there isn't a problem, George?"

"No, it's just a while since we talked." He sounded distant – not distant by miles but as though his mind had drifted to something else.

Why did she feel as though this conversation hadn't really begun.

"Was there something in particular, George? You seem rather upset?"

A pause at his end. "Not wrong, no. But I really would love to see you, Isobel."

"To talk about something?"

"It would just be great to hook up – and catch up. You know."

She really didn't. What was he getting at?

"Well I'll let you know when I plan to be in Paris next."

"Or . . . I could come and see you."

What on earth was he talking about? "Come where to see me? Not here surely?"

"Yes, there. I'm going to be in London for a night or two next week. Could I come and visit? Take you out to lunch?"

"Both of us you mean?"

"I was rather hoping it might just be you. Would Robert mind?"

There was a note of something in George's voice that she couldn't quite pin down. Why was he so desperate to see her alone?

"It might be better if I meet you in London. Rye is quite a trip by train."

"That would be great!"

"And you don't want to tell me why?"

A pause, "I think it would be better if we wait 'til we meet."

"OK. You're being rather mysterious. I can't help feeling there's something wrong."

"Not wrong. Not exactly."

"You're not filling me with confidence, George."

He gave an embarrassed laugh, "There's one other thing. Please don't tell Grace that we're meeting? She'll tell Nina and . . . I'd prefer Nina not to know."

"But they're due here in a couple of weeks. Why don't you all come over together?"

"That's not going to be possible. Not right now."

"I still don't understand. Why the mystery?"

"Complicated issues. I need to talk to you first."

Isobel was irritated. Not more of the 'Nina is gay and in love with Grace' routine, surely? What had got under George's skin? It was no good. He wasn't going to tell her. He rang off soon after that, saying he would confirm all arrangements as soon as he could.

Isobel sat in total bafflement. She realised that anyone listening to that conversation would have thought an affair was afoot. Yet George had never given her that sort of signal. She thought back to breakfast at Le Papillon:

how excited she'd been; how sweatily gauche. She remembered sitting in his suite, catching a glimpse of his bed, wishing and hoping seduction was on his mind. The fact is it hadn't been on his mind – and it was unlikely it was now. George was up to something, but what?

Her phone pinged again. Jean-Luc! She forgot George immediately.

Grace slept badly after the scene with Nina, eventually surfacing late morning and heading for the kitchen for coffee. Nina's door was closed. She paused outside, listening for any sound within, but it was silent. Had she gone out? Antoinette was running the mop over the kitchen floor, but she put it to one side the moment Grace walked in. It was obvious she had been waiting for someone to talk to – an audience for some news. It was *mauvaises nouvelles*, but, she couldn't hide the smirk on her face, "*Katja a été arrêtér.*" Arrested? Even for Katja, that was extreme. What on earth had she done?

In answer to Grace's questions, Antoinette scurried into the drawing room and brought back Madame Chirol's copy of '*Le Figaro*'. She turned the pages and pointed to a picture of a group of topless women being man-handled by police, all of them with writing emblazoned on their breasts. Katja was easily recognisable. Her own black-marker pen message was 'Fuck Your Morals'. She held a placard saying 'Freedom for Women' and wore flowers in her hair. Even wearing flowers, she looked angrier than usual. Before Grace could find out where and why this extraordinary protest had occurred, Antoinette heard Madame Chirol's bedroom door opening and whipped the paper away to return it safely to the coffee table.

Grace sat wondering what to do. She didn't like Katja but she felt bad about Antoinette's malicious gossiping. Madame Chirol was elderly, after all, and this must have upset her badly. Pam would have been mortified if Grace had ever been arrested. It would have been one of the very worse things that could happen. She couldn't just ignore it. Summoning her courage, she tapped at the drawing room door and walked in.

Madame Chirol was sitting in her usual spot underneath the Savonnerie tapestry, her coffee tray laid out before her. '*Le Figaro*' was nowhere to be seen. She looked at Grace and smiled gently, "Ah Grace – I thought you may come to see me."

Grace was touched by this. Had she really been expected? "I came to ask about Katja? Is she all right?"

Madame Chirol sighed, "You've heard already. From Antoinette?"

Grace didn't want to land Antoinette in hot water, but there was no other way she could have known, so she ignored the question, "I was worried when I heard. Are you OK, Madame?"

For a moment Madame Chirol seemed taken off guard, "I am fine, thank you, Grace. What Katja does is nothing to do with me."

The two women looked at each other and Madame Chirol frowned, "Do you know, Grace? Of my relationship to Katja?"

"Yes, Madame."

"I see. Antoinette again?"

"Not exactly. It was something Katja said when my own grandmother died. She is very fond of you, Madame."

"As I am of her."

She sipped her coffee thoughtfully, "I do not deny her existence, you know. It just seemed better for her that my lodgers did not know of our blood ties. Katja is rather embarrassed by all this, you know." She gestured to the fine furniture and family portraits that dominated the room.

"What will happen now?"

"To Katja? Not much. She will be detained by the police today, but I doubt they will press charges. In France, we have a great respect for the right to protest."

"She is lucky to have you."

"I think I am the lucky one, Grace. Katja is, after all, following her convictions. That is to be praised."

Grace felt wrong-footed. She had come to Madame Chirol to commiserate with the old lady, but had not reckoned on encountering such a different viewpoint, "You don't mind then?"

Madame Chirol shrugged, "It is not my own belief – that to bare your breasts is the way to reform – but I do think it is important to stand up and be counted if you see something happening that is wrong. My own husband fought in the Résistance during the War and was lucky to survive. Many of his friends did not. He would have admired his grand-daughter for her lack of fear, I think."

Once again, Grace felt very young. At sixteen, she had thought she knew it all. At nineteen, she was intimidated by how much she had yet to learn.

Then she remembered Nina, and Katja's attempt to blackmail her. Why was this so necessary given the Chirols' wealth?

"What does Katja do for money, Madame?" She hadn't intended to blurt it out. What business was it of hers, after all?

"What does Katja need money for, Grace? Material things mean very little to her. I pay for her keep and give her a small allowance. What she does with that is up to her. The one thing I won't agree to is giving Katja money for her causes. That would be foolish, don't you think?"

She was blind to Katja's lack of scruples then;

had no idea of how low her grand-daughter was prepared to sink for her "causes".

Madame Chirol spoke again, "If Katja has one bad fault, it is in being too judgemental of others. I think you may have suffered from that, Grace. She has not been very welcoming to you, I know."

"I irritate her. I don't mean to, but I do."

"You stand for a lot of things she despises: the product of a happy marriage for one thing. Katja's own childhood was badly disrupted by events."

"She gets on better with Nina, I think."

"Nina's mother is dead. Perhaps in her mind that evens things out."

Perhaps it did. Grace realised how she must look through Katja's eyes – a spoilt child just out of school who had never had one original thought in her life. No wonder she gave her a wide berth.

She got up to leave Madame Chirol to her coffee, but the old lady had a question for her in turn, "Would you like to tell me about Nina? About what has happened? I thought that was why you had come to see me."

Grace was shocked. How could she know?

"Poor Grace. I have taken you by surprise, but I was surprised too."

"In what way, Madame?"

"You arrived back here yesterday afternoon together after a holiday in Miami. Last night Nina delivered a letter to me saying she would be moving out as soon as possible. She would not give a reason. I do not need to be Inspector Maigret to realise something – or someone – has come between you."

"But it's me who will be moving out!"

"I see. That is what you agreed?"

"Yes, Madame."

"She has clearly decided to go instead. Would you like to tell me why?"

Grace began to cry, "I can't, Madame."

Madame Chirol stood up and walked over to the gilt-edged armchair on which Grace sat. She patted her gently on the shoulder, "Don't cry, *ma petite*. It seems to me there is something more serious here than the usual lodger dispute. A case of '*cherchez l'homme*' I suspect rather than '*cherchez la femme*' – you understand?"

Grace nodded, blew her nose, "Come and talk to me if you wish, Grace. I am not a judgemental woman, as you must now surely realise. I will be sorry to see either of you leave in bad odour. No matter how difficult this is, I think you should try to resolve your differences with Nina if you can."

How could she? Nina hated her and rightly so.

Later, lying on her bed surrounded by clumps of wet tissues, she thought how ironic it was that she should have gone to offer sympathy to Madame Chirol and ended up with the old lady trying to comfort her. It also struck her that Madame Chirol must have had a particularly difficult twenty-four hours, first with Katja's arrest and then with Nina's bombshell announcement. For the fortieth time that day, she checked her phone. No word from George.

Isobel was just back from visiting Jack. Robert put the kettle on, "How was it?"

"Fine. The Incomparable Lauren's got him doing *tai chi* now."

"Is that safe?"

"He does it sitting down. Apparently, it's still beneficial. It'll be Tantric sex next."

"That's an image my mind's eye could have done without. Saskia brought carrot cake round. Want some?"

"Just a small piece. Everything OK here?"

"Sort of."

"Meaning?"

"You won't like it."

"Spit it out, Robert."

"Grace. She and Nina aren't coming after all."

"What?!"

"I said you wouldn't like it."

"Grace hasn't been back here for months! What did she say?"

"Not much. She seemed a bit muted, if you

know what I mean."

She did know what he meant; had thought something was up when she talked to Grace on her return from Miami. There was none of the enthusiasm that had followed the first visit – everything was 'fine' and 'nice'. That was two days ago.

She tried to curb her irritation, but disappointment made her shrewish, "Did you ask her for a proper reason, Robert? It's incredibly selfish of her to let us down. What about Nina?"

"I think that may be the problem."

"What do you mean?"

"Apparently Nina is moving out."

"Moving out?"

"Yes."

"Why would she do that? It's an amazing set-up for them."

"Grace wouldn't say much – just that Nina wanted to move on."

They looked at each other.

She spoke first, "Are you thinking what I'm thinking?"

"Probably. You nearly always read my mind."

She ignored the jibe. "Obviously something happened in Miami."

"It does seem the most likely explanation."

"But if she's fallen out with Nina, wouldn't that be more of a reason to come home?"

"You tell me. I never did understand the

falling in and out of girls."

He could be infuriating. "Maybe I should go over to Paris?"

"Don't start that again, Bel."

"What do you mean?"

"Grace is nineteen. You can't go over to kiss her knee, metaphorically speaking. If she wanted our help or advice, she would come home."

"But what reason did she give? She must have said something."

"Just that she had a lot of work on and it wasn't a good idea to miss more classes when she was only just back from the States."

"I'll ring her back myself."

He looked even more uncomfortable, "She asked you not to."

"What's that supposed to mean?"

"She said, if Mum wants to talk to me, please tell her to leave it until tomorrow. I think she knew you would be cross."

"Cross! Cheeky cow."

"Bel, please."

"Did she know I would be out at Dad's?"

"Well you do usually go and see him on Tuesdays."

True, she did. Grace couldn't face her then, knew that Robert would be a push-over in comparison. What on earth had happened to cause this amount of friction?

She and George were due to meet in London the next week. Perhaps he could provide some answers. The more she thought about it, the more it seemed obvious there must be a link between the phone call with George and some sort of problem between Grace and Nina. Then it all fell into place in her head. George had been right all along. She had dismissed him as being an over anxious parent when he had announced that he thought Nina was gay and in love with Grace. Now it made perfect sense. Grace must have found out her friend's true feelings and, unable to reciprocate, they had decided it would be better if Nina moved out. What an idiot she'd been.

"What is it, Bel? Has she said something to you about Nina?"

"It's just a hunch, Robert, but Nina moving out might be for the best."

"Really? Not what you said a moment ago."

"You're right. Girl stuff can be hard to understand."

"Now you've got me worried."

"Why?"

"It's a golden rule in this house that I never get anything right."

◆ ◆ ◆

Grace couldn't ignore what Madame Chirol had told her. When she heard Nina come back and go into her own room, she plucked up courage and tapped on the door, "It's me."

"Go away, Grace." Nina sounded more tired than angry.

"Please, Nina, can we talk – just for a moment?"

"There's no point."

"Please." She took the silence that followed as taciturn acceptance.

Nina was sitting on her bed. She glared at Grace, who stood nervously by the door, half in and half out.

"What do you want?"

"I saw Madame Chirol earlier. She said you were moving out."

"So?"

"We agreed it was up to me to go."

"I changed my mind."

"That doesn't seem fair, Nina."

"None of it seems fair, Grace."

"Please can we talk? Without arguing?"

"There's nothing more to say."

"I would really appreciate if you let me move out. I feel bad enough already."

"I don't want to stay here."

"Why not let me move out?"

"Why not? Jesus!"

She put her head in her hands, a gesture of despair that made Grace want to rush across the room to comfort her.

"I don't want to stay here because you've ruined it for me. I don't want to stay here to put up with Antoinette's gossiping, Katja's taunting and Madame Chirol's determination to coax the truth from me. I don't want to make friends with the next person who takes your room. I don't want to be reminded of the fun we've had or the secrets we've shared. I want a clean break. Get it?"

Grace nodded miserably.

"Can you go now, Grace? I don't want to talk to you. I would prefer not to see you ever again, but I have to work out a month's notice apparently. If you want to make amends over the next four weeks, there's just one thing you can do."

"What's that?"

"Stay in your room when I'm here. Keep out of my way. I don't want to have to see you or speak to you. Understand?"

She understood. Nothing could be plainer.

However, there was one other thing bothering her. She had to ask.

"Are you going to tell my parents, Nina?"

Nina shrugged, "I've thought about that, believe me. But no, not yet. That's not because I want to protect you or George – far from it – but they might want to shoot the messenger. Why should I take the flak?"

Grace was relieved, but she noted the word, "yet".

"Thanks, Nina."

"Just leave me alone, Grace. For the next

month, I don't want to know you're here."

The lunch with George did not go as Isobel expected.

They met in a restaurant just off Golden Square with high booths around each table. It was the sort of place lovers might meet for clandestine lunches. Expensive, seductive, quietly glamorous. She wished she were meeting Jean-Luc.

George looked as handsome as ever, but as he rose to greet her, she noticed how tired and puffy his eyes were. Clearly, too much jetting around the world was taking its toll.

"Isobel, you look wonderful!"

And this time, she felt as though she really did. She was wearing a brightly printed dress that she hadn't been able to get into for years, but since coming back from Paris in March the weight had been dropping off her without too much effort. She felt light – not only in stones and pounds, but in spirit.

As always, they chit-chatted with ease, but Isobel knew there was an elephant seated at one of the booths. Better enjoy the lunch before they dealt with that.

"Was there a particular reason you wanted to meet, George?"

He turned the stem of his wine glass round. The movement reminded her of Jean-Luc playing with the condiment set.

"Has Grace said anything?"

"In what way? I know she and Nina are no longer coming to Rye."

"You must be disappointed."

"Very. Can you tell me what's going on, George? Grace says Nina is moving out?"

He nodded, looked miserable.

She reached across the table and took his hand, "It must be hard, George. You must be so worried."

At this, he looked positively startled, "You know then?"

"Only what you told me yourself."

"When?"

"At Le Papillon."

Silence. What on earth was wrong with him?

"You told me you thought Nina was gay and she might be in love with Grace. I didn't take you seriously then and I'm sorry for it now."

His face was what Pam would have called "a picture". She didn't know whether he was going to laugh or cry, "Thank you, Isobel. You're sweet."

She had the strong feeling there was something else he wanted to tell her, but he was struggling to find the words.

"Was there something else, George? You will tell me if I can help at all, won't you? I'm really very fond of Nina."

He wouldn't meet her eye, "Has Grace said anything else, Isobel? Nothing about me?"

What an odd question. Was he worried that Grace would feel responsible in some way? Would think George would blame her for Nina's unhappiness?

"I've barely talked to her, to be honest. She sounds a bit downcast, but hopefully she and Nina will get through this. It's not the end of the world, is it?"

"I suppose not."

"Nobody can help falling in love, George."

"No."

"It's just unfortunate that Grace doesn't reciprocate. Not in that way."

"I suppose it is."

"Love is where it falls and all that."

"So you wouldn't mind? If Grace were to reciprocate?"

"Not at all." She was pretty sure this was true.

"You would be happy for her, no matter what?"

"Of course. She's my daughter. All I want is to see her happy. You must feel the same, George?"

"Yes, Isobel, I do. Thank you. That is a weight off my mind."

"Happy to help, George." She gave his hand a squeeze. Grace would be happy they'd had this conversation.

She was right. Only not in the way she had intended.

That night, George called Grace from London. It was the first time they had spoken since she left Miami. He had replied to messages she sent, but only in the curtest of ways.

When she saw his name on the screen, her heart nearly leapt out of her chest. She tried to sound normal, but only a squeak came out her mouth, “Hello.”

“Hi Grace. Can you talk?”

“Nina’s out if that’s what you mean.”

“Sure?”

“Yes, I heard her telling Katja she was off to a bar with some friends.”

The walls were thin. Last night, she could hear Nina crying. Presumably Nina could hear her crying too.

“How have you been?”

How had she been? Devastated. Lonely. Heart-broken. Confused.

“OK I guess. How about you?”

“Not so good, Grace. I miss you a lot.”

She wanted to be angry with him, but her heart was melting already. “Have you, George?”

“I’m so sorry, Grace. This wasn’t what I intended.”

“I know.”

“I feel such a rat. Hurting you. Hurting Nina.

Upsetting your friendship."

"Is she talking to you yet?"

"No. She's pretty angry still. What about you?"

"I don't think she'll speak to me ever again."

"Never say never."

"What are we going to do, George?"

He avoided the question. "I saw your mum today."

A tsunami of jealousy engulfed her. "I suppose that was her idea?"

"No mine, as it happens."

"Why would you do that?"

"I was going to tell her."

"About us? Are you mad?"

"I guess I am, Grace. I certainly feel as though I've gone mad."

"But you didn't?"

"No, I screwed it up."

"So what did you talk about?"

"Other stuff. You and Nina. What had gone wrong between you."

"What on earth did she say?"

"She has the wrong end of the stick. It's my fault."

"What's your fault?"

"I said something last year I shouldn't have done."

"Go on."

"I said I thought Nina might be gay."

She had forgotten, but now it came back to

her, "Yes, I know. Mum told me. Why did you think that of all things?"

He paused. "No reason."

Something clicked deep in her mind, "Katja! She sent you pictures of her and Nina?"

"How did you know that?"

"She was trying to blackmail Nina before Christmas, but by the sounds of it she had already contacted you. Did you pay her off, George?"

"Yes. Stupid of me. Never trust a blackmailer, huh?"

"She must have spent that money and decided there was a way of getting more from you, via Nina."

"But Nina said no?"

"She figured that Katja would have sent you the pictures if she was serious. Of course what she didn't realise was that she already had."

"I didn't want to tell her – it would have made an embarrassing situation even worse."

"Poor you."

"I've got big shoulders." That was true.

"She's not by the way – gay."

"No?"

"It was just an experiment."

"I don't need the details, Grace."

"Sorry. Wasn't thinking. You still haven't explained about my mum. How is this anything to do with her?"

"It's not, but right now she's got the wrong

end of the stick."

"Meaning?"

"When we first met, I liked you so much, but it came on the back of Katja's unwanted correspondence and I was worried, not that Nina was gay . . . but . . ."

"But?"

"That she may be in love with you."

"George!"

"I know. Stupid of me. Anyway, I told Isobel about it and she was very nice, but pretty well told me to get a grip."

"Good for her!"

"But when she found out you and Nina had fallen out and that Nina was moving out . . . ."

"Oh my god. She thinks it's because of that? That Nina's in love with me?"

"Apparently, she does."

For the first time she felt angry with him, "And you let her think that?"

"It struck me it might be for the best if that's what she does think."

"Now you are behaving like a rat."

"Grace, think about it. Your mum and dad are bound to be worried, trying to work out what's wrong. I don't think we're ready to share our secret with them, are we? Just gives us a bit more time to work out what to do."

So he did think they had a future? She could barely contain her excitement.

"I love you, George."

"Miss you, beautiful girl."

Yet still he did not say the words she so wanted to hear.

MAY

She would see him once more and that would be the end. She was married to Robert and their lives were too entwined for her to risk being found out. She relied on Robert for help with Jack; they were both committed to Grace's future. Miss Mapp could barely sustain one shared home, never mind two separate ones. She had been reckless and selfish, but she was coming to her senses now. One last trip to Paris and that was that.

Dani listened to this monologue with her usual patience, but as always she went direct to the heart of the matter, "Will you go to bed with him again? For this 'one last time'?"

"Absolutely not! We'll meet for lunch and I'll explain I won't be coming over again. He knows Grace is only there for a gap year, so he must realise it's coming to a natural end anyway."

"But I thought you liked having your doors kicked down?"

"You're laughing at me, Dani!"

"Sorry. It's just the more I listen to you, the more convinced I am you're going to jump straight back into bed with Jean-Luc the moment we get there."

"Why do you say that?"

"The lady doth protest too much."

"Unfair! I'm just trying to explain to you that I have decided to stay with Robert and try to be a good wife."

"This might not be everyone's definition of a good wife."

"Well maybe I'm not 'everyone'. As you said yourself, it's something I have to get out of my system, that's all."

"Like colonic irrigation?"

"Dani! Stop!"

"Sorry, Bel. I understand, really I do. Stuff happens. You move on. Is that it?"

"Sort of. Except for one vital difference."

"Which is?"

"Stuff never usually happens. Not to me. That's why I have to see Jean-Luc one last time."

"Explain?"

"I don't want to block his number again and just disappear. I owe him more than that. I want us to raise a glass of champagne together and say a proper good-bye."

"You are far too romantic for your own good."

"Romantic? I never think of myself like that."

"And what about Robert?"

"In what sense?"

"You've mentioned staying with Robert for Jack's sake and Grace's sake and even for Miss

Mapp's sake. What do you feel for Robert himself?"

"Truthfully? I'm not sure."

"He deserves better than that, Bel."

They were in Dani's garden, Isobel subliminally taking in Saskia's summer composition of viburnum, irises, lamb's ears, larkspur, sedum and ballerina roses.

"I know I'm behaving selfishly, Dani. Believe me, I do."

"I know. It's just we're very fond of Robert, you know. But changing the subject just for one moment, how's Grace doing? Has Nina moved out?" Isobel had told Dani her theory about Nina being in love with Grace. Dani was unconvinced.

"Not officially. Madame Chirol has insisted on a full month's notice, which I think takes it to next week. She could find someone else for that room at the drop of a hat, so I suspect she was hoping Grace and Nina would be reconciled."

"Which, I assume, they haven't been?"

"No. Grace won't talk about it. She seems to have closed the shutters where we're concerned. Have you heard from her?"

"She replies to my messages, but she's not her usual open self. It's the same with Saskia."

"You would tell me, wouldn't you? If she confided something in you and not in us?"

"Truthfully?"

"Yes, of course."

"Grace is nineteen, Isobel. I would no more

betray her confidence than I would yours."

"Oh."

"Sorry, but that's just how it is."

"You're right. I couldn't expect anything else."

"I'm very much looking forward to seeing her next week though. It's been ages."

"Sure Saskia doesn't mind?"

"No, she's cool about it. She's never been keen on big cities and it's hard to drag her away from the garden at this time of year. How about Robert?"

"He's depressed by how much money this gap year has cost us already, but he can see the end is in sight, so he's given up trying to talk me out of it. It did help that I said you wanted to visit. I owe you, Dani."

"You can buy the first Martini then."

"Ha! There's no bar in our hotel. It's a lovely spot in Montmartre, but it's pretty basic."

"How about a drink at Hôtel Costes? I've always wanted to visit."

"Brilliant idea! Now you're talking!"

Before she went to Paris, she drove over to see Jack.

"All this to-ing and fro-ing," he said. "Can't keep up with it all."

"It's coming to an end soon, Dad. Grace's gap year finishes next month."

"Thank goodness. Time you stopped being such a flibbertigibbet."

"Don't you mean Grace?"

"No, you. Always on that bloomin' Eurostar these days."

"I'm fifty next year, Dad. A bit old for words like 'flibbertigibbet'."

He snorted, "Time you acted your age then."

"Dad!"

What on earth did he know? It worried her that Jack's radar had always been finely tuned. She couldn't get away with anything when she was younger; he could smell a lie as easily as sniff out a dead rat.

Lauren must have been listening at the door. She entered holding a bottle of pills and a glass of water, her face a shade too pink for Isobel's liking.

"Hello, dear!" said Jack.

Why was he always charming to Lauren and downright rude to her?

"Time for your medication, Jack," she smiled. "And then you really should have a rest before supper . . . if Isobel doesn't mind?"

"You do look after me well. Doesn't she, Isobel?"

"She does indeed. Lucky to have her."

Jack had put her in such a foul mood, she couldn't wait for him to go for his nap, so she could escape.

When Lauren took him down the corridor to put him to bed, she picked up her bag ready to go.

"Could you just wait one moment, Isobel?" came Lauren's voice.

"Of course. No problem." What now?

A few minutes' later, Lauren appeared, "More tea?"

"Thanks, but no. I really should be getting back."

"I just need to tell you something. About Jack."

"Go on."

"I think he has Parkinson's. A gentleman I used to look after had it and there are similar signs with your father."

Isobel felt her world wobble.

"I don't think it can be Parkinson's – he doesn't have a tremor."

"He does have other signs though: stiffness, slowness, rigid expression."

"He needs a diagnosis then. Shall we take him to the doctor's?"

"I already have." She might have known it.

"It might have been nice to tell me."

"I didn't want to worry you. Know how busy you are." Not another person subtly accusing her of parental neglect. She felt like picking up one of Pam's china cats and hurling it at the French windows.

"I see. And what did the doctor say?"

"He's going to refer Jack to a neurologist, but it can be difficult to diagnose. As you said, most people develop a shake. But on the whole, he thought I was probably right." Of course Lauren was right. Incomparable Bloody Lauren.

"What do we do now then?"

"Nothing for now."

"Nothing at all?"

"There's no cure, Isobel, but it could take years before it disables him completely. We'll just have to wait and see what the consultant says."

"Will he end up in a nursing home?"

"Possibly. At some point."

Her dad drove her up the wall at times, but she was appalled by the news. She thought of her mum, furiously rejecting any notion of having help with Jack. Had her mum suspected something like this?

"How did he take the news, Lauren?"

"Hard to say. To be honest, he hasn't mentioned it since." She looked embarrassed, "I told Mavis, by the way." So Mavis Dawkins knew more about her father than Isobel did?

"Why did you do that?" It was hard to conceal her annoyance.

Lauren looked uncomfortable, "They're good friends, you know. It just came out in conversation. She's been worried about him and his little turns for a while."

"Sorry. Didn't mean to sound snappy."

The fact was she hadn't been worried at all;

had barely noticed his "little turns."

At that point, they heard Jack shouting Lauren's name with some urgency. She jumped up, "He must need the loo. Excuse me, Isobel."

"Of course. I'll let myself out." All her irritation faded away. Thank God someone else was there to do the unmentionable.

◆ ◆ ◆

Grace looked at her phone: four-twelve. Another sleepless night or, to be more exact, sleepless morning. It wouldn't be light for another couple of hours, but she knew from experience she would have little chance of getting back to sleep now. Through her bedroom wall, she could hear Nina gently snoring. It was nearly a month since Nina had stopped talking to her. In three days' time, she was due to move out.

The timing couldn't have been worse. For one thing, her mum and Dani were arriving two days before Nina was due to leave the Chirol apartment. She wouldn't trust her ex-friend not to say something, so she would have to put them off coming here until Nina had gone.

To add to the problem, George had sent her a message saying he would be in Paris at the same time. Although he didn't say so, it was obvious he was coming over to patch things up with Nina and help her settle into her new apartment.

Nina was on a very generous allowance from her father, so she wouldn't want to burn her bridges entirely and George would come to her aid at the click of her fingers. Grace was certain that Nina would give him an ultimatum: Grace or me. There was no doubt in her mind that George would choose Nina. The thought made her stomach contract with fear.

As always, he was staying at Le Papillon.

"Will I see you at all? xxxx" she'd messaged the previous night.

"Of course. I couldn't bear it if we didn't see each other xxx".

That was all very well, but he seemed to be missing the point. How was that to be managed if she were with Isobel and he was with Nina.

"How? Xx".

"Don't worry, honey. We will find a way xxx".

Fat help that was. To make matters worse, she had been really looking forward to Dani's visit. She would have preferred to see Dani on her own; she was the one person she could trust with sensible advice. Her mum would probably irritate her madly. Now the visit was going to be over-shadowed by Nina, George and the whole horrible situation.

It was no good. She couldn't sleep. She tip-toed down the corridor to the kitchen and put the kettle on. She would take a camomile tea back to bed.

Bad move. She heard the front door open

and footsteps down the corridor. A moment later, Katja walked in. As always, she looked magnificently hostile.

"Why are you here, English girl?" Grace assumed she meant 'here' in the kitchen, rather than questioning her existential existence.

"Couldn't sleep. Are you just back?" This was a pointless question given that Katja was wearing her usual uniform of boots, jeans, ripped T-shirt and leather jacket. Her black eye-liner was smudged and her newly bleached hair was dark at the roots.

"Sure. I'm a vampire, you know, I love the night."

Grace hadn't seen Katja much since her arrest. Madame Chirol had been right. She had been released by the police the next day, with no charges pressed. During the day, her door was always shut. Was she asleep or absent? Maybe she slept in a coffin with the lid shut to block out the sunlight.

"But you're a vampire too, aren't you, English girl?"

Katja smiled maliciously at Grace's discomfiture.

"What do you mean?"

"You look so angelic, but you suck the happiness out of those who love you."

"You're drunk, Katja."

"Poor Ninaaaaaaaa. Daddy doesn't love her anymore."

So Katja knew? How?

"I don't know what you mean."

"Bullshit!"

"Please, Katja, keep your voice down."

"So we don't wake Nina? Who hates you now. Because you keep the bed warm where her mummy used to sleep."

"Stop it, Katja. Please."

"Pleeeeeeeeeeese. You know, English girl, I never knew you had it in you. To be such a bitch. I almost like you for it."

"I don't want you to like me."

Katja came up to her face then, eyeball to eyeball, "That's just as well," she said. "I can't fucking stand you."

Grace pushed past her, desperate to get back to her own room and avoid further confrontation. But there was someone else in the doorway: Nina. For a moment, Grace wanted more than anything to put her arms around her friend and plead for them to get back to normal.

"You woke me up," she said accusingly. Grace noticed her eyes were rimmed with pink.

"I'm sorry," said Grace. "Didn't mean to."

Katja was grinning, "Isn't this fun? All of us together. You and your future step-mother."

She looked so delighted at the misery on Nina's face that Grace felt physically sick. The room began to spin. She ran for the bathroom, splashing cold water on her face and taking slow, deep breaths.

From the kitchen, she heard angry voices and Katja laughing - then a sound like the crack of a whip.

Who had slapped who? There was silence for a moment.

"Now why don't you fuck off, you evil bitch!" she heard Nina say.

Then came the sound of footsteps as she walked past the bathroom and back to her room. Grace opened the door and nervously crept into her own bed. Through the wall, she could hear the muffled noise of someone sobbing. She wished her walls were lined with cork like those of Proust.

She lay awake until dawn, but she never heard Katja go to her room.

"It looks like an Edwardian brothel," said Dani.

"I think that may be the idea."

It was their first night in Paris and they were sitting in the bar of Hôtel Costes, watching the beautiful people go by. There was a lot of rich panelling and tall, gilt mirrors; buttoned, velvet banquettes and deep fringing on the chairs. Isobel had a terrible feeling that Pam would have absolutely loved it. 'Outrageously opulent' the guidebooks said. 'Nice and comfortable' her mother would have countered. She would have particularly approved of the gold brocade on the love seats and the intricate pattern of the carpets.

"Maximalist," said Dani.

"Are you talking about the interiors or the Martini?"

"Both. They certainly know how to mix a drink here!"

"I'll drink to that."

Grace was due to meet them soon, having insisted she would make her own way from the apartment. Isobel had expected her to sound more excited than she did, but she seemed particularly distracted.

While they waited, they ran over the planned schedule. Dani was going to offer to take Grace out for lunch the next day on her own; Grace wouldn't be suspicious given she loved having quality time with her godmother. She and Dani would meet in Montparnasse near the CCFS as she had classes that afternoon. This would give Isobel a window in which to meet Jean-Luc – he had suggested the same restaurant as last time, so there would be no chance of them all bumping into each other. Dani would make her own way back in the direction of Boulevard Haussmann, meet up with Isobel and the two of them would go shopping. They would take Grace out to dinner for the final time that night, before heading home the next morning. Isobel would not visit Paris again: Robert would come over in June to help Grace move back.

While they waited for Grace, they made up stories about the people who passed.

"Movie mogul. Never off the casting couch."

"Colombian hooker. As expensive as it gets."

"Disinherited royalty. Planning a coup."

"Professional trophy wife. Out for husband number five."

The Martinis went to their heads and they giggled loudly.

"But who do they think we are, Dani?"

"Cougars?"

"I don't think we look rich enough. Don't you have to be rich to be a cougar?"

"Fashion editors?"

"Don't make me laugh! Of what? '*The Lady*'?"

"Speak for yourself!"

"They probably know we're just here as Martini tourists."

"Shall we give them something to think about?"

"What do you mean?"

"This." Dani put her arm around Isobel, pulled her close and gave her a smacking kiss on the lips.

"Mum! Dani!" At the look on Grace's face, they started laughing even louder.

"Sorry, sweetheart. It's Dani's fault."

"Are you two drunk already? Honestly!"

Dani stood up and gave Grace a hug, "Not

drunk. Just happy. How are you, Grace, darling?"

Grace smiled and gave her a big hug back, then bent down to peck Isobel on the cheek.

Dani called the waiter over, "Three more of your delicious Martinis, *s'il vous plait*."

By the time they reached the Lebanese restaurant Isobel had booked for dinner, Grace seemed more her usual self. The Martini had certainly thawed her out. Isobel tried to avoid the subject of Nina, aware that if she wanted to tell them about it, she would. Grace seemed pleased at the prospect of lunch on her own with Dani, but Isobel felt guilty about all the lies she was telling. She was aware that neither she nor Grace were on good form that night, but Dani entertained her god-daughter with snippets of gossip from Rye and Saskia's obsession with taxidermy.

"I caught her stroking Linden in a very odd way the other night."

"What do you mean?"

"She was sort of feeling for his skeleton as she ran her hands down his body. I don't think she realised she was doing it until I told her not to think about stuffing the cat."

"Hilarious!"

"She'll probably end up preserving me for posterity."

Later, they ordered Turkish coffee and talked about Grace's course.

"Will you be sorry to finish?' asked Dani.

"Yes and no. I won't miss the endless assignments. I thought I would miss Paris and living in Madame Chirol's apartment, but now I'm not so sure." The name Nina hung in the air above their heads, but nobody spoke it out loud.

"But you're off to Durham in the autumn. You might have to write assignments there too, you know."

"Mmmmmmmm . . . ."

The shutters were closing again. Dani made a valiant effort to keep the conversation alive, but Grace grew quieter and quieter. By ten-thirty she was yawning and saying she needed to get to bed.

"Shall we walk you back, Grace?"

"No, Mum – no need – I'll see you both tomorrow. Meet me outside the college at twelve-thirty, Dani? Mum can give you directions."

"You bet. Can't wait."

"Me neither. I'll have to leave for classes by two-thirty, but we'll have a couple of hours. That OK?"

"Of course."

"And I'll see you tomorrow night, Mum. Enjoy the shopping!"

"Thanks, lovely girl. I will."

When she'd gone, Isobel looked at Dani, "Is it just me?"

"Or is something wrong? I'm not sure, Bel. It might be she's just upset by this Nina business. I'm still not sure why Nina's moving out."

"I don't think she looks that well."

"A bit pale certainly."

"She didn't eat much."

"Like I said, she seems a bit stressed by it all."

"I think there's something else."

"What?"

"A man maybe?"

"Yes, that's possible. I thought that at Christmas, funnily enough."

"Did you? Why?"

"An overload of pheromones. They change the whole look of a woman."

"I thought they changed our smell."

"I didn't notice the smell – just the look. Maybe I'm pheromone sensitive."

"Well it would explain a lot. Her reluctance to talk about Durham for one thing."

"True."

"But why wouldn't she say so? I'm her mother. She can trust me."

"I don't know, Bel. For some reason or another, Grace is keeping her cards very close to her chest."

"And you're not going to tell me, even if you find out?"

"Not if she asks me not to. No."

"Damn you for being such a good godmother, Dani!"

"You're welcome, Bel."

For some reason, she felt more nervous about this lunch than the last one. She had decided to wear the same dress she had worn when she met George, knowing it flattered her slimmer figure, but she fussed over her hair for what seemed like hours.

"For God's sake, Bel!" said Dani in exasperation. "Give the hair-dryer to me and I'll do it."

"Really?"

"I do Saskia's every morning."

"I had no idea."

How lucky they were. Saskia baking cakes and doing the garden; Dani on hand to blow-dry Saskia's hair.

"There. What do you think?"

"You're a godsend, Dani. I've never been any good with these hotel hair-driers they keep chained to the drawer."

"You're welcome. You look lovely by the way."

"Thank you. Feel a bit sick to be honest."

"Shame I can't meet Jean-Luc. I am rather curious."

"I wish you could too, but I think it would be awkward."

"I know. Just hope it goes well today, Bel. Do try to behave!"

"I will. Promise."

It had been two months since her last encounter with Jean-Luc. Her heart leapt as she walked into the restaurant and saw him waiting at the same table. He stood up and waved when he saw her; evidently he'd been on the look-out for her arrival. How flattering. She felt her heart thumping as she walked towards him.

"Isobel! More beautiful than ever." A kiss on each cheek.

"Thank you, Jean-Luc. How are you?"

"Relieved, Snow Queen. I thought you might cancel."

"That's what you thought last time!"

"I know. I have so little faith, don't I?" He laughed, his eyes crinkling around the edges and sparkling with good humour. It would be hard to be angry with Jean-Luc given the way he laughed.

When the waiter handed her the menu, she realised her hands were shaking. She held the menu in her lap trying to conceal her nerves. Jean-Luc had already ordered a bottle of the same delicious Sancerre they had enjoyed last time. She knew she must try not to drink too fast and let it go to her head. She was determined to enjoy this lunch and then say a final good-bye.

This being Jean-Luc, her resolve did not go entirely to plan. As the lunch went on, he became increasingly attentive, gazing into her eyes, stroking her hands and arms, telling her how much he'd missed her.

She was determined to remain resolute, "This is my last visit, Jean-Luc. Grace finishes her gap year next month and my husband will be over to pick her up. I won't have a reason to come here again."

"I have been thinking about that, Snow Queen."

"What do you mean?"

"I have a job offer for you."

He delivered this line in a dead-pan way, but she could tell by the twinkle of his eyes, he was enjoying her surprise.

"What do you mean? What kind of job?"

"PA."

"To you?"

"Yes, to me."

She laughed, "My French isn't nearly good enough."

"I love your bad French."

"Is it that bad?"

"Bad French is part of your English charm."

"So why on earth would you want a PA who is twenty years behind the times and speaks terrible French?"

"To help me in Hollywood."

"What!"

He grinned, "My next project in fact, and my first for a major Hollywood studio. I will be there for at least six months. I have a French PA, but she needs to stay here and run my Paris office. For America, I need someone who speaks fluent English."

"Is that the only qualification?" He had to be

winding her up, but he sounded sincere.

"That and good organisational skills. The same ones you used before you had your daughter."

"I'm hopelessly out-of-date when it comes to computers and stuff."

"We would be leaving in September. You have a few months to brush up on that sort of thing, and anyway you would have your own assistant."

Her head was spinning. A job. Hollywood. Her own assistant. It couldn't be happening.

"Is this just about sex, Jean-Luc?"

He laughed, "I knew you would think that. In fact I would try very hard to resist you while we worked together. This film is a big deal for me. I don't want the crew gossiping."

She wasn't sure she would be able to resist him, but she admired the sentiment.

"It's kind of you, Jean-Luc, and I am very touched by your generosity, but I couldn't possibly accept."

"Why not?"

"You just said it yourself. It's a big deal. I would let you down."

"You don't think you could do it?"

"I'm afraid not. It's all too long ago."

"I don't agree. I think you should trust my judgement on this and embrace the challenge. Life is not a dress rehearsal, Isobel."

"You barely know me. How can you be so

sure?"

"I know you better than you think. And what have you got to lose? If it is a mistake, it will be *my* mistake, not yours."

His confidence in her was intoxicating.

"It's a shock, Jean-Luc. I'm incredibly grateful, but I need time to think about it."

"Of course you should think about it, but you haven't asked the most important question yet."

"Which is?"

"The pay." And then he named a figure that seemed so outlandish she really did think he was either mad or playing a cruel joke.

She laughed, "I thought we were meeting today to say good-bye for ever. Now this!"

He grinned at her, "We're not in Hollywood yet and we have a room waiting for us at Le Papillon. Let's go and celebrate your new career."

There was nothing she wanted more right then but a post-lunch tryst with Jean-Luc, but should she give into temptation after everything she had said to Dani?

"I was determined not to go to bed with you again. Told myself it just wouldn't feel right."

He laughed at that, "I don't think you would complain, you know, about how it felt."

"Stop it, Jean Luc! You know what I mean." Now they were both laughing.

"I might not see you until September. I would be sad not to wish you a tender good-bye, Snow Queen."

How could she refuse?

Grace reached the restaurant where she and Dani were due to meet a few minutes before her godmother. She was excited that it would just be the two of them. Much as she loved her parents, her relationship with Dani was special to her. She loved Saskia too, but Dani and she had always had an intimacy that was precious. She'd always thought she could tell her anything, but could she tell her this?

They ordered omelette and frites and two large glasses of house red. Dani made her laugh with tales of the Incomparable Lauren and Jack's new found love of fine cuisine.

"Your poor mum – she doesn't know whether to be relieved that Jack's being so well cared for or to stab Lauren in the eye."

"It must be pretty infuriating. Is Lauren to be trusted, do you think?"

"She seems nice. What did you think when you met her?"

"Same. If she's after Grandad's millions, I think she'll be disappointed."

"True!"

After a second glass of house red, Dani gave her a searching look, "How are you, Grace? Really?"

"What do you mean?"

Dani sighed, "Do you remember when you were little, you were staying with me and you tried to get dressed on your own and then shouted out, that you were 'all in a tangle'?"

Grace laughed. This had been one of their jokes for years. Grace had only been about three at the time. She didn't remember it herself, but Dani had often made her laugh with her description of walking in to find Grace with two legs in the same hole of her dungarees and a very puzzled expression on her face.

"Are you in a tangle now, Grace?"

What a very Dani way of putting things.

"Meaning?"

"I know you well enough to know that something is wrong. You might not want to tell me about it, but then again, a trouble shared is a trouble halved."

"You sound like Granny."

"Is that a bad thing?"

Grace shook her head.

"You still haven't answered my question, sweetheart. Are you in a tangle?"

"I guess I am."

"Do you want to tell me about it?"

"You'll tell mum."

"No, I won't. When have I ever betrayed your confidence, Grace?"

That was a fair point. It was Dani who Grace had told when she lost her virginity. Dani who knew about her first joint. Dani who she'd rung when she needed picking up from a club in Brighton that had been raided at three in the morning, after she'd told Isobel and Robert she was staying the night with a friend in Tunbridge Wells.

"You're not going to like it, Dani. Even you."

"Maybe it's not a question of whether I like it or not. It's not my life, is it? You're nineteen now. You're entitled to make your own choices, for better or for worse."

"I feel so miserable."

"Go on. Is this to do with Nina?"

"Sort of. It's more to do with George actually."

"Ah."

"I wish you'd met George, Dani. Then you might understand."

Dani gave her a searching look, "Are you saying that you and George are having an affair?"

"I'm saying that I love him. And he loves me."

"That's quite a lot to take in. Why don't you start at the beginning, sweetie?"

So she did. She poured out her heart to Dani: the meeting at the carousel; the messages that followed; new year in Miami; the inevitability of what happened at Easter; Nina's fury at finding out on the plane home; her sorrow and guilt at hurting her friend; her love for George.

"When did you see George last?"

Grace looked uncomfortable, "Not since Miami but . . . "

" . . . but you have plans to see him again soon? When?"

"This afternoon actually."

"What!" Dani had remained so calm throughout their conversation, but now her composure was shattered, "You said we only had a couple of hours to meet because you were due at class."

"I lied. Sorry."

"You lie disgustingly well, Grace. Where are you meeting?"

"George's hotel."

"Le Papillon?"

"Did mum tell you he always stays there? Yes, Le Papillon. I said I would be there about three."

"Does Nina know?"

"Not about this. Hope not anyway. She's moving out tomorrow, so I'll make myself scarce then."

"Grace, this is not a good idea."

"Which bit exactly?"

"None of it, to be honest. Surely you don't want to risk hurting Nina further if she does find out you've spent the afternoon in bed with her father?"

"It won't make any difference. She hates me anyway."

"But what are you planning to do? For the future?"

"My future is with George."

"Grace, really? Are you sure? That's a huge

step."

"It's the only one I can take. Like I said, I love him."

"When are you going to let your mum and dad know?"

"George and I need to discuss it. Frankly, the sooner everyone knows, the better. I'm sick of tip-toeing around."

"But what are you going to do when you finish your course? What about Durham?"

"I won't be going to Durham, Dani."

"Grace, this is madness. You can't throw your whole life away in this manner."

"Is that what you think I'm doing? Throwing my life away? I thought you of all people would understand."

She pushed her chair back and picked up her bag, "I need to go. I'm going to be late. Sorry to disappoint you, Dani."

"Grace! Wait! Please. Sit down."

Sulkily, Grace did as she was asked.

"I'm sorry for what I said, Grace. Truly I am. It's a shock, that's all."

"I knew it would be."

"But I'm always going to be here for you, no matter what. I'm not going to break your confidence and I'm going to respect whatever you decide to do."

The brittle expression on Grace's face was replaced by one of relief, "Really, Dani? Thank you! That means a lot to me."

"I ask only one thing."

"Go on."

"Don't make any hasty decisions. Keep all your options open."

"You mean Durham?"

"I mean everything: your parents, your home, your studies. Go to Miami if you must, but at least consider the possibility that you may change your mind in the future."

"I really don't think I will."

"I know, sweetheart, but you might. That's all I am saying."

"Anything else?"

"One leg in each hole." She was straight-faced as she delivered this line.

Grace began to laugh, "You're ridiculous!"

"I try."

"I really do have to go, Fairy Godmother."

"OK. I'll see you tonight then."

"And you won't tell mum?"

"I won't. Promise. But you do have to tell her and Robert soon."

"I know. Just one other thing."

"What?"

"Try to be happy for me, Dani. I know that's a big ask, but please try."

◆ ◆ ◆

Isobel lay in Jean-Luc's arms, looking up at the

ceiling, “That was another very expensive lunch, Jean-Luc.”

“You mean the room? It was worth every moment, my love.”

“I should go now.”

“I know.”

Reluctantly, she sat up and reached for her shoes. Her hair was a mess and her mascara was running, but she felt beautiful and desirable.

Automatically, she checked her phone. One message from Dani:

“On no account go to the Papillon xx”. It wasn’t like Dani to sound so bullying. Isobel was irritated by the message. It was true she’d promised Dani she wouldn’t go to bed with Jean-Luc, but it was a bit late now.

She quickly pinged back a reply, “Will fill you in later. See you at Galerie Lafayette, three-thirty”. It was now two-fifty-two.

Once she’d tidied her hair and re-done her make-up, they walked down the corridor together and pressed the lift button. There was no-one else in sight.

“Just one more kiss,” said Jean-Luc and he wrapped his arms around her and kissed her lovingly. They quickly pulled apart as the lift door opened. Out of the corner of her eye, Isobel saw a couple stepping out, arms entwined. One of them was George. For a fraction of a second, her brain couldn’t make sense of the fact that Grace was the other.

"Mum! What are you doing here?" At the word 'mum', Jean-Luc murmured, '*putain*' and stepped away from her.

Grace looked furious. George looked terrified. The lift doors closed with a whisper, leaving the four of them standing in the hotel corridor.

"Shouldn't you give me the answer to that question, Grace?"

"I asked first. Who is this exactly?" Grace gestured towards Jean-Luc.

"This is my friend, Jean-Luc. He helped me when I fell in the snow." What else could she say?

"Your *friend*? You were kissing him, mum, I saw you." She looked vitriolic. Anger stripped the beauty from her face.

George cleared his throat, "Grace – Isobel - can I suggest we talk in my room, rather than out here. Seems like there's a few things you need to say to each other."

He was right, but Isobel turned on him with a generous dose of self-righteous sarcasm, "How very thoughtful of you, George. Lead the way. Then you can tell me exactly what you are doing with my daughter."

She turned towards Jean-Luc. He looked mortified, "There's no need for you to come with us, Jean-Luc. It's a family matter."

"I'll wait for you downstairs."

"There's no need."

He nodded and for one terrible moment, she thought he would reach out to shake George by the hand or give Grace *la bise*, but he turned away and pressed the lift button. Isobel followed George and Grace down the corridor.

It was the same suite as last time. Isobel felt as if she had been picked up and flung into a parallel universe. How stupid she'd been. Stupid to have had her head turned by Jean-Luc. Stupid not to have seen what was happening with her own daughter. Then she remembered Dani's message. "On no account go to the Papillon". Grace had confided in Dani then. For a moment, she bitterly resented her friend.

She sat down in an armchair, Grace on the sofa. Isobel was suddenly overcome with tiredness. She felt as if the life she had known was draining away. There had to be another reason for Grace being here, not the one she feared. George poured out two large glasses of white wine and a hefty vodka for himself.

"Are you going to go first or am I, Grace?"

"You obviously! Who the fuck is Jean-Luc? How could you do that to dad!"

George intervened, "Grace, that's no way to talk to your mother. Please."

Isobel thought Grace would bite his head off too, but her voice dropped a register, "OK, sorry."

She must stay calm. "I don't actually owe you any explanation about Jean-Luc, but I regret you saw what you did."

George looked uncomfortable, "Maybe I should go. This is really none of my business."

Isobel was sharp, "No, it's not. But I think, given the circumstances, you should stay, don't you?"

Grace was brimming with malice, "What if I tell Dad?"

"That's your choice."

She would have to brazen it out. Robert was a problem for further down the line.

She took a deep breath, "I think the bigger question here is what you and George are up to?"

"You know what we're up to."

"Grace!" This from George again.

"How long have you been . . ."

"Sleeping together?"

At this, George looked as though he might die of embarrassment. Isobel almost felt sorry for him, but not quite, "I was going to say, 'seeing each other', Grace. But yes let's discuss sex too while we're here."

"It's not just about sex."

"I don't think it was me who implied it was."

"George and I are in love. We're planning a future together, aren't we, George?"

It was obvious this was far from how George had wanted to break this particular news. He didn't answer. Couldn't even look at Isobel.

"What do you mean, 'a future'? You're going to Durham in the autumn."

"No. I'm not."

"Yes! You are!"

"Now who's shouting?"

"George, can you tell me what's going on? You can't be serious about this."

George was holding his head in his hands, as if willing the gods to transport him elsewhere. Grace was frustrated by his reticence, "Go on, George. Tell her!"

"This is not how I wanted you to find out, Isobel."

"I'm bloody sure, it isn't!"

"Don't speak to George that way!"

"Shut up, Grace! I'll speak to him how I want to!"

George slammed his glass down on the table and stood up, "Please stop shouting, both of you. This conversation is less than helpful given how difficult the situation is."

He sighed, "I think you'd better leave, Isobel."

"You're throwing me out?"

"I think you and Grace both need to calm down. I don't think that's possible while you're in the same room."

"Does Nina know?" And at that, the final piece of the jigsaw fell into place in her head. Stupid, stupid, stupid.

"She does. As I said, it's a difficult situation."

"You talk as though it is a situation not of your own making."

"I didn't plan to upset you, Isobel."

"Really George? Was it all Grace's doing?"

"Mum!"

"Don't worry, I'm going." She stood and

picked up her bag.

"Lover boy will be waiting for you downstairs, remember?"

George intervened, "Grace, stop this! I'm sorry, Isobel, but I think we need to talk things through when emotions aren't running quite so high."

She couldn't bring herself to say good-bye to either of them. She opened the door and walked briskly down the corridor to the lift, trying hard not to cry.

In the bar, she looked for Jean-Luc, but he had gone. Not surprising. On her phone were two unread messages.

From Jean-Luc, "I'm so sorry. Please say you'll still come xxx".

From Dani, "Where are you? X".

She rang her number and Dani picked up straight away, "Bel, are you OK?"

"No. I'm not."

"Where are you?"

"Le Papillon."

There was a long silence, "With Jean-Luc?"

"Jean-Luc isn't the problem, Dani, I think you know who is. Please come quick." She was holding back the tears, but the dam would break soon.

"There?"

"No." She couldn't stay here. What if George and Grace came down?

"Where?"

"There's a carousel in the Tuileries. Meet me there. Ask for directions, can you do that?"

"Sure. I'll get there as soon as I can."

◆ ◆ ◆

While they walked, Isobel talked and cried and talked again, aware she was giving Dani a stream-of-consciousness account of Jean-Luc, the lunch, the hotel, the lift and the sudden realisation of what was going on from both sides. Only much later did she realise the offer of a job and a trip to Hollywood had flown clean out her head.

"You both had a shock then?"

"You mean me and Grace – or me and Jean-Luc?"

"You and Grace. Although it doesn't sound like Jean-Luc or George had the best day of their lives either."

"George is a total bastard. I don't care about spoiling his day."

"Bel, don't get angry with me, but you do have to consider the possibility that George has real feelings for Grace."

"What did she tell you over lunch?"

"I knew you'd be cross with me over that. I wasn't going to tell you, but it seems a bit late for keeping confidences now."

"How true!"

"Grace says she loves him – and she believes he loves her. Certainly he took his time before they went to bed, which implies he was wrestling with the whole dilemma."

"She's nineteen, Dani! Barely more than a child."

"She's nineteen, Bel. Technically an adult."

"Not even old enough to drink in the States."

"But old enough to get married, Bel."

This literally stopped Isobel in her tracks, "Married? You surely don't think they'll get married?"

"It's a possibility, isn't it?"

"No! We have to stop her, Dani! She's still my daughter, my little girl."

"She's a woman, Bel. Who knows where it will end?"

Isobel sat down on a bench, white with grief, "How am I going to tell, Robert? And how on earth am I going to tell Dad? It's going to break both their hearts."

Dani sat next to her and put her arm gently round her shoulders, "This too will pass," she said. "This too will pass."

JUNE (1)

"We need to talk."

"Ah. The four words that strike most dread into the male heart."

"Even so. We do."

"I thought we were all talked-out, Bel."

"We've barely even begun, Robert."

They'd eaten in almost total silence, but now he stood to clear the plates away, while she topped up their wine glasses. They had drunk a lot recently.

"Now?"

"If not now, when?"

"I'm not sure Primo Levi meant it in this context."

"Forget fucking Primo Levi!" She hadn't meant to shout, but wine made her irritable and Robert's obfuscation was maddening.

He had his back turned to her, carefully rinsing each plate before loading it into the dishwasher. She felt like picking up the bread knife and driving it deep into his neck.

"Robert, leave the dishes. Please. We do need to talk."

"This won't take a moment."

"It's an avoidance strategy."

"What if it is? Do I always have to do what you say, Bel? Since when did that become law?"

"Fine. Suit yourself." She picked up her glass and marched into the garden. It was a beautiful summer evening, baby clouds scudding across the blue sky like skiffs across the sea. She tried to breathe deeply and calm herself, focusing on the smell of honeysuckle that clambered over the garden shed. This had always been her favourite month, but now it was tainted and poisoned by everything that had happened in Paris.

After a while, he came out, holding his own glass in one hand and the bottle in another, "You said you wanted to talk?"

"Here?"

"Why not. It's a lovely evening."

They lived cheek-by-jowl with their neighbours in this higgledy-piggledy street in Rye, most of whom would also be sitting outside to enjoy the long and balmy summer evening. Presumably, Robert thought that might be insurance against more shouting, swearing and trading of insults. Most likely, he was right.

She nodded and sat down on one of the rickety iron chairs on their tiny terrace. Robert pulled up a chair next to hers, so they sat side by side facing the garden, the silence between them almost companionable. At this time of year, it was a mad scramble of roses, irises, day lilies, hollyhocks, delphiniums, foxgloves and red hot pokers, far removed from the beautiful compositions that Saskia achieved. It looked glorious in its anarchy, but by August it would be a dismal and desiccated display.

"Go on then."

It was now or never. She was grateful for the lack of eye contact.

"I haven't told you everything about Paris. I think you need to hear it from me, not Grace."

She felt his body stiffen beside her, without turning her head. "Is this also to do with George?"

"No. Why?"

"I just wondered. Go on."

She took a deep breath, "I met someone in Paris. Back in January."

"You mean you've been having an affair?"

He had turned to look at her, but she couldn't meet his eye. She stared fixedly at a clump of hollyhocks.

"Sort of."

"Sort of? Christ, Bel! What does 'sort of' mean? Have you been sleeping with someone else or not?"

"It's only happened three times. The affair."

"Are you seriously saying that you think you can have just a little bit of an affair? Three points on your licence, not nine?"

"No of course not, but . . . ."

"Well that's what it sounds like! For the

record, I worked it out a while ago. Your dirty little secret."

"You knew? How?"

"So many clues."

"What do you mean?"

"The way you look, the way you move, the way you smile. But none of it for my benefit."

Had she really been so transparent? Those bloody pheromones Dani was always banging on about.

His tone sharpened, "What's Grace got to do with it though?"

There was no point trying to gloss it over. "She found out. Saw us."

"What exactly did she see?"

"It was in the Papillon. We were kissing. Saying good-bye."

"Right."

She still didn't dare turn her head. There had been a lot of pent-up misery seeping from that one word.

"Would you like to know what I think?"

The tempo of his voice was calm and unchanged, but instinctively, she braced herself.

"You're a horrible, selfish, immature floozy who's caused maximum embarrassment to Grace and maximum distress to me. I blame you for the fact that Grace is running off with George to America. It's your vanity that seeded the idea of a gap year in Paris in her head and your reckless and stupid profligacy that's brought Miss Mapp to near ruin. And to cap it all, you're a liar and a tart."

He stood up, "Is that enough talking for you this evening?"

She still couldn't meet his eye. He poured the dregs of the bottle into her glass and then walked back into the house. She stayed sitting where she was until the dark and the chill drove her back into the house that was no longer a home.

Grace was counting the days until her course finished and she could start her new life in Miami. There was a new girl in Nina's room, a Spanish nanny called Lena. She seemed sweet enough, but Grace hadn't made much effort getting to know her: there seemed little point. Katja seemed to have disappeared into thin air.

Every time she thought of Rye, her mum and dad, her grandad, Dani or Saskia, she tried to obliterate them with memories of lying in George's bed on Sunset Island Two. After the scene with Isobel in George's suite, she had refused point-blank to talk to her mother again. Dani had tried her hardest to mediate, but Grace was having none of it, "I can't forgive her, Dani. She has the nerve to be angry with me after doing god knows what with that prat. It makes me feel sick to think of it."

The worse ordeal had been the conversation with Robert. He'd phoned her as soon as Isobel got home and broke the news. Grace had intended to spit out everything she knew about her mother and Jean-Luc, but her father sounded so broken by the news of her and George that she couldn't find it in herself to hurt him even more. He had listened to everything she had to say without interruption, casting no stones in George's direction, but he had pleaded with her to think again.

"Come back just for one month, Grace. If you still feel the same way, we won't stand in your path."

"I can't, Dad."

"Why not, sweetie? Just one month."

"I've made up my mind."

"You won't be able to stay in Miami, you know. They're very strict about visas."

"I'll be there for three months and then . . . ."

"Then?"

"That's a matter for George and me."

"Has he asked you to marry him? Is that it?"

The truth was, he hadn't, but she was sure he would. How else could they build a future together?

Robert had coaxed and wheedled, but she'd refused to budge, "I'd still like to come to Paris and help you pack. I could bring back anything you don't need."

"There's no need."

"But I'd like to. Please say I can come."

What could she do? In the end, they agreed he would come out for a weekend in the middle of June. It was only later, she realised he would be there for Father's Day.

The one person she really missed was Nina. Ironically, Nina was the person to whom ordinarily she would have spilled out all her troubles and anxieties. Had Nina not been George's daughter, she would have had someone to talk to about the whole situation. She could have shared the misgivings she hid from her parents and Dani about their relationship and their future. It wasn't the twenty-three year age gap that bothered Grace; it was the ghost of Maria. Deep down, Grace feared she would never live up to Maria. She felt like the second Mrs de Winter, doomed always to be in the first wife's shadow.

It wasn't just she missed Nina as a confidante; she missed her entirely. Nina was smart and funny and passionate. She was also loyal. She would never have done anything to hurt Grace. Yet Grace had done something inexcusable and low to someone who had shown her nothing but kindness and generosity. The one person she could have talked to about how crap she felt about *that* was her mother, but now that relationship lay in tatters too.

She had Dani of course, but how could she turn to Dani with all these problems when her godmother was also her mother's best friend? It was obvious by her attempts to be a peace-keeper that she had a great deal of sympathy for Isobel, as well as concern for Grace. "She's still your mother", she said. "She loves you very much." None of this was what Grace wanted to hear. It was easier not to think about Isobel at all.

Which left George. After that terrible afternoon in Le Papillon, George had been unusually silent. She had curled up next to him on the sofa and he had stroked her hair, but they didn't talk about what had happened and they didn't make love. He had arranged to take Nina out for dinner that night and she'd wanted to stay in the suite and wait for him to come back, but he had refused on the grounds Nina might want to come up for a night-cap. The next day, he had come to the apartment to help Nina move to her new lodgings and Grace had made herself scarce before he arrived. From there he'd travelled direct to the airport without them meeting again, giving no indication of how he and Nina had got on or what they had discussed. He had replied to her messages, but they were neither as frequent nor as affectionate as previously.

In two weeks' time, her gap year in Paris would be at an end. George had promised to book her flight to Miami and she had her ninety-day ESTA sorted, but in truth she was sad not to be going back to Rye, at least for a short break.

Every time she thought of her grandad, she felt anxious. What if something were to happen to him while she was in the States, just as it had to her granny? What must he be thinking of her? She wished she could lie in her old bedroom listening to the bells of St Mary's, pack a picnic to Camber Sands, ride her bike along the estuary. At times, she wished she had never come to Paris at all.

But when she thought of George, her heart sang. If Rye and everything and everyone in it was the sacrifice she had to make for George, then so be it. They fitted together completely, two pieces of a puzzle that were made to be interconnected for ever. People thought George was too old for her, but they were wrong. He was perfect in every way.

◆ ◆ ◆

Robert was giving her the silent treatment. Every time she walked into a room, he walked out of it. If he cooked, he cooked only for himself, meticulously tidying up afterwards. If she cooked and invited him to join her, he pretended not to hear. He slept in the tiny spare room, getting up early to open the shop and staying until late. He made it clear that she was neither needed nor welcome in Miss Mapp, even on days he was out searching for new stock. Once she walked past and saw Saskia sitting in the familiar captain's chair. She waved when she saw Isobel, but she looked embarrassed and timid. Isobel waved back and walked on. Her heart was pounding in her chest with jealousy and shame.

"Do you think he's waiting for me to pack my bag and go?" she asked Dani.

"Do you want to go?

"Where would I go to?"

"That's a practical answer to an emotional question. Do you want to go or do you want to stay?"

"I can't stay with someone who hates me."

"I don't think Robert hates you. It's you who've changed."

"What do you mean?"

"Admit it, Bel. You don't love Robert in the way you once did."

Bulls-eye.

"Is it that obvious?"

"It has been for a long time."

"There's something I haven't told you."

"Go on."

"My lunch with Jean-Luc . . . he offered me a job."

"What sort of job?"

"He's going to Hollywood in September for six months to make a film and he wants me to go with him as his PA."

She had carried these momentous words around her for the last week, but they sounded as unreal when said out loud as she had feared.

Dani couldn't conceal her astonishment, "Is PA an euphemism, Bel?"

"I know how it sounds, because that's what I thought too. No, I think he's serious."

"You haven't had a full-time job for nearly twenty years."

"I know. It's ridiculous, isn't it? I couldn't possibly do it."

"Why do you say that?"

"I wouldn't know what to do or how to do it. As you say, it's all too long ago."

"I think you could do it."

"Do you?"

"You're wasted here. You always were, but when Grace was young and you were still in love with your husband, maybe it didn't matter so much."

"You never said so before."

"I wouldn't have wanted you to feel bad. Going back to work is exactly what you need to do. Don't waste an opportunity like this."

"What if I mess up?"

"You won't, but what's the worse that could happen? Jean-Luc would have to find another PA – can't imagine that would be hard for a film director in Hollywood."

"I'd have to get up to speed with the tech side of things."

"There are plenty of courses for women wanting to return to work."

"I'd need a better wardrobe."

"We could go shopping. I'll lend you the money and you can pay me back when your first wages come through. How much is he offering?"

When Isobel named the figure, she practically fell off her chair.

"And you still haven't said yes?"

"I told him I would let him know for sure by the end of the month."

"What are you waiting for?"

"Come on, Dani, it's not easy. How am I going to break that to Robert – or Grace – or my Dad for that matter?"

"That's where you've been going wrong, you know."

"What do you mean?"

"Time to put yourself first, Isobel Peters."

The fates had other ideas. Later that day, Jack called, "Isobel, something's happened." By the tone of his voice, it was something bad.

"What is it Dad?"

"It's Lauren. She says she has another job. She's leaving."

Just what she bloody needed.

"Did she say why, Dad? Have you fallen out?"

"No, nothing like that. Can you come over? Soon?"

"I'll come now."

Driving over, she thought how miserable her father had been when she told him about Grace. She hadn't wanted to give him the whole story, fearing it would upset him too much, so she'd said that Grace had an American boyfriend and was going to stay with him for a few months. Jack found this incomprehensible. Why was she not coming back for a holiday at least? Why the rush? Who was this young man? Did she plan to stay there for ever? What about University? He was slightly mollified when Grace rang to see how he was and to promise she would be back in the autumn to see him. Isobel had been relieved to learn that Grace had said very little about "her young man". Jack had grumbled about the lack of information, "Lives in Miami apparently. Must have met him when she stayed with that friend of hers." Isobel had agreed this probably was the case.

Lauren must have heard her car on the drive, because she was waiting at the door, "I suppose Jack rang you?"

"Yes he did. He seemed rather upset. Is he awake?"

"No, he's gone for a lie down. Just as well. Thought we could talk first."

They went through to the sitting room, tidied of most of the kitsch and clutter. A couple of years previously, Miss Mapp had benefited from a surprise hit by a Japanese author about the joys of tidying up. Isobel suspected Lauren might well have bought that book. She could write her own version by the looks of it.

"I wish you'd told me before you told Dad, Lauren."

"Yes, but Jack's my employer – technically."

That was true. Her wages were paid direct from Jack's account.

"Even so. He's an old man and it was clearly a shock."

"I know, Isobel, but I felt I owed it to him to be honest about the situation."

"You've found a new job? Is it a question of more money?"

"It's not another caring role, no."

"So?"

"It's a catering job. A cook to be exactly. For a family in London."

"Oh." That made perfect sense.

"It's always been my dream, you see. I love cooking, but I don't have any actual qualifications in catering. The agency weren't sure I could make the transition."

"But you have?"

She nodded, "Mavis helped."

She might have known. That bloody Dawkins woman.

"In what way?"

"Confidence, Isobel. She gave me confidence. That's something you can't buy"

"No, I don't suppose you can."

"Turned out I could take the basic courses online, hygiene and so forth. Then this job came up and I got it. I was walking on air when they told me."

Isobel had spent the last six months complaining about Lauren, mimicking her voice and mocking the pretentiousness of her cooking, but now she felt like throwing herself on her knees and pleading with her to change her mind. The fact was Lauren was brilliant with Jack. It was going to be impossible to find someone half as good. With horror, she realised that she would have to move into the bungalow herself. Wasn't that the obvious thing to do now her marriage was on the rocks? It would be up to her to get Jack up in the morning and put him to bed at night; to cook his meals and accompany him to the loo; to oversee his inevitable slide into physical decline. After gadding around Paris for the last year, it was the ultimate payback. There would be no Hollywood job for her. This was Compensation Theory with knobs on.

She tried to smile, "I'm happy for you, Lauren."

"Thanks very much. I can still barely believe it."

"How long 'til you go?"

"I'm on a month's notice, but I haven't taken any holiday since I got here, so it's a fortnight."

Two weeks. Impossible. This couldn't be happening.

"I've told the agency. I'm sure they will try to find a replacement as quickly as they can."

From the bedroom, they heard Jack calling Lauren's name.

"Make yourself a tea, Isobel. I'll get him up and we'll be back in a jiffy."

Jiffy. One of Pam's words.

She put the kettle on and laid the tray for three. From the bedroom, she could hear Lauren's voice, gentle and coaxing. How did she remain so patient? How had her mother managed not to go mad?

She had just put the tray on the coffee table when Jack shuffled in on his Zimmer frame. Lauren followed in his wake.

For once, he looked pleased to see her, "You came straight over then?"

"Yes, Dad, I said I would."

"What am I going to do without her?" From behind him, Lauren's eyes met Isobel's and she gave a small shrug of apology.

"Why don't you sit down and we can talk about it."

It took a while for Lauren to ease him from the support of the Zimmer into the arm-chair, carefully placing the mug of tea into his hand, "There you are, Jack. Lovely cup of tea that Isobel's made."

"I don't want someone new in the house. I won't like it." His tone was belligerent and combative.

Lauren said nothing, sipped carefully at her own cup of tea as if they were discussing something far removed from her own life.

"I agree it's a shock, Dad, but I have a solution."

They both looked at her. Jack with suspicion and Lauren with surprise.

"I'll move in here myself."

There. It was out. Too late to unsay it. In her mind's eye she saw a long corridor with every door slamming shut.

"Don't be bloody stupid, Isobel. What about Robert and the shop?"

"I think Isobel just meant until the agency find a replacement, Jack."

"Even so. It won't work for me."

Charming.

"What do you mean, Dad?" Stay calm, calm, calm.

"No bloody good."

"Could you just stop all the 'bloodys' just for one moment? Why won't it work, Dad?"

"You! I couldn't stand you here all the time, Mrs Head-In-Air."

Lauren looked mortified, concentrated even harder on sipping her tea.

"I'm trying to help, Dad. You could be a little more grateful. I seem to remember you wanted me to move in after mum's funeral."

"That was then – before I got used to having Lauren around. It won't work. Sorry, but no."

Irritation rose in her voice, “What do you suggest then?”

“Mavis.”

“Mavis from over the road?”

“How many Mavises are there?”

“What are you suggesting, Dad? She might not want to help out.”

“That’s where you’re wrong. She often keeps me company when Lauren’s not here, doesn’t she Lauren?”

Lauren nodded, sipped more tea. Surely her mug was empty by now?

“I’ll pay her of course. It would all be properly arranged. Will you ask her?”

“Me? Wouldn’t it be better if you asked her?”

“You could sound her out first. Pop over now in fact. She’s bound to be in at this time of day.”

She couldn’t believe she was being asked to do this ridiculous thing, but with two weeks to go, it didn’t seem as though she had a choice. Presumably Mavis Dawkins would not be such a fool as to say yes. She walked over the road and rang the doorbell, willing herself to keep smiling.

Mavis knew all about Lauren’s job of course, “Thrilling to land a job like that. Good for her. But what are you going to do about Jack? Two weeks isn’t long for the agency to find someone new.”

“That’s the trouble.”

“Don’t suppose it’s practical for you to move in either.”

“I offered, but Dad had a better idea.”

"Really?" And then the penny dropped, "You'd like me to step into the breach?"

"We realise it's a big ask. He would pay you of course. And I would be on hand to cover if you needed time off."

"And your husband's around too, I suppose?" Isobel nodded. Another untruth to add to all the rest.

"Why not!"

"You'll do it?" She wanted to weep with gratitude.

"Just 'til the agency finds someone suitable of course."

"Of course."

"I'll come over with you now. Put Jack out of his misery."

"It's incredibly kind of you, Mavis. Thank you." Someone else of whom she would never again speak or think ill. Why had she been such a gold-plated snob? In the space of one day she felt as though she had been trapped inside a kaleidoscope and shaken violently around so that first one unexpected pattern emerged and then another. All this time she had clung to her narrow perspective, but from now on she would never take anything or anyone for granted again.

On her way home, she stopped off to buy a bottle

of wine. Robert was in the kitchen when she walked in and put it on the table. He was beating eggs in a bowl, presumably for an omelette. This struck her as a sad and solitary meal.

She took two glasses from the dresser, opened the bottle and poured the wine. He made no comment.

"There's something else I have to tell you."

Silence.

"The man I told you about is a film director. He's going to Hollywood in September for six months and he's offered me a job as his English-speaking PA."

Silence.

"I know what you're thinking, Robert – it's what I thought too – but I think he just wants to help me."

Silence.

"I'm going to say yes."

She had made up her mind on the drive back from Jack's. The prospect of losing the chance to go back to work had made her realise how much she wanted not just this job, but any job. She couldn't let it slip through her fingers.

He didn't turn around, "Two eggs or three?"

"What?"

"As you can see, I'm making omelette. Two eggs or three?"

"You're making me an omelette?"

"If you'd like one, yes."

"Oh. Two's fine, thanks."

"Cheese?"

"Lovely."

"Lay the table then. It won't be a jiffy." Jiffy. That word again. Was Pam channelling through both Lauren and Robert?

Over omelette and red wine, she talked to Robert for the first time in a long time with as much honesty as she thought he could bear.

"I can't remember the last time I was really happy. I was once, but not for the last couple of years."

"I know."

"Grace going to Paris just made me realise how empty my life had become, how monotonous and predictable."

"I should have tried harder to make you happy."

"It's not your fault, Robert. I was twenty-six when we met – I'm nearly fifty now – I've changed that's all. There was nothing you could do about that."

"I haven't changed."

"No, I don't think you have. You probably won't believe me, but I do still love you, just not in the same way."

"I bore you."

"*I* bore me, Robert. That's the real problem."

"I'm sorry I never realised . . . how much you missed your job, your other life. I should have seen that."

"I didn't realise it myself until quite recently.

Please don't feel guilty."

He seemed to be struggling to find a response. Then, "Are you leaving me, Bel?"

She took a deep breath, "I don't know. That's something I have to find out. I don't want to hurt you, but I don't want to lie to you either."

"I appreciate that. I hate it when you lie." He looked at her with such sadness, she nearly lost her resolve.

"You're my best friend, Robert."

"Don't cry, Bel. Come here."

They stood up and he folded her into his arms, making a space next to his heart into which she fitted perfectly.

"Whatever happens, we'll stay friends, I promise," he said. "We have Grace and that means we'll always play a part in each other's lives. Whatever happens."

She nodded, blinking back her tears as best she could.

"The worst is over. I know where I stand and I thank you for that."

"You don't hate me?"

"I did. Earlier this year. Not now."

"Will you be OK? Without me?"

"I'll miss you, but we can't go on like this, can we? You so miserable and me pretending not to notice?"

She shook her head.

"There's only one thing I can do for you now, Bel, and I promise I will do it to the best of my ability."

"What's that?"

"Let you go. I need to let you go."

"I'm not sure this is a good idea."

"I have to try. I can't just let her disappear."

"But she's only expecting me."

"I know, Robert. But we need to tell her – and that would be better coming from both of us."

"I suppose you're right, but I think I should see her on her own first. At the apartment."

"Fine. Talk to her while you help her pack and then, with luck, you can cajole her out to dinner with both of us."

"No creating a scene about her going to Miami with George?"

"Absolutely not. I'm over all of that. If she really thinks her future lies with George, then the best thing we can do is accept it. I don't want to drive her away."

"Agreed."

The weather in Paris was beautiful. They checked into a bland, three-star hotel close to Grace's apartment – a double room as no twins were available - and then Robert hurried away to meet Grace. It was Saturday and Grace was flying to Miami the following week.

Isobel wanted to make the most of the June

weather, so she walked all the way to the Île Saint-Louis, enjoying meandering down the narrow streets exploring art galleries, boutiques and markets. She stopped for coffee and crêpe, then began retracing her path, pausing on the bridge over the Seine to enjoy the view of Notre-Dame. How much had happened during this extraordinary year. She thought back to the day she and Grace had arrived in rainy Paris, laden with luggage, struggling up the platform of Le Gare du Nord. Nothing could have prepared her for how Grace's gap year had altered not just her daughter's future, but her own.

The day before, she had driven to the bungalow to check up on Jack and Mavis. Jack was far from happy to hear about Isobel's new job.

"Mrs Gadabout. Ants in your pants, are there?"

"I want to go back to work, Dad. This is too good an opportunity to turn down."

"You haven't worked for years. Sure you're up to it?"

"I suppose that's what I have to find out."

"First Grace, now you."

"It's only for six months."

"What does Robert make of it?"

"He's fine with it, Dad." Now was not the moment to have that particular conversation.

"Well, I wouldn't have let your mother do such a thing."

No he certainly wouldn't have done. Had Pam ever wanted to escape? Bang the bungalow door behind her and head for the hills?

"Things are different now, Dad."

"Isobel's right, Jack." Goodness. Was Mavis becoming her newfound ally?

Jack snorted. Pam would have understood the snort to be a sign for her to stop talking, but it had no effect on Mavis.

"You might not like it, Jack Wilson, but times are different now. Women need some financial independence. Never know what's coming at you."

"If you say so."

"I *do* say so."

She turned to Isobel, "Never mind him. It's you that counts. Your life, isn't it?"

Jack would have viewed this as gross impertinence had her mother expressed a view so opposite to his own with such confidence. He glared at Mavis in sullen fury, but she simply brushed him away, "We've had our day, Jack. Let the young have theirs."

The young? Was Mavis talking about her? It struck her then that people twenty or thirty years younger would always be "the young" no matter how old you were. One day, she would look back and think forty-nine very young indeed. For the first time, she felt grateful for all the years she had ahead of her. It made her decision feel far less absurd.

When she left, she hugged her father good-bye.

"When will you be leaving?" His tone was brittle. Anxious.

"Not until September. Try not to worry."

"Do you need money?" She was touched, recognising it as the question every parent asks when they want to express how much they care.

"No, Dad. I'm fine for money, but thank you."

Mavis walked her to the door, "He's a funny old stick. Can't seem to get the right words out."

"Which words?"

"You know. That he loves you. That he's terrified of something happening to you."

"Is he terrified?"

"'Course he is. The sun shines out of your backside, my girl." Did it? Her dad never showed approval for anything she did. Never had done.

"Look after him when I'm away." Should she be going? It felt the height of selfish irresponsibility.

"Don't you worry, I will. Enjoy Paris in the mean time."

"Thanks, Mavis. Appreciated."

As she drove back to Rye, she felt a mountain lifting from her shoulders.

Isobel felt guilty about not seeing Jack on Father's Day, but he disliked it anyway, "Bloody American nonsense. Shops just want to sell more cards."

She had left a card for him with Mavis

regardless, and chosen a blank one for Robert that showed a shelf of Penguin books. In it, she had written, "To the Best Father in the World - Grace is a Lucky Girl" and signed it with a row of kisses. It was the very least she could do.

◆◆◆

When Grace heard Antoinette ushering Robert into the apartment, she could hardly contain her excitement. She hadn't seen her father since her granny's funeral and so much had happened since then, she felt like a different person. When he put his arms around her to give her a deep hug, she breathed an audible sigh of relief.

"I've missed you, Grace."

"Missed you too, Dad." She hadn't realised just how much until now. She stayed with her arms round him and her head on his chest for what seemed an age. He stroked her hair and she felt as if she were six again, sitting on his lap at Miss Mapp's, pretending it was her bookshop and not his.

"Goodness, a lot to do then?" He was looking round at the room, clothes thrown on the floor, a knot of tights tipping out of one drawer.

"I know. It feels as though I've got three times as much stuff as when I got here. That can't be true, but just look at it!"

"I've brought an extra suitcase just in case.

It's in the hall. We can pack your winter stuff in that and I'll take it back to Rye. Can't imagine you'll have much need of jackets and jumpers in Miami."

He mentioned Miami in such a matter-of-fact way she felt wrong-footed. Why had she been so worried about Robert coming to Paris? It wasn't as if he were going to play the Victorian father and threaten to cast her out. Not his style at all.

"Make me a coffee then? I'll start sorting that cupboard over there. Anything I'm not sure about I'll put on the bed."

"Thanks, Dad."

By the time she walked back in the room, it already looked different. Robert was making neat piles of winter clothes, testing them out for size in the suitcase.

"We're going to need another case, Grace. Is there anywhere local we can buy a cheap one?"

"There is, but how will you manage two large cases yourself on the Eurostar? You must have an overnight bag to carry too?"

"I'll work it out." Something in his voice sounded uncertain.

Grace knew her father too well. It was obvious he couldn't manage three suitcases on his own.

"Mum's here, isn't she?"

"Please don't be angry, Grace."

"She is! Why?"

"Is that my coffee? Thanks. Shall we just get

on with the packing and then talk it through over lunch?"

Grace knew how maddening Isobel found Robert's ability to change the subject. She could see why, "No, Dad. I think now you've dropped that particular bombshell, we need to discuss it. I don't want to see her, OK? I only want to see you. You had no right to bring her."

He sat on the edge of her bed and gestured for her to sit next to him, "It's not what you think, Grace. She's completely accepted things about you and George. As have I."

"It's not just that actually." How on earth could she tell him? He'd only just got here.

There was a silence. Robert seemed to be struggling for words.

"I know all about it. I know what you saw."

Wrong-footed again. "She told you? About . . . . him?"

"Yes."

"Are you going to get divorced? Is that why she's here, so you can tell me together?"

"We're going our separate ways for a while, but she has something to tell you about that herself. As for her and me, I don't know what the future holds."

"I don't understand. Don't you hate her?"

"I don't expect you to understand. Other people's marriages . . . relationships . . . are often not predictable to those looking in. Not even to the children of those relationships."

"You've forgiven her? But it's a horrible thing to do to anyone."

At the memory of her mother breaking free from Jean-Luc's embrace, her eyes filled with tears.

He ran his fingers through his hair in the familiar way he had whenever upset, "Do you know when someone truly grows up, Grace?"

"When?"

"When they realise their parents are just two fallible people, struggling along in life, making mistakes, cocking stuff up . . ."

"I still don't want to see her."

"Let's not talk about it right now, OK? I'm sorry to have given you an unwelcome surprise, but I'm here to help. Really."

He stood up and began folding jumpers and scarves again. It was a clear signal that he didn't want to talk about him and Isobel any more.

As they worked, he asked her about her course results, how she felt about leaving Paris, what she thought she'd most gained from the year. It was so nice having him there that Grace couldn't stay annoyed for long. She chatted away about college friends she'd made and her favourite Parisian haunts. She didn't mention Nina's name, but Nina was there in the undercurrent of her thoughts.

Something Robert had said earlier bubbled to the surface, "Is that why Nina can't forgive George?"

He looked at her, clearly surprised at the mention of her name, "What is?"

"Is it because she hasn't accepted George as a person rather than her father?"

"Probably, Grace. But you must see how hurtful this situation is for Nina."

"Because of me?

"Because of both of you. Let's face it, she must feel you've both let her down."

"Have we?"

"I'm not here to cast stones, Grace."

Whenever she thought of Nina, she felt sick. The taste of bile in her mouth. "I wish I could make it better between them. I miss her so much."

"Unfortunately, you can't. Only Nina has that power."

"Dad . . ."

"Yes?"

"Am I making a terrible mistake? Tell me the truth."

"It's not what we would have wished for you, Grace, but only you know how you feel."

"Dani was right. I'm in such a tangle."

"If you find out it was a mistake, just promise me you will come home. Don't let pride keep you away."

"OK, Dad. I promise."

◆ ◆ ◆

Grace had refused to invite Isobel to the apartment, but when she and Robert walked into the restaurant she'd chosen for dinner, her mum was waiting for them both. She looked so happy and pretty that Grace's anger and hurt began to melt away. It was an awkward greeting between them, the briefest of hugs, but Isobel was clearly relieved she'd agreed to see her at all.

They ordered a bottle of wine and then Robert made an excuse that he needed the loo. Grace wasn't fooled. He was a terrible liar.

Isobel leaned over the table and took her hands.

"I can't put things right, Grace, but I can say how sorry I am. Please don't think the worse of me."

"It was a shock, mum." It was a sledge-hammer to her childhood, splintering everything she had thought true.

"I know. In fairness, it was a shock for me too . . . but that doesn't excuse anything." At least she acknowledged that.

"I'm sorry too. Not about George, but about the fact you found out in the way you did."

"You have my blessing now – and Dad's. You can tell George I'm off my high horse."

"Thanks! He likes you, you know." It was true. She knew he liked Isobel a great deal, a source of jealousy for some considerable time.

"Time is a great healer, Grace. We all just need

some time to adjust."

Over dinner, Isobel told her about the offer of a job and a six-month trip to Hollywood.

"But you haven't worked properly since having me."

"So people keep reminding me."

"How will you cope?"

"I don't know, Grace, but I have to try."

"Who's offered you a job like that out of the blue?"

Hesitation. "Jean-Luc."

"I don't fucking believe it!"

"Don't swear at your mother, Grace."

"I'm not actually swearing *at* her – more *about* her."

"Even so."

She turned to her dad, "How can you let her do that? Rock off to America with *him*?"

"In the same spirit I can let *you* rock off to Miami with George. Sometimes you have to let go and hope the person you love doesn't fall."

A grateful smile from her mum. "Thank you, Robert."

Her mum and dad seemed in perfect harmony, which was doubly confusing.

"You don't sound like people on the brink of divorce."

"We don't know if we are yet," said Robert.

"But even if we do," said Isobel, "we are still both your parents. We're here for you whatever happens."

"I just want things to stay the same."

"You're going to Miami. Nothing will be the same."

In the taxi, Grace sat between them, her head on Robert's shoulder. None of them spoke.

They turned into the street adjacent to Madame Chirol's to find their way blocked by fire engines, police cars and ambulances.

"*Pas de route*," said the cab driver.

"OK," said Isobel. 'We'll get out here."

When they stepped out of the cab, they could smell smoke in the evening air. At a distance, flames were leaping into the sky. Uniformed men and women were running from one end of the street to the other, some manoeuvring thick hoses and extendable ladders. Whatever had happened was clearly serious.

They tried to reach Madame Chirol's, but as they turned the corner into the tree-lined avenue, *gendarmes* angrily waved them back.

"*Entrée interdite*," one shouted.

"*J'habite ici*!" shouted Grace.

"*Entrée interdite*," came the command again.

Through the yellow smog of smoke, Isobel tried to find the source of the flames. When she did, her heart lurched.

"I think it's your building, Grace," she said.

"Look."

Halfway down the street, just by the door that led through to the courtyard was the epicentre of activity. They could see a growing cluster of people on the pavement opposite, the frightened and confused faces of the recently evacuated, some already dressed for bed. The only people going through the door were those with breathing apparatus strapped to their backs.

"I think we can get a bit nearer if we keep to the other side and move slowly," said Robert. "Just don't step out into the road where the police can see you."

They inched towards the growing crowd. Suddenly, they saw someone flying from the other end of the street, screaming like a banshee, "*Baboushka*!"

The police tried to hold her back, but she kicked, bit and spat, determined to break free and reach the burning building. Just as she reached the door, two women were escorted through the waiting crowd. One, old and grey, was leaning on the arm of the other. It was Madame Chirol and Antoinette.

"*Baboushka*!" Katja flung herself at her grandmother, nearly knocking her off her feet. She was sobbing with relief. Isobel saw Madame Chirol standing on tip-toes to reach up to her gangly grand-daughter and pat her gently on the cheek.

"*Maman*!" Now a man was pushing through the crowd to reach Madame Chirol, insisting the *gendarmes* let him through. She willed herself to wake up from this bad dream. Even in profile, she would have known Jean-Luc anywhere. She slid to the other side of Robert and Grace, her mind racing with shock. Had she really been going to bed with Madame Chirol's son? She prayed Grace wouldn't recognise him.

Grace, however, had seen someone else in the crowd.

"George!" Isobel saw Grace frantically waving to him, but he was deep in conversation with one of the *gendarmes*. What was he doing there when Nina had moved out? Checking Grace was OK presumably. It was no good; he clearly couldn't hear anything above the din of sirens, whistles and shouts.

"Did you know he was in Paris?"

Grace shook her head miserably.

"George!" It was no good. He still couldn't hear.

Isobel saw Jean-Luc go up to him and lead him over to Madame Chirol. The old lady was telling him something. They called two of the *gendarmes* over and she could tell by the body language that George was saying something that Jean-Luc was translating to the police. Whatever it was, was causing concern.

"I think we'd better find out what's going on," said Robert. "Maybe they think you're in your bedroom, Grace."

Grace hesitated and Isobel knew why. She had finally recognised Jean-Luc and, like Isobel, couldn't understand what he was doing talking to George.

"Ignore him for now," whispered Isobel. "Dad's right. They need to know you're safe."

They pushed through the crowd, Grace shouting George's name until he finally heard and turned. He didn't smile.

Isobel saw on Jean-Luc's face the same look of blank incomprehension that must have been on hers a few moments ago. He looked at George again, a dawning realisation of where they had met. Trying to stay calm, she walked to Madame Chirol's side. She was aware of Katja's frightened sobbing; of Jean-Luc's appalled silence.

"Are you OK, Madame?"

With her coiffed hair dishevelled and her face flecked with ash, Madame Chirol looked ancient and shrunken: a female Dorian Gray whose portrait in the attic had been destroyed by the fire.

She barely seemed to recognise Isobel, "Everything is gone, Madame Peters."

"But you are safe, Madame. Hopefully, they will rescue what they can."

"They can't find the girl."

"Which girl?"

"Nina."

She started to cry. It shocked Isobel to see

someone as proud as Madame Chirol reduced to crying so publicly. Jean-Luc moved protectively closer.

"But Nina doesn't live with you any more, Madame." Perhaps this was the start of senility brought on by shock.

"She was with me tonight. We were cataloguing my old clothes. She wouldn't come unless Grace were out, so I told her tonight would be a good time."

Isobel had no idea what she was talking about. Old clothes? Had Nina really been there?

She started to cry again.

"But you left together, surely?"

"I smelled smoke. From the tenants' quarters. It all happened so fast, Madame Peters. I thought Nina must have got out before me."

Jean-Luc put his arms around his mother, murmuring gently "*Viens avec moi, maman. Nous devons partir.*" He led her down the road to a waiting ambulance, Katja following like a frightened puppy. He never acknowledged Isobel, nor she him.

This could not be happening. Nina had surely found a way out. George was still standing a few feet from them, Grace by his side. She saw her daughter shoot terrified looks at his face, but he never acknowledged her existence, never acknowledged theirs. He was rooted to the spot, scanning the Chirol building for signs of his daughter. What could they do, but keep silent vigil by his side?

Suddenly, there was a commotion near the front of the building and a fireman appeared holding a limp figure in his arms. Gently, it was placed on a stretcher and driven off by ambulance, sirens blazing. Two of the *gendarmes* walked slowly towards them, checking who was Monsieur Miller. George stepped forward and they said something he clearly didn't fully understand. Grace ran over to help, but he turned his back on her and followed them to the waiting police car, which drove off at speed. Smoke still filled the warm June night, but the flames were vanquished, leaving the jagged silhouette of the burned building against the night sky.

JUNE (2)

Grace had been desperate to follow George to the hospital, but Robert had said he should go instead and Isobel had persuaded her back to the hotel, where her daughter had crawled into her arms as if she were a child of four and cried for what seemed like hours. Isobel lay on her back, staring up into the gloom, turning the events of the day over and over in her mind. The more she tried to make sense of what had happened, the more impossible it seemed.

The next morning, Robert rang her from the hospital.

"Can you talk, Bel?"

"Grace is in the shower, if that's what you mean. How's Nina?"

"Not good. She went into cardiac arrest in the ambulance. She's hanging on in there, but they've intubated her."

"What does that mean?"

"Put a tube down her throat to help her breathe. She's in an induced coma."

"Will she make it, Robert?"

"I don't know. The doctors don't say much."

"Has George been able to see her?"

"Only once. For a few moments."

"How is he?"

"How do you think? The worse thing is his silence. I have no idea whether he wants me here or not."

"He can't be on his own."

"That's what I think."

"Should I bring Grace over?"

"I'm not sure. To be honest, he hasn't mentioned her once, but then he hasn't really acknowledged me either."

"I still can't believe it. That poor girl."

She heard Robert drawing his breath in, trying to hold it together.

"It's terrible. How's Grace bearing up?"

"In an awful state: blaming herself for Nina being there. Thinks George will hate her."

"What shall we do?"

"You mean about today? I don't know, Robert. You must be exhausted."

"It's been a long night."

"Why don't we swap? I'll take over at the hospital and you come back to rest and be with Grace."

"Grace isn't going to like that. She'll want to be with George herself."

"I know, but if George wanted to see her, he'd have said so."

When she gave her the news about Nina, Grace started crying again, "George hasn't replied to any of my messages, mum."

"I'm sorry, sweetheart."

"Nina might die and George hates me and I've lost everything. Do you think it's because I'm wicked?

"Of course not. Don't talk like that."

"Katja was right."

"What do you mean?"

"She said I was a vampire sucking happiness out of the people who loved me".

"What a horrible thing to say."

"Is it? From where I'm sitting, she seems pretty spot-on."

Isobel sat in the waiting room with George. Outside it was another beautiful day. Such beauty made cruel events even crueller.

George sat on the armchair opposite, his head back, looking up at the tiles on the ceiling. Since she'd arrived, he had barely acknowledged her.

"Have you eaten anything, George? Shall I get you something?"

He shook his head.

"A drink then? Or why don't you go back to the hotel for a while and rest? I'll stay here."

He shook his head again.

"Do you want to talk about it, George? Shall we talk about Nina?"

Again the gentle shake of the head. She felt as if she were making everything worse with these inane questions, but she didn't know what to do for the best.

"Grace is in pieces, George." She could visualise her now: checking her phone for the fiftieth time that day.

He seemed genuinely uncomprehending, "Why?"

"Why! Because her best friend is fighting for her life in hospital. Because she blames herself. Because she thinks you hate her and blame her."

"Why would I hate her?"

"George, please. I know you're in pain – I can't for one moment imagine what this must be like for you - but could we just at least acknowledge Grace exists?"

He rubbed his eyes, "Why would I hate her?"

"I don't know. Do you?"

"I don't hate anyone, Isobel. I just want Nina to be all right."

"I know. I'm sorry."

"I'm in Paris. It's Father's Day. And Nina might be dying. I just can't get my head around that."

"No. I'm sorry."

"It's such a waste, Isobel. She has her whole life ahead of her."

"Yes." The unbearable sadness of that made the word choke in her throat.

"I wasn't even supposed to be here this

weekend."

She had wondered that. Grace had clearly not been expecting him.

"What happened?"

"I was in Berlin pitching for a new job. Nina called. She sounded calmer, more like her usual self. Asked if I could come here for Father's Day."

"But you didn't tell Grace?"

"I knew Robert was coming over to see her and I didn't want to get in the way. Wasn't sure how he would feel about me, to be honest."

"No."

"She didn't mention you were coming, Isobel."

"She didn't know."

"A surprise, huh? All I wanted was to see Nina, take her out for dinner, clear the air . . .

"And ask her for your blessing to live with Grace." She hadn't intended for it to sound bitter, but it did.

"Don't hate me, Isobel."

"I don't hate you. I'm sorry."

"But we never had a chance to have that talk, you see."

"To clear the air?"

"Exactly."

"But that's not Grace's fault."

"No."

Silence descended.

"Has it affected how you feel about her, George?"

He sighed, "I don't know. Maybe. But if it has . . . ."

"What?"

"Surely that would be a good thing from your point of view."

Until yesterday, she would have agreed him over that. Now their positions seemed entirely reversed.

"She loves you, George."

He put his head in his hands, "I thought I might have loved her too, but now I'm not so sure. This changes everything, you see. It feels as though Nina might been taken from me as a punishment for me trying to take your daughter from you. I can't do that."

"But the phone call Nina made? It sounds as though she wanted to be reconciled."

"But how do I know for sure? The plane landed late. She told me to meet her at the apartment . . . that Robert and Grace would be out for dinner . . . but by the time I got there . . ."

"Please don't just walk away from Grace without a word."

"I don't know what to say to her."

"She's expecting the worst. You owe it to her to tell her yourself."

"Not today, Isobel. I know she's your daughter, but I can't face her today."

◆ ◆ ◆

Isobel and Robert managed to book Grace a room in the hotel on the Sunday night, but in the end she slept in Isobel's bed again while Robert took the second room on his own. He looked so exhausted, this was probably just as well. George had insisted Isobel left him alone at the hospital, promising to get in touch if anything changed.

At seven in the morning, she woke to see two messages flashing on her phone.

The first was from George, "Nina out of coma and off ventilator. My girl is a warrior."

She didn't wait to check the second message, but shook Grace awake to tell her that Nina was going to be OK. They lay in bed, arms entwined, and sobbed with relief. Then she sent Grace up the corridor to wake Robert, and rang George's number.

He was a different man.

"Isobel! You got my message."

"I did. We can't tell you how relieved we are. How is she?"

"Very weak, still on oxygen, but breathing independently."

"Can she speak?"

"She's in and out of consciousness, but she tried to say my name when she saw me."

"Are the doctors happy?"

"Ecstatic. To be honest, I don't think they thought she was going to make it. Too much carbon dioxide in her lungs apparently."

She was aware of the door opening and Robert and Grace tip-toeing into the bedroom so as not to disturb her conversation. They climbed into bed next to her and Robert held Grace tight against him.

"Is she allowed visitors?"

"Not yet. Only me and even then not for long."

He started laughing down the phone, "The nurses say that Christian Dior saved her life."

"What do you mean?"

"Apparently, when they pulled her from the apartment, she'd wrapped something around her face to protect her from the smoke. That's probably what made the difference. It was one of Madame Chirol's old blouses."

"Saved by couture! That's something to tell her children."

"Isn't it! Better go now. Just in case she asks for me."

"Hadn't you better go back to the Papillon and sleep, George? You must be completely done-in."

"I couldn't sleep even if I tried. My girl's alive. It's a beautiful day."

When she ended the call, the three of them sat in dazed silence.

It was Grace who spoke first, "Do you think I'll be allowed to see her, Mum?"

"Not sure. Doesn't sound like it at the

moment."

"She wouldn't want to see me anyway."

"You don't know that."

A pause, "Did George mention me at all?"

Isobel shook her head.

There was a long pause. "It's over, isn't it?"

She and Robert said nothing. It was obvious what she meant.

It wasn't until she came out the shower that she remembered there had been two messages flashing on her phone.

Jean-Luc: "Can you call me?"

Brief. No Kisses.

She waited until she heard Grace in the shower before ringing him. Robert was back in his own room getting dressed. They might both know about Jean-Luc, but she would have been embarrassed to have a conversation openly in front of them.

He answered straight away, must have been anxiously waiting her call.

"Isobel! Are you all right?"

"Yes. As well as can be after everything."

"It was a shock to see you in that way."

"A shock to me too."

"Your poor daughter. How is she?"

"As well as can be expected."

"We heard from Nina's father today. Apparently, she is out of danger. For that, we thank God."

"As do we." She would go back to Montmartre and light more candles.

"But now I am calling on behalf of my mother, you see."

"How is she?"

"Still in shock. Losing her home in that way at her age is a tragedy."

"Unimaginable."

"The reason for my call is that the authorities have given permission for us to return to the apartment and see what has survived the fire. I thought your daughter may like to meet me there later this morning. My mother is in no state to make the visit."

"Should I come too?"

There was a pause, "Or your husband?"

He was right. Now that Grace knew about her and Jean-Luc, it would only make a bad situation worse for her to go too.

"Will it feel odd for you to see Robert?"

"Not at all. Does he know who I am?"

"He does now."

"So long as he does not punch me, it is probably better he comes."

She smiled, "He won't punch you."

It had only been a week since she'd called Jean-Luc and told him she was taking him up on his job offer, but now everything felt so different.

"Does any of this affect us, Jean-Luc? Do you still want me to come to Hollywood?"

"I was going to ask you the same question, dear Isobel."

"I think so. Yes."

"*Moi aussi*. Yes."

She heard the bathroom door opening, "Better go. I'll call you again when I've talked to Grace and Robert."

Over breakfast, she relayed Jean-Luc's call as calmly as she could.

"Can't someone else meet us there?" said Grace petulantly. "Plenty of other Chirols around."

"The authorities are doing everything through him. We can't interfere with that."

"I don't want to go."

"All your stuff was there, Grace. There might be something you can save."

Robert leaned over and took his daughter's hand, "Your mum's right, Grace. I'll be with you. It'll be OK."

They should have been travelling back to Rye that morning. She needed to tell Jack they were delayed, but without going into the details.

She rang the number, but Mavis picked up the phone.

"Everything OK, Isobel, dear?"

"Hi, Mavis. All fine, thank you." Nina was in hospital. Grace was heart-broken. Her husband and her daughter were on their way to meet her lover. Everything was absolutely fucking fine.

"Are you back in Sussex now?"

"Not yet, Mavis. We're staying in Paris a little longer than planned. Is that OK with you?"

A surprisingly girlish laugh. "No problem at all, Isobel. You make the most of it."

"Thanks. Is Dad there?"

"He is. Hold on. I'll carry the phone over."

"Dad?"

"Hello, Isobel. How are you, dear?"

How to answer that? That she had been fine when she left him, but that she was not the same person she had been two days' ago. That she felt maimed and battered and dreamt of children burning in empty rooms. That she woke with the smell of smoke in her nostrils.

"Fine, Dad. Everyone sends their love."

"Grace still going to the States with this boyfriend of hers?"

"Yes." No. Almost certainly not.

"Pity."

"Dad, we're staying a few days longer. Is that OK? Mavis says she doesn't mind."

"No problem at all, dear. In fact, we have news." A chuckle from him and a giggle in the background.

"What sort of news?"

"No need for the agency to send someone new. Mavis is moving in. Permanently." She could hear more laughter in the background.

"Really?" How confusing. What about her own house?

"Yes, it's all arranged."

Something in his tone gave her to understand he was giving her momentous news. Her mum had been dead less than six months.

"Are you saying congratulations are in order?"

"I suppose I am. Not getting married though." Well that was a blessed relief.

"As Mavis says, we'll be living in sin." More laughter in the background.

Wasn't that what they were all doing? Living in sin? Living *with* sin?

"Great news, Dad! Congratulations to you both! Can't wait to hear all about it when we get back." She felt she could not get off the phone quick enough.

"I said you'd be pleased. Mavis was worried you might object."

"Not at all. Happy for you both."

"Shall I put Mavis back on the phone?" She couldn't face more of that saccharine laugh.

"Losing signal, Dad. Sorry. Love to you both. See you soon."

"OK. Bye, dear."

"Bye, Dad."

She felt too old to be gaining a step-mother.

Even one of the unmarried variety. The world tipped on its axis by another degree.

Nothing could have prepared her for the sight of the apartment. They stood in the drawing room, the parquet floor soft and squelching underfoot. It was like seeing a fine watercolour redrawn with blunt charcoal: blackened walls, blackened ceiling, a limp, grey rag that had once been the Savonnerie tapestry, furniture reduced to stick-like frames, a wasteland of soot, smoke and ash.

Jean-Luc had met them at the door, giving a little bow to Robert and a nervous smile to Grace. Isobel was a spectre in the grey dust that filled the rooms.

Robert seemed struck dumb by shock. He took off his glasses and wiped them carefully. Grace sensed he was trying to pull himself together.

"How sad to see this room destroyed, Monsieur Chirol."

"Indeed it is tragic. However, I should say I am not Monsieur Chirol. It is understandable you would think so, but when I married I took my wife's name – Valette. We divorced many years ago, but the name has grown on me and it is the name by which I am known."

"In the film world?"

He looked embarrassed, "*Exactement.* However, I would prefer it if you would call me Jean-Luc. I think you both know my name."

Grace didn't know what to say, but Robert – usually so scrupulously polite - ignored the request.

"Where is your mother now, Monsieur Valette?"

"She is staying with me, near the Luxembourg."

"This must be a terrible shock."

"At her age, yes."

"At any age."

"True."

"Do they know how it started?"

"One of the lodgers left an appliance plugged in. It over-heated and the electrics caught fire. It took hold very quickly" Surely it hadn't been her? She used hair straighteners, but she was always careful to unplug everything. She'd never trusted the rickety old electrical power sockets in the apartment.

He must have read her mind, "It was not you, Mademoiselle. Even if it had been, it would not have been your fault. The fact is the apartment needed updating many years ago, but my mother was always so stubborn. It was, as you say, an accident waiting to happen."

"Which room was it?"

A slight pause, "Katja's. My niece. She is devastated of course, but we have tried to comfort her as best we can. It was a simple mistake, but terrible consequences."

"Poor Katja." This would eat at her conscience for the rest of her life.

He nodded in acknowledgement. "Shall we go through?"

They followed him down the corridor where only two days ago, she and Robert had packed up her bedroom. Three horribly misshapen and charred suitcases stood by the door: the two that Robert and Isobel had planned to take back to Rye; the third, smaller one that Grace had packed for a hot Miami summer. Grace's bed was a black coffin on which lay a pall of silver ash.

One look told her that nothing could be saved. What was she doing here? Why had he asked her? As if reading her mind he said, "My mother thought you should see for yourself. That it should be your decision whether there was anything here you want."

She shook her head. Felt dizzy.

Robert spoke, "Do you want to try to open the suitcases, Grace? See if anything can be salvaged?"

"No, Dad. There's no point. Look at them."

"We would need metal-cutters probably." The two men looked at each other and Jean-Luc shrugged.

"No. I don't want anything!" She was horrified at the prospect of opening the suitcases and having to look through the charred remnants of her life. Better to leave it all behind. She gave a sob of despair.

"Grace, are you OK?" Robert put his arms around her, holding her tight.

"I want to go."

"Yes of course."

She started to cry, "Now. We need to go now." She tugged at Robert's sleeve like a small child.

Jean-Luc began to apologise profusely, "I am so sorry, Mademoiselle. We thought it was for the best. She didn't want you to think we had kept anything we should not."

At the door, Robert held out his hand to shake Jean-Luc's.

"Please tell your mother we are so sorry and we wish her well."

"Thank you. I will."

He didn't let go of Jean-Luc's hand, "I wish you well too, Monsieur Valette."

There was no mistaking those words.

Jean-Luc nodded, mumbled something in French, and came towards her as if wishing to say good-bye, but she waved him away, burying her face in Robert's jacket. Her father guided her carefully down the stone stairs, now layered with soot, both of them averting their eyes from the twisted frame that was all that remained of the lift.

◆ ◆ ◆

The next day, George sent Grace a message asking her to meet him in his suite at Le Papillon. Robert and Isobel had both offered to go with her, but she wanted to go on her own. Robert insisted on waiting for her in the hotel lobby.

George was as distant as she had feared. Could barely meet her eyes. He poured them both a drink and asked her how her parents were.

"They're fine, thanks - but how's Nina doing? Is she out of danger?"

"Much better, thank you. She'll be in hospital for at least another week and the doctors have advised no long-haul flights until her lungs are stronger, so I'm going to take her down to the south of France to recuperate."

"And then?"

"Then she'll come back to Miami with me. I don't think I can let her out of my sight again."

"No Milan?"

"No Milan."

She knew what he wanted to say. He just didn't know how to say it.

"What about me, George? Shall I join you in Miami later this year?"

He looked up at the ceiling and then out at the window. "No."

Two letters. One word. A lifetime of heart-ache.

It was hopeless, but she couldn't believe her future was evaporating in this way.

"Please, George. I still want to be with you."

"No, Grace. It's best you go back with your parents to England and go to college as planned."

"Don't you love me, George? Don't you want me?"

Still he could not meet her eyes, "It's not that simple."

"Isn't it?" Tears were running down her face now, splashing into her wine.

"Grace, please."

"You blame me for Nina nearly dying. I knew you would."

"I promise you, I don't."

He put his glass down, walked over to her, knelt on the floor and took her hands in his.

"Grace, honey, there's no future for us. You must see that. I don't know why I thought it was OK to do what I did and I'm sorry for it now, but it ends here."

"You're *sorry* for it! How can you say that? You love me!" Yet he had never actually said those words.

She began to shake with grief then, not caring that snot was falling from her nose and that tears were turning her face to pink blotches. George stayed kneeling in front of her, stroking her arms and murmuring how sorry he was to hurt her, how she would be OK in time.

Eventually she managed to speak, "Do you think you might change your mind? In a few months?"

"No, Grace. It won't work."

"Does Nina hate me?"

"Nina's very sick still. She's in no state to hate anyone."

"Can I see her before I go? I'd like to say goodbye."

He ignored the question, patted her on the arms and stood up, "Are your parents here, Grace?"

"My dad's downstairs – I said I'd call him."

"Maybe we should ask him up here?"

"To take me away, you mean?" It came out more bitterly than she intended.

George walked over to the window, looking out over the Tuileries. A clammy silence descended.

Out of the corner of her eye, she caught sight of someone else sitting in the chair where George had sat. Pam. In the split second that passed, Grace took in the fact that her Granny was wearing her favourite cardigan and looked just as she always did, smiling at her as though they were back in the bungalow having tea. No hint of a ghost. Then the chair was empty again. A calm descended on Grace as though she and Pam had just had a long heart-to-heart about the whole situation. George was still at the window, staring blankly out at the park. She knew what she had to do.

She picked up her bag and walked over to where he stood.

George turned towards her. His relief was palpable, "I'll walk down with you. I'd like to say good-bye to Robert."

"No, George." She couldn't bear to see the two men shaking hands and exchanging pleasantries as though Grace were not broken, as though life would ever be the same again.

"Tell Nina I'm sorry for everything. I should have been a better friend."

"And I should have been a better father."

Then she walked out the door and towards the same lift where she had seen Jean-Luc kiss her mother a few short weeks' before.

SEPTEMBER

Now that the day had arrived, she very much wanted to cancel the whole enterprise. Her suitcase was in the hall – a smart, new one to match the smart, new her. For the twentieth time that day, she checked her handbag – a present from Dani – for passport, visa, money and phone. The taxi would be here in a moment.

Grace and Robert had wanted to wave her off, but she'd insisted they drive to Jack and Mavis's for the day instead.

"If you're both here, I'll cry and mess up my make-up."

It had been hard enough to hug them goodbye a couple of hours earlier, but once they'd left she was free to admit to herself how terrified she was. Automatically, she reached for the flight-checker app on her phone again. In a little over four hours' time, she would be *en route* to California. She wondered whether business class was all it was cracked up to be.

Since they arrived back at the end of June, life had been a roller-coaster. For a while, she'd put Hollywood clean out her head, because her priority was helping Grace through the heartbreak of losing both George and Nina.

Grace said little, ate little, slept little. She showed no interest in going anywhere or seeing anyone, even refusing to accompany Isobel on her trip to congratulate Jack and Mavis. During the day, she was either in her bedroom with door firmly closed or curled up in front of the television watching old episodes of American sit-coms. She never smiled at the well-worn catch lines or echoed the canned laughter. Isobel doubted she even knew what she was watching, so absent was she from the little house in Rye. Was suicide a possibility? This played on Isobel's mind to a point where she dreaded leaving her daughter in the house alone.

Every time she tried to break through this wall of silence, she was knocked back. Then one day, a small glimmer of light.

"Please let's talk about it, Grace." She waited for the inevitable rejection.

"What exactly?"

"Any of it. George. Nina."

"There's nothing to say."

"There's a lot to say – and it would do you good to say it. Don't bottle it in, sweetie. I can't do anything to put things right, but I can listen to how it's made you feel."

The tears began to fall, "I don't know what I'm *for*, Mum. What's the point of me exactly?"

"Sweetheart!"

"I'm a bad person. That's why Nina nearly died. Why George doesn't love me. I'm a horrible person and I deserve to be dead!"

"No, no! None of that is true. Come here."

Isobel held her close while she sobbed and sobbed. At one point she was aware of Robert coming in the kitchen door, but he must have crept back into the garden again for when the crying eventually stopped, there was only her and Grace once more.

She made them mugs of tea and took her daughter's hands, "Grace, I could offer you a lot of platitudes at this point, but the truth is I don't know the answer to that question, because you haven't started to find out yourself. You feel as though your life has ended, but it's only just beginning. That may be a cliché, but it doesn't make it any less true. I know it's not what you want to hear, but listen to me. Go to Durham. Take your degree. Seize life."

"I can't just forget about it all."

"I'm not asking you to do that. But I am saying that the way forward is to go to a place where nobody knows about Nina or George or what happened in Paris. Make new friends, new relationships – create new stories to weave into your life."

"I'm too sad, Mum. Nobody will like me."

She had to bite her tongue then. How much Isobel would have loved the opportunities that lay open to Grace. Twenty-three years had slipped through her fingers since she met Robert. In twenty-three more she would be seventy-two. Old age was no longer inconceivable, but something definite outlined on the horizon. How could she make her daughter understand how fleeting time was?

"Just think about what I've said. You still have your place at Durham. That was your future once – make it your future again."

"And George?"

"I would love to say 'forget George', but sadly it's not that simple. Please trust me on this though. One day you will wake up and realise that although you can't erase George from your memory, you can put him in a box high up on a shelf where he can't torment you."

"And Nina?"

"The same. Try to remember Nina with love and the way you were together, but don't let what happened between you destroy your own happiness."

"You make it sound easy!"

"It's anything but easy, Grace, but Dad and I are here to help."

"Even though you're separating." A note of bitterness.

"It's bad timing I know, but yes – even though

we're separating."

"Are you still going to America?"

"Let's see, shall we?"

"Don't blame you. It must be awful living with me."

"You can't help being sad, sweetie. Nobody can. Granny would have told you to pull your socks up though."

Grace smiled at that, "I miss her."

"I know. Me too."

"You're going to think me mad, Mum."

"What?"

"I saw Granny in Le Papillon. In George's suite. It was only for a moment – when I knew it was all over between us - but I felt as though she were telling me something."

Isobel found she wasn't nearly as surprised by this revelation as she might have been. Since Pam's death, she had often felt her close at hand. At times caught the scent of her perfume in the air.

"What did she say?"

"To let George go."

"Wise woman."

"I didn't really see her though, did I?"

"You said you did."

"But I couldn't have done. Do you think I'm crazy, Mum?"

"Not at all. In many ways, I think it's completely possible you saw what you thought you did. And if you didn't . . . "

"Yes?"

"It was still good advice."

It was starting to rain. Isobel stood up, "Your poor Dad. He's probably sheltering in the potting shed rather than disturb us. I'll give him a wave."

It would be nice to think that this pep talk had marked the beginning of Grace climbing out of despair, but in truth she knew it was more to do with an email she received a few days later.

Her daughter walked into the kitchen smiling for the first time in weeks.

"Nina emailed me."

"What! How is she?"

"Getting stronger. She's back in Miami with George."

"What did she say? Can you share?"

"Here."

She held out her phone. Isobel reached for her glasses.

It was a very sweet and generous message, reassuring Grace that she was fine and she should never blame herself for what happened. She didn't hide her relief that it was over between Grace and George, but she finished by saying she just wanted Grace to know that – even after everything – she would always have lovely memories of her and Paris and Rye. She sent her love to Isobel, Robert and Jack. There were two kisses, but no request to stay in touch.

"Have you seen the attachment?"

Isobel clicked and opened a beautifully

drawn portrait in ink of a girl standing at a tall window looking out at the Eiffel Tower. It was unmistakeably Grace.

"That's stunning. Did you know she'd drawn it?"

"No idea at all."

"Do you think she'd let us have the original?"

"I'd feel awkward asking."

"It's a lovely email to write."

"Isn't it? More than I would ever have hoped."

"What are you going to write back?"

"Not sure yet. I won't mention George directly, but I will say sorry for all the hurt we caused her. Other than that, I'll try to keep it light and friendly – give her the gossip, that sort of thing."

"Gossip?"

"The fact my mum's leaving my dad and running off to Hollywood with Madame Chirol's son. Nina's going to love that!"

And before Isobel had a chance to protest, she was gone again, taking the stairs two at a time up to her room.

◆ ◆ ◆

Dani had been proved right with her assertion that Compensation Theory should work both ways.

Dealing with Grace's heart-break had been

draining, but a couple of weeks after coming back to Rye, something momentously good happened.

"Do you know which day it is?" asked Robert.

"Tuesday." Why couldn't he check his phone like everyone else?

"I'm talking about the date." What was he talking about now? He was grinning at her in a particularly vexing matter.

Then the penny dropped.

"Is it tomorrow? Really?"

"It is. Do you fancy a trip to London?"

"No. You go." She couldn't face any more disappointments; felt as though she would jinx things with her presence. For tomorrow was the day of the book sale. It was the moment of truth for the first-edition Dickens.

She kept her phone by her side all that afternoon, anxious she might miss Robert's call. When it finally rang and she answered it with trembling fingers, she could tell by the way he said, "It's me" that it was good news. '*The Tale Of Two Cities*' had come up trumps. An American college had dug deep and out-bid a private collector, with the tenacity of the private collector pushing the price up dizzyingly high, well into six figures. When Robert gave her the exact figure, she had to sit down. Financial good fortune was a stranger to their marriage. How ironic it was paying a visit to them so late in the day.

That night they cracked open champagne and shared the news with Grace.

"How did you keep that one a secret?"

Robert handed her a flute of golden bubbles, "I think your mother had forgotten all about it, to be honest."

Isobel smiled and clinked her own flute with his, "Not exactly forgotten, but there has been rather a lot going on."

"It's nice to have something to celebrate," said Robert. "Goodness knows, we need it."

"What will you spend it on?" asked Grace.

"A lot of boring things like clearing the overdraft and giving Miss Mapp a face-lift. What would you like to do with your share, Bel?"

"My share?" She was completely thrown. Everything was paid for out of the joint current account. She only had a small savings account to call her own where she squirrelled away anything she could to buy the family birthday and Christmas presents each year.

Robert smiled, "I'd like you to have half of it. It's not as if I've been able to give you much in the way of spare cash over the years."

Later, as they washed the champagne flutes, he put his arms around her, "I'm serious, Bel – about the money – spend it on whatever you like. You deserve it."

"It wouldn't feel right, Robert. Not with things being the way they are."

"I still want you to have it."

"A quarter then, not a half."

"We'll see. The offer's staying firmly on the table."

As the weeks passed, the idea of going to Hollywood seemed like a childish fantasy, but Dani urged her on.

"Give me one good reason not to go, Bel."

"It's so selfish for one thing."

"Bugger that! If more women learnt to be selfish, there'd be far fewer anti-depressants being prescribed."

"Even so."

"Come on. Be honest. How do you really feel about it?"

"Exhilarated. Terrified. I'm beginning to realise how anxious Grace must have been this time last year."

"This is proper, grown-up work. Far more exciting and far better paid!"

"I did find a summer course to bring me up to speed with IT skills."

"That's great. Good for you."

She paused, "How's Robert coping with it all?"

"He's being very Robert . . . decent, unprotesting."

Dani gave her a searching look, "You can't

expect him to play by a different set of rules, you know."

"What do you mean?"

"What's sauce for the goose is sauce for the gander."

She hadn't really considered that.

"Fair point. I'll just have to live with the consequences."

Easy to say, but deep down she was shocked. Could Robert really fall in love with someone else? Take another woman to bed?

"He has quite a fan club, you know. Saskia noticed it when she was helping out. Not sure Robert has noticed himself, but once you're out the picture . . ."

"Out of sight, out of mind?"

"Just don't say you weren't warned."

"Please don't take this the wrong way, Dani, but I can't stay with Robert just to keep you and Saskia happy."

"Of course you can't."

"I can't keep being responsible for other people's happiness. I need to find my own."

Dani grinned, "Exactly the words I have been longing for you to say."

"Look after him for me though. I do love that man, just not in the way I did."

"I know."

She leant over and took Isobel's hand in hers, "I hope you find what you're looking for, Bel. More than anything, I really hope you do."

◆ ◆ ◆

Towards the end of June, Jean-Luc made contact again. To be exact his French, PA, Camille, made contact. She spoke impeccable English.

"Monsieur Valette is very anxious to know if you will be taking up the position offered to you, Madame Peters?"

She had thought it odd he hadn't been in touch since she'd left Paris. Wondered why he wasn't asking her this himself.

"Yes, thank you. I will." She could barely believe she was saying the words.

"Then we will be working together very closely! I look forward to it, Madame Peters."

"Isobel, please."

"I look forward to it, Isobel. Going forward, I will be making the arrangements for you, such as visa, travel, accommodation and so forth. Please can we begin with you scanning me a copy of your passport and sending it over?"

"Of course. Thank you."

"If you give me your email address, I will send over details of what we require shortly. Monsieur Valette has suggested a start date of the fourteenth of August."

"I thought the job was from September."

"You will be relocating to Hollywood in September, but he wants you on hand remotely from then as there will be a lot to discuss before your arrival."

"Of course."

"You will have a junior assistant to support you. Monsieur Valette would like to know if you are happy for us to arrange that or whether you wish to appoint her yourself?"

"I'm happy for you to do that, thank you."

"Very good. I will also sort your office email address later today and send you the password."

"Thank you."

"And I will send you the draft contract to read. Please come back to me should you have any queries."

"Thank you."

"Do you have any questions for me, Isobel?" Where should she start? This one phone call had made her feel totally inadequate.

"No, thank you."

"OK. We will be in touch again soon. *Ciao*!"

"*Ciao*!"

She went to the kitchen and poured herself a large glass of white wine. Her phone began flashing again: Jean-Luc.

"Isobel! Camille just gave me the good news!"

"She seems very nice."

"She is wonderful. You will get along beautifully."

"She seems very organised."

"Indeed. As you will be."

"Jean-Luc . . . ."

"No protests, please. Now you are wondering why I did not ring you myself?"

"I suppose I was."

"Because now we start with the clean slate, Isobel. No complications. This is important for both of us. We have serious work to do in America, *non*?"

He had meant it then. Their affair was over.

Again, he seemed to read her mind.

"Six months will go in the flash, as you say. Six months very business-like. After that . . . who can predict?"

She laughed, "OK, Jean-Luc. We will both concentrate on our work."

"Monsieur Valette."

"What!"

"You must try to remember, Isobel. Always Monsieur Valette when we are working."

"Got it." This was going to be even harder than she thought.

He began laughing, "I was not serious. Only to other people must you remember I am Monsieur Valette. To you, always Jean-Luc."

"I must admit that is a relief! So Valette is your first wife's name?"

He hesitated, "Yes. We divorced a long time ago." Yet the photos she had seen in his apartment were clearly recent.

"Does that mean your second wife is also Valette?" How very confusing.

There was a long pause.

"In fact, there is no second wife."

"I don't understand. You're married, surely?"

"As we are working together, it is best I be honest with you. I have been married only once. I let you think that the photographs of the woman you saw in my apartment were my second wife. In fact she is my girlfriend of a long time, but we never actually married."

"But you are still together?"

"We are – like you and your husband – separating for a while. She does not wish to come to America and neither does she wish to be bored in Paris while I am away."

"I see."

He laughed, "I do not expect you to understand, but we are free agents in that respect"

"I'm glad you told me. Might have put my foot in it."

"She knows to go through Camille if she wants me." That was a relief.

"I am grateful to you, Jean-Luc, for giving me this opportunity. Thank you."

He laughed, "You might not feel the same way at the end of six months. Do you realise, Snow Queen, you have not even asked me which film they want me to direct?"

"Go on."

"'*The Loved One*'. Evelyn Waugh. Why they want a French director for this most English of novelists I do not know."

"The one about the funeral parlour?"

"*Exactement.*"

"It's very funny. Very dark too."

"Then maybe a French director makes good sense, after all."

"You will do a brilliant job, Jean-Luc."

"And so will you, dear Isobel."

She saw the taxi draw up outside and the driver walk up to the door. A moment later, he was manoeuvring the heavy case down the steep garden path, while she checked her handbag one last time.

A last, nervous glimpse in the hall mirror and she was out of the door and locking it behind her.

The driver smiled at her as she slid over the back seat.

"Work trip, is it?"

"Yes, how did you know?"

"You don't look like a tourist, love. Taking you to business check-in, am I?"

"That's right."

She gave him the name of the airline and the terminal required, then sat back a smile on her face. She might not appreciate the 'love' but she felt as though she had passed her first test.

Whatever life held for her, she was going to give it her best shot.

BEFORE YOU GO

Thank you for reading *Gap Year*. I hope you enjoyed reading Isobel and Grace's story as much as I enjoyed writing it. As you can imagine, it takes a long time - years usually - for anyone to write a novel. Books come to existence through dedication, passion and a deep love for writing. Reviews help persuade readers to give a book a shot and so support new writing. It will take *less than a minute* and can be *just a line* to say what you liked (or what you didn't) about *Gap Year*. Please leave me a review wherever you bought this book from - it really does help. A heartfelt thank you,
Helen Chislett

ACKNOWLEDGEMENTS

With thanks to my Faber writing group - in particular Alexandra, Angela, Barbs, Geraldine, Jenny, Kathryn, Michelle, Naomi, Sophia and Tara. And to Nicole for all those cups of tea at the Corinthia while we compared our writing journeys. Thanks too to Carolyn Quartermaine for patiently correcting my French.

My biggest gratitude as ever to John for all his encouragement, support and unwavering belief.

ABOUT THE AUTHOR

Helen Chislett

Helen began work as a writer on Good Housekeeping magazine aged just nineteen. Since then her work has been published in every UK broadsheet newspaper and numerous lifestyle titles, women's magazines and design publications. For fourteen years, she was a contributor to the FT 'How To Spend It' magazine. She has written over twenty design and decoration books to date. 'Gap Year' is her first novel.

Printed in Great Britain
by Amazon